I AM LEMONADE LUCY!

KENNETH WOMACK

Black Rose Writing | Texas

First printing

ISBN: 978-1-94471-538-0
PUBLISHED BY BLACK ROSE WRITING
www.blackrosewriting.com

I Am Lemonade Lucy! is printed in Palatino Linotype
Author photo by Marissa Carney
Drawing by Takamin

For Ryan:

The Real One

I AM LEMONADE LUCY!

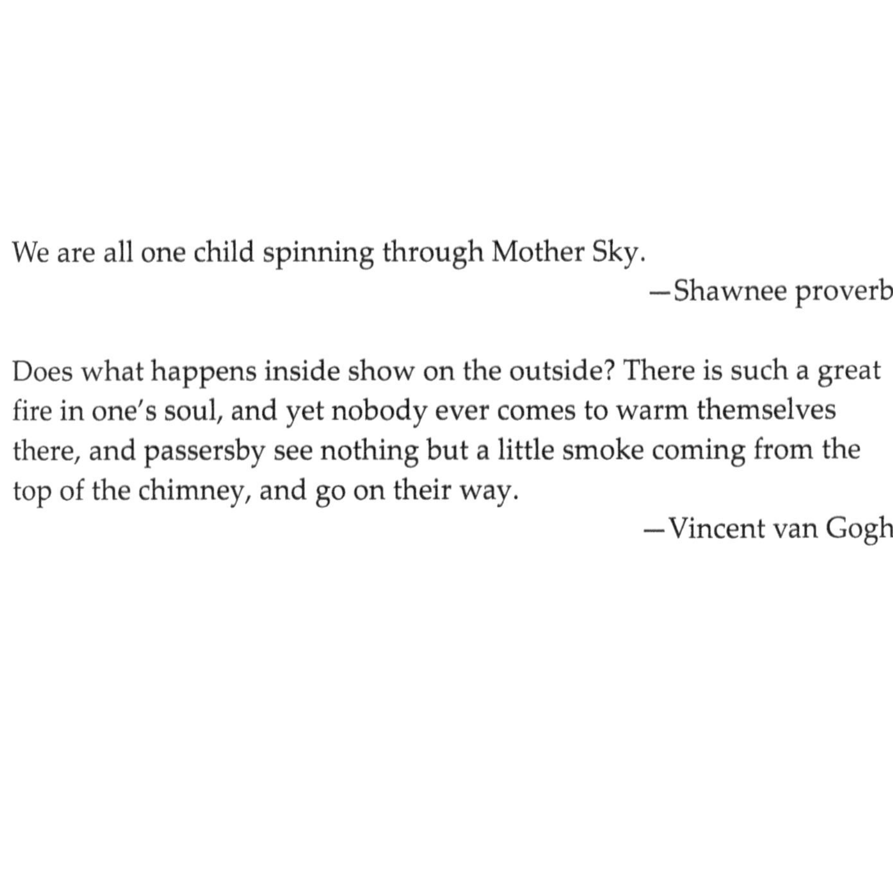

We are all one child spinning through Mother Sky.

—Shawnee proverb

Does what happens inside show on the outside? There is such a great fire in one's soul, and yet nobody ever comes to warm themselves there, and passersby see nothing but a little smoke coming from the top of the chimney, and go on their way.

—Vincent van Gogh

CHAPTER 1: NINETY-SEVEN THOUSAND, EIGHT-HUNDRED SEVENTY-TWO

The ladies in the Registrar's office were thunderstruck by the sight of her—or, to be more precise, by the sight of *it*.

For them, the very spectacle of the young Middle Eastern woman's hijab was utterly disquieting. They simply couldn't take their eyes off of it: the long, cape-like headscarf with its brilliant folds of purple and peach fabrics that had literally walked in off of the street with its wearer only moments before.

If they could have seen Azza beyond the hijab—if they had taken in the emotional contours of her face—those formidable women who comprised the grey-haired staff (they preferred to think of themselves as *mature*) would have glimpsed the fear in their most unexpected visitor's eyes, would have seen it written upon the lines of her olive cheeks.

Unbeknownst to herself, Azza had become, in that very instant, the unsettling sensation of tiny Fremont, Ohio. By nightfall, people across the hamlet would know about her astonishing appearance in their environs. She would be the stuff of local legend and great exaggeration, a presence provoking both fear and wonder. And for her part, Azza was just as flustered, in her own way, by those mature ladies of the Registrar's office, their jaws agape at the sight of the whole of the Islamic world having seemingly intruded upon their workaday lives.

And they knew what the hijab meant all right, they most certainly did. They were at Northwestern Ohio State College, after all—where folks like Mrs. Beckelhymer, the Assistant Registrar, insisted that they comport themselves as progressively as possible, this being Higher

Education and everything. If it weren't for Mrs. Beckelhymer, the ladies of the Registrar's office would still be referring to themselves as the *girls* of the Registrar's office. And while Mrs. Beckelhymer was no shill for political correctness, she admonished them, time and time again, about acting appropriately and respectfully of their station at the college. So it would be that they were ladies instead of girls.

Yes, they knew what the hijab signified, and they knew that Islam was supposed to be the religion of peace. But even still, they weren't mindless dolts, those ladies of the Registrar's office. They caught the headlines when they could on FoxNews.com, even read a newspaper every now and again, same as any other American. Besides, they had seen those towers burn and collapse into ruins on that bright September morning just like everybody else.

As the ladies of the Registrar's office looked on, Azza crept up to the bold yellow line painted across the linoleum floor in the waiting area. And there she stood, as if holding vigil, as one flip-flop wearing student after another passed in front of her and loped up to the reception desk. With the new semester set to begin come Monday, they were there to pay their tuition, carefully writing out checks or presenting credit cards to settle their bills.

Her chin held up high in defiance, Azza might very well have been waiting there still if not for the young man in the red-and-blue cap, his boyish face framed by a shock of blond hair. As he strolled in from the bowels of the Registrar's office, he saw her holding her ground on the yellow line as the other students passed her by on their way to be served. Not missing a beat, he walked up behind the reception desk, whispered in the ear of old Agnes, the matronly attendant on duty, and gestured in Azza's direction. Flashing a warm smile at the young man as he strode out of the Registrar's office, Agnes motioned for Azza to come forward.

When she finally stepped up to the reception desk, Azza's hijab was shortly to become a secondary notion to all concerned as she struggled to lift a lumpy, threadbare valise in the direction of the countertop. The ladies of the Registrar's office had been so enthralled by the sight of Azza's getup that morning that they had failed to notice the heavy cargo that she had been dragging behind her until the moment it landed, with a thud—her headscarf bobbing and weaving with her exertions—on top of the faded Formica reception desk. Quite suddenly, the ladies' attentions were fully drawn to the mysterious valise, which lingered on the countertop as if it were some kind of ticking time bomb, waiting to go off.

For her part, Azza emitted an audible sigh of relief as she released the weighty bag from her clutches. In truth, she was happy to be rid of the wretched thing. She had lugged it all the way from Orly Airport on a transatlantic journey since yesterday—having watched her dear father vigilantly pack the valise himself before he drove her away from their tiny apartment in Bobigny, possibly forever, in his rusted-out Citroën pickup. Standing there in the Registrar's office, she found herself wondering if she would ever see her home again—the dusty tenement on the Rue Maria Callas that she had shared with her family for as long as she could remember. What a thing, she thought to herself, to be reminiscing so fondly about a place that most Parisians derided as Department 93—that Godforsaken *Quatre-vingt-treize!*—or, worse yet, as one of the much-reviled No-Go zones. But she missed that grubby apartment just the same.

Not surprisingly, it was old Agnes who saw it first—who saw the contents of the valise that would shortly have the ladies of the Registrar's office forgetting all about the disturbing sight of the purple and peach folds of Azza's hijab. When the young woman stepped up to the counter, Agnes announced in the most solicitous, most welcoming voice that she could reasonably muster under the circumstances, "May I help you?"

Ignoring her, Azza struggled to unzip the mighty valise, finally managing to pry the metal jaws of the bag open. And that's when the older woman saw it: the veritable mounds of cold, hard cash that spilled before her onto the countertop. Twenties, tens, and fives, mostly small bills—with a smattering of hundreds to round out the lot. And what a lot it was.

Perhaps it was Agnes's silence that caught their attention, as she stood there agog, staring at the heaping pile of money. But soon the other ladies of the Registrar's office gathered around her to gaze at what amounted to more American currency than any of them had ever seen before in their lives—and, without a doubt, far more than any of them had ever glimpsed in the Registrar's office, of all places, where students normally trafficked in the commerce of late-add credits and the occasional unpaid parking fine.

In nearly the same instant that Azza unveiled all of that moolah, Mrs. Beckelhymer, her hair done up in a tight blonde bun, strolled in from her cubicle in the bowels of the building. She hadn't seen so much cash in one place either, but while the rest of the staff looked on in a kind of stunned disbelief, she knew exactly what to do.

"I'll get the Registrar," she said in a hushed voice to no one in particular as old Agnes, her eyes still glued to the wads of money on the reception desk, began to nod in agreement. Yes, it was definitely time to fetch the Registrar all right.

In a few moments, Dr. Smyth breathlessly arrived on the scene, his wire-rimmed glasses bizarrely perched atop his balding head.

"My God!" he exclaimed in a halting British accent. "What do we have 'ere?"

For Azza, Dr. Smyth's words bordered on the ridiculous. She knew perfectly well what had been stashed away in her valise, which in turn, had been lodged inside the steamer trunk that had arrived, along with Azza and her disturbing headgear, at the John Glenn Columbus International Airport only a few hours earlier. A U.S. customs agent had dutifully counted and recounted the money, and issued her a receipt, which she now held aloft in her hands.

Clearing her voice, Azza replied, in her clipped Tunisian accent, "It is my tuition, sir."

"Most students pay by check," said Dr. Smyth, having regained his composure, "and in installments."

For a moment, Azza stared back at him quizzically and then, pursing her lips, replied:

"It is my out-of-state tuition, yes?" she said, glancing at the receipt. "It is ninety-seven thousand, eight-hundred seventy-two American dollars."

"Come again?" said Dr. Smyth.

"It is ninety-seven thousand, eight-hundred seventy-two American dollars," she said. "That is the amount of your out-of-state tuition, sir. I read it on your website, the one where you publish your fees. Out-of-state tuition is twenty-four thousand, four-hundred sixty-eight American dollars per annum. When you multiply it by four, the total is ninety-seven thousand, eight-hundred seventy-two American dollars."

"That's a lot of money," said Dr. Smyth, stating the obvious.

"Yes, it is, sir," Azza answered. "It is equivalent to eighty-seven thousand, seven-hundred eighteen Euros. I am paying in American dollars in full for four years of study at your institution, where I would like to take my baccalaureate degree in chemical engineering. Please, will you help me, sir?"

"You are registered at the college, Ms.?—"

"Azza Amari, sir. Yes, I am registered as baccalaureate student at Northwestern Ohio State College in the School of Business and Engineering. But I have no interest in business, sir, only in engineering. My studies begin on Monday, do they not?"

"Dr. Smyth," said Mrs. Beckelhymer, who had begun organizing the dollar bills into loose stacks on top of the reception desk, "there is no standing college policy about specific means of payment. We take personal checks, and, for a small processing fee, Master Card, Visa, and American Express. There's no rule against cash. It's legal tender, after all."

"It sure is a heck of a lot of legal tender," said Dr. Smyth. "But you're correct, of course, Mrs. Beckelhymer. Agnes, please ask a campus security officer to accompany you to the bank. We'll be making our deposit a little earlier than we expected this afternoon."

"Yes, Dr. Smyth," Agnes replied, as she began assisting Mrs. Beckelhymer, who was already making short work organizing the wads of cash on the countertop into neat stacks by denomination.

"Thank you," said Azza, regaining her composure as Agnes and Mrs. Beckelhymer began transferring the dollar bills into a plastic postal tote. "Now, sir," Azza continued, "if you will please escort me to my dormitory so that I can prepare for my studies."

"Come again?" Dr. Smyth answered, as he rubbed even deeper creases into his well-lined forehead.

"I have paid ninety-seven thousand, eight-hundred seventy-two American dollars in full, sir. Your website promised an all-inclusive collegiate experience. I was recruited by Mr. Harley Vinson, who spoke with my father by telephone, making all of the necessary arrangements for me to attend Northwestern Ohio State College in your international program, no?"

"Young lady, we don't have residence halls," said Agnes, looking up from the plastic postal tote. "We're a commuter campus."

"A commuter campus?" said Azza, her eyes wrinkling in confusion.

"Yes, ma'am," said Agnes. "A commuter campus. Our students live at home, usually with their parents, and attend classes during the day."

"But Mr. Vinson said—" Azza replied, fumbling uncertainly for her words. "He said that I could have the full American collegiate experience at Northwestern Ohio State College. That I would have a dormitory room and a meal plan. That I would be given a library card and have access to the student bookstore and also to the learning center in case my English is not so good. That Northwestern Ohio State College is melting pot of diversity where I can gain experience through co-op programs and internships. That there would be dorm mixers, although I don't know what is dorm mixers, but he said that I would have that. Mr. Vinson also told my father that I would have the option of a study abroad opportunity, although my father explained to him that Northwestern Ohio State College would be study abroad opportunity enough for me. That Northwestern Ohio State College would be living abroad from Bobigny—"

"From *what*?" said Agnes.

"From Bobigny," Azza replied. "It is one of the *banlieues*—one of the suburbs, as you might call them, of Paris."

As Azza continued her furtive discussion with Agnes, Mrs. Beckelhymer pulled aside Dr. Smyth, who was now rubbing the lines of his forehead in utter consternation.

"You know what this is," she whispered to him.

"It's total disaster is what it is," he answered.

"But Ms. Amari isn't necessarily wrong," said Mrs. Beckelhymer.

"Of course, she is. We don't have international programs at

Northwestern Ohio State. We barely have collegiate sports."

"Maybe not," Mrs. Beckelhymer replied, "but I know all about Harley Vinson. He's our international rep. A shady character, for sure, but he's ours. Admissions is under the gun to improve enrollment numbers, and they go out and hire charlatans like Vinson, who offer the world to get students to sign on the dotted line. He's probably never set foot on our campus, but that wouldn't stop him from promising scholarships, dorms, the whole shebang."

"But we don't have dormitories," said Dr. Smyth. "We don't even have so much as a guest house."

"But like it or not, we have Ms. Amari over there in the flesh, and she has no balance due, which puts her ahead of just about the entire incoming freshman class. I suggest that we scramble the folks over in Admissions into action and get some sort of international program in place by close of business today."

"All right then," Dr. Smyth replied, wiping his brow. "I guess we'll have to fake it till we make it, as you Americans say."

And with that, Dr. Smyth and Mrs. Beckelhymer turned back towards the reception desk, where their visitor from another world awaited them, her chin held high and her demeanor prideful and resolute for the express benefit of those ladies of the Registrar's office. But for her part, Mrs. Beckelhymer glimpsed something very different in Azza's eyes—something that nobody else saw that day, an aspect of Northwestern Ohio State College's newest freshman that no one else could see beyond her hijab and her olive skin.

Oh, Mrs. Beckelhymer could see the terror that lived inside of the bulging ovals of Azza's eyes. She recognized that the young woman's irises were awash with fear all right, and that her sense of fear betrayed everything about her otherwise steadfast appearance in the Registrar's office that morning.

For Mrs. Beckelhymer, there was something else altogether about Azza that she couldn't shake. And that something else, something utterly unmistakable from the Assistant Registrar's vantage point, was *despair*.

CHAPTER 2:
TO BE CONTINUED

Kip Beckelhymer just stood there and took it. Like always.

As his throat tightened and his eyes began to water, Kip knew better than to try and speak. Talking would only serve to unleash the floodgates, and there was no way he was going to break into full-on tears right there in front of Domino's Pizza, with a whole world of people streaming by that afternoon on their way to the CVS next door or the campus just across the street.

And worse yet, there was no way he was going to cry in front of Birdie, his girlfriend with the funny name. Or could it be his *ex*-girlfriend with the funny name?

As it happened, there was nothing funny at all about Birdie, who was trying, without being too gentle about it, to break up with him right then and there in front of Domino's. For her part, Birdie stared at him with a look of contempt verging on disgust. Her chestnut brown pigtails hung limply beside her bronze face, deeply tanned from too many lazy days in the summer sun.

What's the hurry? Kip wondered to himself. Couldn't she have texted him later—when he wasn't at work? Or better yet, perhaps she could have tried *not breaking up with him at all*. Was being tethered to him in high school—what was left of it anyway—such a terrible fate? It's not like they were married.

"I think we should see other people," said Birdie, as Kip looked this way and that, bracing himself for the waterworks. As Birdie stared him down in front of the strip mall, a posse of incoming college freshmen and their parents passed by on their way to the bookstore. With classes set to begin on Monday, everyone was making a mad rush to meet the new semester.

And that's when Kip got his reprieve in the form of Jim Doody, Domino's slacker of a store manager, who stepped outside of the pizza joint and made a beeline in his direction.

Girding his courage, Kip took advantage of the moment, looked Birdie straight in the eyes for the first time since she had accosted him in front of Domino's, and muttered through gritted teeth, "So, um, are we good here?"

But before Birdie could so much as utter a single word, they were joined by the store manager, unkempt as always with his unruly mane of red hair and his scruffy apron mottled with grease stains and splotches of bright orange tomato sauce.

"You don't look so chipper, Kipper," said Jim, laughing uproariously at his own joke and gingerly balancing a pizza box in his hands. "Seriously, though, should I get another driver?"

"I . . . I can do it, JD," Kip replied, inhaling a deep breath, his voice cracking ever so slightly. "Where to?"

"2234 Augusta. This here's an extra-large Honolulu Hawaiian, so be careful," he said, placing the wobbly, oversized pizza box in Kip's outstretched hands and leaving the couple, such as they were, alone at the storefront.

"So, uh, we're good, then?" Kip asked, steadying the pizza box in his arms.

"To be continued," said Birdie, acidly.

• • •

Truth be told, Kip didn't need GPS to find 2234 Augusta. He frequented there almost as often as he went to his own home—almost as much, if you can believe it, as he spent trolling the halls of Fremont High, which was saying something.

Driving away from the strip mall in his rusted-out Subaru, Kip steered the powder-blue hatchback onto the old highway that bisected

Fremont. With each arduous shift, the car's ancient gears crunched as Kip coaxed the feeble vehicle into an awkward forward momentum. He could see the Sandusky River stretching out ahead, with the wooded tufts of Brady's Island visible just around the bend. As he crossed the river, the faded brick veneer of Woody's Drive-In came into view, followed closely on its heels by Tal's Bait and Tackle Shop and the Kroger, where Kip had toiled the previous summer as a cashier before Domino's—and the promise of endless gratuities from the hamlet's pizza-loving hordes—presented itself. During his brief tenure at the pizza joint, he had met plenty of pizza aficionados among the townsfolk, but scarcely little in the way of actual tips.

As he passed the Fremont Bible Church and took that hard right turn that he knew so well onto Masters Way, Kip choked back the sob that had been gathering in his throat since leaving Birdie back at the storefront. For Kip, her change of heart had been truly sudden and unexpected. How, indeed, had her eyes so easily transformed from unchecked adoration into bitter indifference in the space of a single week? To say that he was blindsided by her disavowal would be an understatement.

After all, it had been only the previous weekend when they had made the five-hour drive to Gurnee, Illinois, to take in the sights, sounds, and thrills of Six Flags Great America. Against his better judgment, Kip had braved every last one of the amusement park's stomach-churning roller coasters for Birdie's benefit. Afterward, he had sunk a succession of basketballs—not to mention, some 20 bucks from his paltry Domino's earnings—in an absurd carnival game. Birdie had squealed with delight when his basketball prowess in the arcade had delivered a giant SpongeBob SquarePants stuffy into his arms, which he dutifully transferred to his girlfriend's eager embrace. She had even gone so far as to post a picture of the stuffy on her Instagram account, which amassed tons of likes from her girlfriends. Surely, they were meant to be a couple—Kip reassured himself at the time—having scored such an enthusiastic response from the social media world?

They capped off their visit to Six Flags with a romantic carousel ride, after which Kip presented Birdie with a gold promise ring in the shape of a heart. For the longest time, she stood by the carousel and stared at the ring, her eyes overflowing with tears of joy. On the long drive home, Birdie fell blissfully asleep in the passenger's seat, the gold band safely ensconced on the ring finger of her left hand as she gripped the oversized yellow doll with nary a care in the world. Or so Kip thought.

As he steered the Subaru along Masters Way, the houses quickly shifted from the rust-belt doldrums of Fremont proper into the comparative opulence of the professional class. In concert with the homes, the yards suddenly became much larger and more well-kempt, particularly as Kip neared the rolling green lawns of the golf course that lived in the heart of the neighborhood, a planned community with street signs that boasted the stately names of golf's most famous locales: Pebble Beach Road, St. Andrews Lane, and, finally, Augusta Drive.

By the time that Kip eased the Subaru in front of number 2234, he had mostly regained his composure. He caught a glimpse of himself in the rearview mirror as he brought the hatchback to a stop near a red brick mailbox. A sprinkler head sputtered and choked on the far side of the yard, spewing water droplets on the verdant lawn, with its rich shades of hunter green gleaming in the late afternoon sun.

Staring intently at his reflection, Kip adjusted his red-and-blue Domino's cap and flicked a stray blond hair away from his face. His eyes may have been a little red around the edges, but Birdie hadn't succeeded in breaking up with him just yet. All he needed to do, Kip reasoned, was avoid seeing her until after graduation. Then he would be off to college and a new life, if he were really lucky, in another city far removed from Fremont's relentless gravitational pull. To accomplish that, he would have to knock his SATs out of the park and earn a lucrative scholarship if he hoped to enroll anywhere other than lowly Northwestern Ohio State, where his mother's fringe benefits promised to give him a steep tuition discount.

Of course, he very likely wouldn't be in this predicament at all if his dad hadn't up and died when Kip was in the first grade. In truth, he could hardly remember the guy—not even the tenor of his voice or the sound of his laugh. The only evidence of his dad's one-time presence in Kip's life were a few random pictures from holidays and birthdays, the scattered images of smiling relatives and frosted cakes. His father had left very little behind in terms of personal effects, save for a bound copy of his master's thesis, which he had completed as a student in the Department of History at the University of Illinois long before Kip was even a gleam in his eye. The well-thumbed volume was one of Kip's most treasured possessions. He had committed many of its finest passages to memory, including a thrilling section on Manifest Destiny.

Otherwise, it was as if his dad had never existed at all—as if he had vanished into thin air, leaving his mother's subsistence income and Kip's fatherless status as his only mark on this lonely planet. At least, that's how Kip saw the whole crummy state of affairs. But Birdie came along and changed all that, comforting him with the idea of a loyal girlfriend standing by his side through thick and thin. Yeah, he liked that idea a lot. Even now—after that terrible scene back at Domino's, no less—Kip liked to believe that one day he would put Fremont in his rearview mirror forever. And that Birdie would be right there beside him, steadfast and true, as they embarked upon a new life together *somewhere else*.

As Kip climbed out of the Subaru in front of 2234 Augusta, he carried the steaming pizza box in his arms, gagging slightly as he took in the aroma of the oversized pie, its ample slices chockfull of ham, bacon, and pineapple chunks. Whatever happened to the simple pleasures of pepperoni and extra cheese, he wondered to himself?

Kip balanced the pizza box awkwardly in his arms as he made his way up the regal front walk, stopping dead in his tracks as the Tudor home's massive oaken door creaked open.

And there he was: Ryan Langham, Kip's sorry excuse for a best friend.

"Beckelhymen!" Ryan boomed as he loped in Kip's direction. Wearing a pair of garish purple Crocs, Ryan sported a pair of oversized green walking shorts on his lanky frame, along with a black muscle tee-shirt with the word LIFEGUARD stenciled on the back.

"Seriously, Ry?" said Kip. "You had the nerve to order the Honolulu Hawaiian? My car will need to be fumigated before I can go home tonight."

"The Powder Puff doesn't look any worse for wear," said Ryan, peering at the hatchback as he deftly removed the pizza box from Kip's arms in a single motion. "Besides, you're just worried that Princess Birdie won't ride with you in your smelly old car anymore."

"Ry—" Kip gulped, struggling to hold back the tears that had threatened to flow back at the strip mall.

"Dude, did I hit some kinda nerve?"

For his part, Kip could only purse his lips, shake his head, and stare down at the pristine, brick-lined path.

"Wait," said Ry, "did you and Miss Pigtails break up?"

"I . . . I don't know just yet—"

"You don't know just yet? I call bullshit on that, dude. Go the distance!"

"Go the distance?" said Kip, his mouth agape. "Why are you suddenly channeling *Field of Dreams*?"

"You gotta see this thing through!" said Ry. "This is cause to celebrate!"

"*Celebrate*?" said Kip. "Why would I want to do that?"

"You just got your life back, dude!" Ry continued, setting the pizza box on the ground beside the mailbox. Reaching into its metal bowels, Ry produced a six-pack of Bud Light from deep within its innards.

"*My life back*?" Kip asked.

"Drinks are on me!" said Ry, lifting up the six-pack aloft in his arms.

"But I'm working," said Kip.

"So am I," Ry replied, gesturing towards the sprinkler. "I'm watering the yard."

"Fine," said Kip. "But here's a newsflash for you: I'm 17, I'm standing in broad daylight with my knucklehead friend, and, should one of Fremont's finest drive by at this particular moment, we'll both be filling out our college apps with criminal records hanging over our heads."

"Maybe so," Ry answered, cracking open one of the Bud Light

bottles and taking a long swig of beer. "But at least it will give us something to list under community involvement, right? Sounds like a win-win to me." With his thirst quenched for the moment, Ry settled down on the curb near the pizza box, pried open the cardboard jaws, and removed a thick slice of Honolulu Hawaiian. The pineapple chunks gleamed in the sunlight like yellow globs of rubber nestled among the greasy morsels of ham and bacon.

With seemingly nothing left to lose, Kip settled next to Ry along the curb. With a shrug, he pulled one of the remaining Bud Lights out of its cardboard carrier.

"I still don't know what we're celebrating," he said.

"Dude, you just won back your freedom—and right in time for senior year!" said Ry. "You're finally gonna get into the game, play the field!"

"What's with all of the baseball metaphors?" Kip asked as he prepared to crack open his brew. But before he could so much as dislodge the bottle cap from his Bud Light, his phone buzzed into life with an incoming text:

"ORDER UP!"

"I've got to get back," said Kip, glancing up from his smartphone.

"That blows," said Ry, shaking his head as he quickly dispatched with a slice of Honolulu Hawaiian before greedily removing yet another from the Domino's box. Meanwhile, Kip stood up from the curb, gently dusting the stray grass clippings off of his khaki pants.

"Freakin' Doody has you on a short leash today," Ry continued. "Aren't you even gonna stay and finish your beer?"

"Apparently, your lifetime of joblessness hasn't prepared you for the standard expectations of the manager-employee relationship, wherein he calls and I respond," Kip replied.

"Joblessness?" Ry asked. "Do you think this kickass yard takes care of itself?"

"Looks like ChemLawn and your dad's landscaping service to me," said Kip, staring at his friend with a look of disbelief verging on all-out disgust. "You have knocked back, like, five slices since I've been here," Kip added, shaking his head back and forth. "You are going to be the fattest kid at Fremont High—"

"Dude, dude, dude!" said Ry, easing up from the curb as he balanced a slice of Honolulu Hawaiian in one hand and a beer in the other. "You know how well I play with the ladies. I'll have this worked off by sundown!"

"And all those beers aren't lo-cal either."

"Shut the eff up!" Ry replied. "Those are fightin' words."

"I'm serious," said Kip. "Did you know that President Rutherford B. Hayes was a lifelong supporter of temperance—"

"Of temper *what*?" Ry interjected.

"Temperance," said Kip. "You know—moderation and self-restraint in terms of drinking alcohol."

"Oh, please, Professor Beckelhymen. Kick back and have another brewsky—"

"Seriously, Ry. President Hayes wasn't just merely aligning himself with the Women's Christian Temperance Union, which may have been the politically astute thing to do at the time. He wasn't afraid to be honest about the dangers of alcohol, and not merely on moral grounds. For instance, in an 1878 speech, the President—"

"Dude, dude, dude—don't geek out on me! I drink for the taste. I can quit anytime!"

"Good God," said Kip, as he climbed back into the Powder Puff.

"Forget all about Miss Pigtails!" said Ry, as he pried another slice of pizza out of the box. "We're gonna be killin' it this year. Two playas on the loose!"

Preparing to pull away from the curb, Kip could only stare in astonishment as his wayward friend, all footloose and fancy-free, whiled away the last embers of summer in a hot mess of pizza and beer. Shifting the car into gear, Kip offered a tiny, forlorn wave in his friend's direction. In buoyant response, Ry raised a fresh slice of Honolulu Hawaiian aloft, awkwardly saluting Kip as he made his way back up Augusta Drive.

• • •

As he piloted the Powder Puff back towards the strip mall, Kip watched the dilapidated Fremont environs take on a rusty glow amidst the encroaching summer twilight. Nearing the silty banks of the Sandusky River, he observed as Woody's Drive-In, its sad blight rendered even bleaker by the growing dusk, came into view.

And that's when he saw it: the lime-green VW bug that he knew so well, that selfsame vehicle in which he had ridden with Birdie to the Junior Prom scarcely three months earlier. And the very same car that they had driven up to Adena Point for an after-party that Kip wouldn't soon forget. She had seemed so passionate that night—so *into* him. Well, not *that* passionate. To be honest: it was not like they had gone all the way or anything. At the time, she had seemed so devoted to him—as if they had some kind of future together. Was it all just a sham? Kip wondered to himself. And now, after the terrible scene that had unfolded in front of Domino's earlier that afternoon, prom night felt like three years ago, much less three months.

Leaping out of the Powder Puff, Kip scanned Woody's parking lot for any sign of Birdie before resting his hand on the hood of her VW.

Still warm.

As he made his way to the entrance of the drive-in, Kip girded his courage for the sight that most certainly awaited him inside: Birdie heartlessly sharing an order of barbecue ribs—Woody's mouth-watering specialty—with some unknown, equally callous rival for his beloved's affections. Oh, it promised to be quite a scene all right—

But before he could so much as cross the restaurant's ramshackle threshold, Kip's phone buzzed into life yet again.

"DEFCON 1. PIE'S GROWING COLD!"

As his innate sense of responsibility kicked in, Kip turned on his heel for the Powder Puff, but not before shaking a fist in the direction of the faded brick building.

"To be continued," Kip muttered through gritted teeth.

CHAPTER 3: RELAX, IT'S HOLIDAY INN

Later that day—as the summer sun began to set on that particular Friday evening in Fremont, Ohio—Azza stepped curtly out of a Northwestern Ohio State College utility van. Two brawny student workers followed in her wake, hauling her ancient steamer trunk into the lobby of the aging Holiday Inn on the outskirts of town.

The trio was met at the front desk by Mr. Skakel, the college's septuagenarian Admissions director, who awkwardly presented Azza with a plastic key card.

"Thank you, sir," she replied.

"You'll be in room 19, young lady," he added, gamely tipping his felt hat in her direction, as he prepared to make a hasty exist.

"Room 19," she said to herself, a smile slowly creeping across her face.

"What about it?" Mr. Skakel asked, pausing in his effort to make a clean getaway from the hotel lobby.

"It is nothing, sir," she replied, as she secreted the key card into the folds of her gown. "Now about my meal plan?"

For a moment, Mr. Skakel stared, dumbstruck

"There's your meal plan right over there," said Mr. Skakel, gesturing with his fedora towards the hotel's snack bar. "Just charge it to your room. It's on the house."

"What is 'on the house,' sir?"

"Why, it's your international program, ma'am," Mr. Skakel replied with a twinkle in his eye. "Sleep tight, ya hear, and don't let the bedbugs bite!"

Much later that night, as Azza unpacked her steamer trunk, she tried desperately not to think about Mr. Skakel's warning about the bedbugs. As she glanced about her hotel room, dimly lit by a rack of failing fluorescent lights suspended overhead, she imagined the fearsome insects lying in wait for her, preparing for their bloodthirsty onslaught the moment she succumbed to sleep. But worse yet, she couldn't stop thinking about the untold numbers of people who had previously stayed in room 19—the legions of unmarried couples who had fornicated in her hotel bed in the days and months and years before she ever set her eyes upon the Fremont, Ohio, Holiday Inn that would be her home for the foreseeable future.

But the exhaustion wrought by her transatlantic journey notwithstanding, sleep would not come easily for Azza that night, as she toiled until the wee hours of the morning, scouring the hotel room's every surface, her gleaming hunter green eyes on perpetual lookout for the bedbugs secreting themselves in the darkest corners of her room. But for Azza, the room's most deplorable of horrors were hidden in plain sight. Wearing her fingers to the bone, she poked and prodded at the layers of mildew in the mini-fridge, worked to dislodge the corrosion of meals gone by that lined the interior of the microwave oven, and scrubbed to no avail at the dark rings that stained the bathtub. And while she never saw a single bedbug during her nocturnal onslaught, it didn't alter the fact that the Holiday Inn was a terrible, disgusting place—far worse than her family's apartment back in Bobigny—of that there was little doubt.

And then she remembered the sacred promise that she had made before escaping the *banlieues*. A promise to make contact, in spite of the risks that it seemingly entailed, with the folks back in the ghetto. But a telephone call simply wouldn't do. For one thing, a phone call could be easily traced, possibly even recorded. And besides, a transatlantic telephone conversation, no matter how brief, would be prohibitively expensive. Azza knew perfectly well that she had scarcely little in the way of money for such frivolities, having left almost every last precious American dollar back in the Registrar's office. But there was another way, of course—a fairly covert means for staying in touch, relaying instructions, what have you, that was well known among the Parisian refugee community.

Pulling her old Anova laptop out of her valise, Azza booted up the decrepit machine and logged into the hotel's Wi-Fi. Finding the Middle Eastern chat room took only a few seconds. After googling "Little Tunisia," Azza hastily registered as Anna Karenina, the name she had taken from a book that she and her father adored. They had read it many times together back in their days in the *banlieues*—and much earlier still, when Azza's mother was alive and well back in their homeland.

As her fingers dashed across the keyboard, Azza made her way into the deep recesses of the chat site, where she scanned a list of benign threads ranging from "Alchemy" to "Sufism." Then she found it, the subthread buried deep within the "Halal" chat room devoted to "Lifestyle and Tourism." Just as they had told her, clicking on the "Lifestyle and Tourism" subthread as Anna Karenina opened up a blank page, save for a solitary word, rendered in Arabic, that was awaiting her and her alone:

ابنة جميلة

At first, Azza was stunned, as if she were surprised that the page really existed and that its contents had been waiting there all along for her discovery—hidden, as they were, in plain sight. Smiling quietly to herself at the familiar term of endearment, Azza typed in the first thing that came to mind—this being her new life in America and all—the emoticon that she had seen countless Western kids use on Facebook and social media of nearly every other stripe: :-)

Now he would know, she thought to herself. He would know that she had arrived, that she was safe, that she was good and ready to start this new American life.

Azza checked the time on her old Anova. 2:00 AM. She had made it. *Just in time.*

Without so much as typing another word, she logged out of Little Tunisia and fed the laptop back into the jaws of her valise. But something didn't feel quite right. For the briefest of moments, Azza felt a tiny frisson of fear. She allowed her eyes to take in the contours of the room, scanning this way and that into the haze. But nothing, really, had changed. She was still alone, *entirely* alone among the stillness of the night and the quietude of her thoughts. Nobody had been the wiser for her furtive visit to Little Tunisia.

Almost nobody, that is.

As her eyes adjusted to the darkened room, Azza caught a glimpse of her only witness: a tiny spider perched on the corner of her nightstand. Lying in her bed, she watched as the arachnid shuffled away and disappeared into the gloom.

Everything will be fine, she reasoned with herself. She could be safely content with the knowledge that she was fulfilling her promise to her father.

But it was more than that, of course.

Although room 19's deeply unsanitary nature had scarcely improved after Azza's labors across that long night, she couldn't help settling into a kind of peace for having obeyed her dear, most devoted father's wishes and made the seemingly impossible voyage from the *banlieues* to this inexplicable place. While leaving him back in Paris had left her with a nearly inconsolable sadness, Azza knew in the most solemn place in her heart that he was correct to have sent her away from everything she had ever known—and even if it meant putting his own self in danger.

Oh, Azza understood that he had been right to banish her to this unfamiliar land. She had known this fact even back in the Registrar's office as she endured the stares of those awful Western women. Oversexed and besotted with their freedom and their equality. Could there be anything worse, Azza wondered, than being tried and convicted in the minds of those most unjust women who had no business judging her in this world or the next one?

But Azza stopped herself just as quickly as she had started down that awful path, remembering that it was Allah's will to forgive and that those infidels in the Registrar's office surely knew not what they do.

If only Azza could be charitable and say the same for the Frenchwoman she had encountered as she stepped out of her dear father's old pickup truck yesterday at the curbside near the Orly Airport's departure gates. Taking in the measure of Azza's hijab and what little dark skin her clothing managed to reveal, the woman stepped back, with her smart, fashionable haircut and impeccable outfit in full flower. Gathering all of the fury that she could amass, the Frenchwoman stared at her with the eyes of an unforgiving God and spat in Azza's face, pausing for the briefest of moments to watch the sputum drip, molasses-like, from the younger woman's chin onto the folds of her elaborate scarf.

Taking one last look around her tiny corner of the Holiday Inn before turning out the lights on her first day in America, Azza knew beyond a shadow of a doubt that room 19 had nothing in common with the spacious, brightly-arrayed dormitories that she had seen advertised on the virtual pages of American college websites.

But for Azza, the relative luxury of room 19, or lack thereof, hardly made a fig of difference in the course of her life. And neither, for that matter, did those unknowing women back in the Registrar's office. Allah would forgive them, and so must she.

Azza already knew that Northwestern Ohio State College, such as it was, was easily the best thing to happen to her since she boarded that massive jet at Orly and left Paris behind—along with that hateful Frenchwoman and everyone like her—in another distant hemisphere.

CHAPTER 4: PLASTER OF PARIS

By the time that the end of his shift had mercifully rolled around, Kip had made his final delivery for the evening, a large pepperoni and cheese pizza with a side of buffalo wings—sweet BBQ bacon, extra spicy—to an address on the far side of Stony Prairie. As he made his way back to town after the delivery, Kip gagged at the lingering odor of the hot wings, which commingled inside the tiny hatchback with the countless other smells that comprised Domino's menu of high-octane, garlic-infused cuisine. Gasping for breath, he rolled down the old car's front window in a desperate bid for fresh air. For a red-hot second, he considered driving by Birdie's house over in Ballville to see if her VW was parked out front where it belonged. But the thought of his wayward girlfriend not being home—or, worse yet, parking with some other dude out by the Point—made Kip sick to his stomach. As he steered the Powder Puff in the direction of his mom's place in downtown Fremont, thriving metropolis that it was, his phone spit out yet another text for the umpteenth time that night.

"KIP, COME QUICK. TO THE HAYES. NO TIME TO LOSE!"

It was a disembodied voice that Kip knew all too well. Those telltale monosyllabic bursts of speech.

"Dear God," Kip muttered to himself. "Why, Fletch, why?"

"CAN IT WAIT?" he texted back, glancing at the faded LED clock on the Powder Puff's dashboard. 2:13 AM.

"NO! NO! NO!" came the reply—swift and staccato. And then, like a locomotive following closely on the heels of the previous text:

"CAN'T SAY WHY. NOT SAFE. COME NOW. PLEASE."

Kip groaned in surrender as he made a wide U-turn and drove the

Subaru onto Buckland Avenue, the main thoroughfare linking downtown Fremont with the townlets that dotted its perimeter. With a gentle turn of the steering wheel, he piloted the Powder Puff along tree-lined Hayes Avenue.

And there it was: Spiegel Grove. A majestic estate nestled in a copse of trees. With its ochre-colored brick veneer gently lit by spotlights mounted in a pair of flower beds, the main house was fronted by a wide veranda. Just a few paces away, rising up out of the rolling lawn, sat the foreboding grey edifice of the main exhibition hall.

Even now—in the wee hours of the night as he brought the Powder Puff to a rest in front of the great hall—Kip could feel the makings of a lump in his throat, the pangs of excitement that invariably accompanied his visits to the Rutherford B. Hayes Presidential Library and Museums. For a history geek like Kip, there was simply no denying it: he couldn't get enough of the place.

But Fletch was another story altogether. Kip had tolerated more than his fair share of Fletch's eccentricities since joining the museum's board of governors as a junior member way back in the eighth grade. Truth be told, Kip had been pointedly avoiding Fletch—and Spiegel Grove, for that matter—all summer long. The spring executive session had ended in all-out disaster when Mel Donahue, the chairman of the museum board, threatened a devastating series of budget cuts if Fletch didn't improve the Hayes's fading revenues—*and fast*. With his giant shock of jet black hair moving in rhythm with his rant, Donahue chided Fletch over the museum's microscopic visitor tallies. As it was, the Hayes was only open a few days per week. This last fact really stuck in the craw of Donahue, the owner of the local Ford dealership—as in "Donahue Ford, Driving Fremont Since Y2K!" For the past several meetings, Donahue had harangued poor Fletch over the prodigious visitors' stats from the Clinton Museum down in Little Rock. As if somehow the lingering power of Rutherford B. Hayes was going to compete with the larger-than-life persona of Slick Willie.

For Fletch, Donahue's threats were simply too much to bear. He bitterly resented the chairman for his wildly successful run at Fremont's sketchy local business scene, which had been depressed for nigh on decades. But worse yet, Donahue had somehow mustered the temerity to marry Fletch's ex-wife Emily. For the museum director, it was an unforgivable offense, notwithstanding the fact that the erstwhile couple had been divorced for longer than anyone could remember. While she had a soft spot for her quirky ex-husband, Emily could hardly stomach Fletch's obsequiousness, as he attempted, time and time again, to preen his way back into her good graces. Over the years, he had even been known to show up uninvited at family gatherings, a bouquet of flowers in hand, as if nothing had changed. When Emily had the nerve to go and marry Donahue, those family gatherings weren't so welcoming anymore.

As the spring executive session fell into total disarray, Kip could only watch in horror as Fletch lapsed into hysterics while Donahue, arms stoically crossed in front of him, abruptly called for a vote of no-confidence. When the dust had settled, Fletch's directorship survived thanks to a single vote—Kip's, as fate would have it. But Donahue was not to be deterred, promising to revisit the issue at the winter board meeting. For Fletch, the writing was once and truly on the wall: without a clear financial turnaround at the Hayes, his directorship would be over. But for Kip—history nerd, through and through—the implications were even more dire. Without a steady stream of paying customers, the future of the museum itself might very well be in jeopardy. If they shuttered the Hayes, where would he get his history fix? Surely, not at Woody's Drive-In or Tal's Bait at Tackle. There was plenty of history to be found at those establishments, Kip had to admit, but certainly not of the more sophisticated ilk that he had come to know at the museum. How could the lineage of a greasy spoon or the shifting technology associated with fishing lures really compare to the life and times of the nation's 19th president, the man who single-handedly oversaw the end of the Reconstruction Era?

It couldn't. That's how.

Climbing out of the Powder Puff, Kip loped across the dewy lawn. When he reached the majestic entrance to the exhibition hall that he knew so well, Kip rapped on the vestibule door. As he waited by the entryway, he could see the ghostly image of Marv, the museum's elderly night watchman, materialize as he slowly emerged from the haze of the darkened lobby.

"Well, if it's not President Rutherford B. Hayes, Junior," said Marv, pushing open the door to the vestibule. "How's things at the Kroger?"

"I don't work at the grocery store anymore," said Kip. "I work at Domino's now."

"Kinda funny outfit you're sporting there, sport," Marv replied, laughing at his own joke and gesturing with his nightstick at Kip's red-and-blue Domino's cap and smock.

"Like I said, I work at Domino's these days."

"So ya told me," Marv answered, grunting to himself as Kip made his way past the older man and into the vast expanse of the two-story lobby. "The boss is waiting for you in the back. And he's in a mood, son. Consider yourself warned."

Heading towards the museum's administrative wing, Kip gingerly passed through the darkened expanse of the main exhibit hall, his tennis shoes gently shuffling across the facility's timeworn linoleum floor. After navigating his way among a maze of haphazardly arranged exhibits, Kip found himself at the entrance to the Hayes Café, and just beyond, the building's administrative nerve center. But in truth, the Hayes Café was a café in name only, given that it consisted of a pair of old, mostly empty vending machines. By the same token, describing the administrative wing as any kind of nerve center would also be an exercise in exaggeration, given its current occupant.

When he finally arrived at Fletch's sad and disheveled office, Kip knew that Marv had been right to warn him. Fletch was in a mood all right, sitting alone in front of a vintage rolltop desk and sulking among the clutter.

"Where's the fire?" said Kip, interrupting the silence. With his giant horn-rimmed glasses perched upon his nose, Fletch glanced up at the museum's junior board member, the older man's moon face and preternaturally bald head taking on an eerie glow in the poorly lit room.

"Not here!" Fletch barked, gesturing vaguely towards the ceiling, as if to suggest that the Hayes was infested with an elaborate scheme of bugging devices and hidden cameras.

"Really?" Kip answered. "Is this necessary—"

But before he could so much as finish his sentence, diminutive Fletch barreled past Kip in the direction of the vending machines, where the rotund older man waited for him in the darkened hallway, panting as he attempted to catch his breath.

"For crying out loud," Fletch seethed, "how many times have I told you that the walls have ears? You know that the board is looking for just about any doggone reason to defund me—"

"You mean defund the museum," said Kip.

"I *am* the museum! And you outta know that by now. If there's no Fletcher P. Clawson, BA, MA, at the helm, then what's the point of having Kip Beckelhymer as a junior member of the museum board?"

"Sometimes, you sound just like a talking résumé," said Kip, already exasperated with the older man's demeanor.

"Be that as it may," said Fletch, scanning up and down the hallway for any sign of ne'er-do-wells, "but we're both clean out of luck if the Hayes goes out of business."

"That sounds like a stretch to me," said Kip. "Sure, I'd miss the museum dearly if it closed down, but as you already know, I plan to go away to college next year and never set foot in Fremont again."

"Oh, Kip—"

"But more importantly, the museum isn't going out of business in the first place. It's just about the only reason people even bother coming to Fremont—well, that and the college. Sure, they may fire you, but the Hayes will go on just fine—"

"Oh, yeah?" Fletch hissed. "Whaddya think's gonna go down when they find out that the First Lady's pear has gone missing?"

"The *what?*"

"Oh, Kippers. You know what I'm talking about!"

He didn't.

"Mrs. Hayes's plaster of Paris pear—a reverential gift from the French government—is *gone,*" he moaned.

At this point, Fletch was actually pulling at his scalp, as if he were trying to rip out his hair. But there was no hair to rip out, so it looked, for all intents and purposes, like he was trying to violently massage his shiny forehead. Worse yet, he seemed as though he were on the verge of tears.

"Where was it?" Kip asked, ignoring Fletch's gesticulations.

"In the main exhibit hall," he sighed. "Near the International Achievements display."

"Right," Kip answered, trying desperately to recall the International Achievements exhibit. "Is that the one with all the anti-Hayes political cartoons associated with the Chinese Exclusion Act of 1879—the one that led to his near-impeachment by the Democrats?"

"Well, yeah," Fletch admitted. "But he was cornered by the Dems. You know that, Kip. Sometimes, I can't tell whether your allegiances to the President are very firm. Try to show some fortitude, will ya? You're a leading Hayes scholar, for God's sakes."

"I'm a junior scholar at best," said Kip, correcting him. "So when did the pear go missing?"

"Oh, that's just the worst part, Kip."

"How's that?"

"I don't have the foggiest idea."

"You *what?*"

"Could have been today or six months ago. I couldn't tell you when the pear disappeared from the premises."

"But what about the cameras?" said Kip. "Just rewind the tape or whatever outdated format you use and catch the culprit in the act."

"Oh, the cameras? They don't work."

"Then what are we doing, hiding out here in the hallway?"

"Just 'cause the cameras are out doesn't mean that the Hayes isn't bugged."

"But why are they out?"

"I had to save money somewhere, Kip. Whaddya think pays my salary? Or yours—"

"I'm a volunteer. The Hayes hasn't so much as provided me with vending machine money," Kip replied. "So the pear is gone. So *what?*"

"There's an audit coming. There's your *so what*. Oh, Kip, all of my dreams for the museum are going up in smoke. You know that I'm on the verge of starting my Young Docents program, which the townspeople are just going to *love.* And when that pear doesn't show up in the inventory, I'm as good as done. That dreadful car salesman will see to it for sure. As far as the museum board goes, you're the only friendly vote I've got. The others will see that my goose is good and cooked, and we both know it."

"Should we call Marv over?" said Kip, following Fletch into the exhibit hall. "We might need a professional on this case."

"Are you bent on destroying me, Kip? Marv is one of Donahue's confederates. They'd sooner join forces and run me out of town on a rail if it's up to them."

"Oh, they're just going to fire you, Fletch. Nothing so barbaric as running you out of town on a rail." And then just as suddenly, Kip's annoyance transformed into full-on geek mode. "Did you know that back in President Hayes's day townspeople would sometimes tar and feather their victims in addition to strapping them onto a rail and dumping them at the city limits?"

"You gotta help me, Kip!" Fletch exclaimed, grabbing him by the neck of his Domino's smock. As Kip looked on, the older man began to convulse right there in the hallway, before breaking into a coughing fit.

"Are you seeing a doctor about that?" Kip asked.

"I'm seeing a whole platoon of them, actually," Fletch replied, still struggling to catch his breath. "They've been running a battery of tests, hooking me up to all sorts of devices. And they tell me I've gotta start exercising—"

"Oh, exercising is the worst," said Kip.

"Tell me about it," Fletch answered, scratching at the plastic blue band around his wrist. "Try exercising in my weight class for a while. It's brutal, Kippers, just brutal. But listen up, pal: if we don't find that pear—and *soon*—then it's . . . it's curtains for me. Then Emily won't ever have me back," he added, his face cast downward in unmitigated shame.

For the first time during that long strange night, Kip felt truly sorry for the older man. To be perfectly truthful, Kip had to admit that Fletch had devolved into a figure of fun as much as a genuine friend to him.

But given the events of the previous afternoon, Kip knew a thing or two about lost love. And although he was pretty sure that Emily would hardly throw over the owner of Donahue Ford and Fremont's reigning favorite son to make time with forlorn Fletch, he wasn't going to be the one to extinguish the museum director's dreams. No, Kip wouldn't have a hand in casting Fletch's already miserable fate into the permanence of concrete.

With nothing left to do but help a brother Hayesian out, Kip blindly ran his hands along the walls of the exhibit hall until he happened upon the master light switch, powered up the fluorescent fixtures as they blinked and buzzed overhead, and started looking for the First Lady's pear.

CHAPTER 5: CHEMISTRY 101

Azza awakened with a start, straining her eyes to take in the unfamiliar surroundings of room 19. Kicking off the bedclothes, she anxiously studied her arms and legs for any telltale bedbug bites. But thankfully, she had made it through a second long night as a guest in the Holiday Inn without any evidence of infestation. Not so much as a single welt was visible. *And no itching either.* A hasty internet search the day before had informed her that bedbug bites are accompanied by red rashes and a malingering itchy sensation. But even now, the very act of thinking about itching sent phantom tingles up and down her willowy limbs. She shivered in disgust at the thought of all of those tiny parasites nibbling at her skin and raging to ferret out and suckle upon her blood. As her body shuddered and quaked, she leapt out of bed with a start, staring back at the dent that she had left in the mattress for signs of any of the loathsome creatures scurrying for cover. But there weren't any, of course.

It was all in her head.

Making her way into the cramped hotel bathroom, Azza stood before the miniscule sink and began performing the sacred *wudzu*, her morning ablution. Clad in her blanched white nightshirt, she carefully cleansed her hands, washing them up to the wrist with warm water. After brushing her teeth, she turned to her nose, gently dabbing her nostrils with water before cleansing her face, which she dabbed with the hotel's bleached white washcloth. Then she rinsed off her arms in the warm water, finally moving to her feet, which she ministered to by dangling them under the stainless steel tap at the end of the bathtub, with its inexorable stains glaring up at her.

Having completed her *wudzu*, Azza nervously dressed for her first day of classes at Northwestern Ohio State. All the while, she found herself glancing at the stack of textbooks on her bureau. Yesterday, she had spent much of her long lazy first Sunday in Fremont huddled in her room and thumbing through her massive *General Chemistry* book, which was now overbrimming with heavily annotated yellow sticky notes bulging from its voluminous pages. For Azza, it had been a revelation. To think that almost the entirety of the human body—some 96 percent of every person's mass—is made up of just four elements: oxygen, carbon, hydrogen, and nitrogen, and mostly in the form of water at that. That everyone who has ever lived has consisted of the very same stuff. Just imagine it!

For Azza, reading the textbook felt like time-traveling into her future dream life as a chemical engineer, a working, productive citizen who would enjoy the privilege of thinking about the mysteries of the universe every single day. It was as if she were on the precipice of an exhilarating new adventure. But at the same time, perusing *General Chemistry* had left her with a deep sense of apprehension. As if being able to pass Chemistry 101 would be a litmus test—*pun surely intended!*—on her plans for a future that didn't include the *banlieues*. Meanwhile, her *Introduction to Cultural Anthropology* sat idly by, still sealed up tightly, untouched in its shrink-wrap cocoon.

With her ensemble nearly complete, Azza carefully removed the magazine that she had secreted away in her battered valise. Flipping through the pages of *Aquila Style*, she leafed through articles with titles like "Why McDonald's Is Not Halal," "My Hijab, My Choice," and "The World's Most Eligible Muslim Royals" before settling on a dog-eared page headlined as "The College Girl Look." A young Muslim woman in a hip denim jacket peered out from the pages of *Aquila*, her stylish pea-green hijab fashionably cascading in billowy folds below her neckline. With the magazine balanced in her lap, Azza stared intently into the mirror above the bureau and began arranging her purple and peach headscarf about her face like the model in *Aquila*. After several attempts to get the folds of the headscarf just right, she succeeded in a fairly precise imitation of the model's look, save for the denim jacket, of course. Azza smiled back at her reflection in the mirror. As if to say, "That's right. I'm a college girl now!"

With her formal wear set for the day, Azza unrolled her prayer rug. Not so different from the *mihrab* that you can see in mosques on any given day the world over, Azza's prayer rug featured a niche at one end, the frayed fabric threadlings that unfailingly guide the worshipper towards Mecca. Arrayed upon a field of burgundy, the cloth depicted a series of mosque lamps representing the Verse of Light from the Qur'an, along with decorative pitchers symbolizing the place of cleanliness in the sacrament of prayer.

With her prayer rug splayed out before her, Azza directed her body eastwards, in the tradition of *Qibla* towards the holy shrine of Mecca, to say *Salat al-Fajr,* the morning prayer. Kneeling upon the rug, she began to recite the *Fajr,* her voice breaking the long silence that had descended upon the room since she had said *Salat al-Lail* late Sunday night.

"Allahu Akbar," she sang out into the stillness of the tiny room. "Subhanaka allahumma—"

But just as suddenly as Azza had begun reciting the *Fajr,* the door to room 19 sprang open with a start, revealing a startled Latina housekeeper with a mountain of fresh linens and towels piled high in her arms.

For a moment, Azza stared blankly at the housekeeper, framed by the doorway in her bewilderment, her silver crucifix dangling about her neck. But slowly her look of puzzlement transformed into a gentle, knowing smile.

"*Excusa,*" the housekeeper muttered, gently backing into the hallway and easing the door closed behind her in the same motion.

• • •

Azza stood on the faded, grey macadam in front of the Holiday Inn, head held up high as she cradled her textbooks in the warmth of the morning sun. As the white Northwestern Ohio State College utility van pulled up beside her on the streetscape, Azza waited several moments before the driver, old Mr. Skakel, put the vehicle in park and came around to greet her.

"Good morning, Ms. Amari," he said, doffing his felt hat as he slid open the back-seat door for her.

For her part, Azza nodded as she settled into the utility van and Mr. Skakel shut the door behind her.

"It's gonna be a busy day at the college," said the Admissions director, clearing his throat. "Nothing like the first day of school, I always say."

As Mr. Skakel steered the utility van across Fremont, Azza took in the landscape of her new hometown, a collection of tiny, clapboard homes, interspersed with steepled ivory-colored churches, and schoolhouses. Children trudging along the sidewalks, burdened by an assortment of brightly arrayed backpacks as they made their way to school. There were plenty of shacks, too, along with ramshackle restaurants and storefronts that had clearly seen better days. But Azza was charmed just the same. To her, it looked just like she imagined a small town would.

For Azza, Fremont looked exactly like America.

As the van veered ever closer to the college, the neighborhoods were increasingly pocked by mature homes with well-kempt lawns, an unbroken series of green spaces, save for the strip shopping center across the street, the one with the pizza delivery joint and the drug store.

Mr. Skakel finally brought the utility van to a stop in front of the Registrar's office, the very same place where Azza had alighted only a few days earlier. But the entire campus had been transformed, teeming as it was with older versions of the children that she had seen outside of the schoolhouse. With their backpacks and messenger bags slung across their shoulders, the commuter students made their way from the parking lots that marked the perimeter of Northwestern Ohio State College to the clutch of classroom buildings at the center of the campus. For the most part, the male students were dressed in cargo shorts and printed tees, dark socks and athletic shoes, while the women revealed a much wider array of fashion choices, ranging from the casual—yoga pants and flip-flops—to jerseys and jeans, and, for the more reverential among them, this being the first day of school and all, an assortment of summer dresses and pantsuits.

As Mr. Skakel slid open the door, Azza stepped into the brave new world of her freshman year as an honest-to-goodness coed on U.S. soil. And in the Heartland, no less. Could there be anything more authentically American than this? she wondered to herself.

"Do you have your schedule?" Mr. Skakel inquired, falling into a bracing coughing fit as he eased the utility van door shut behind her. After he caught his breath, Azza handed him the crumpled paper that old Agnes had given her during her very first visit to the Registrar's office. After studying it intently, the Admissions director shaded his eyes and pointed towards a limestone building on the far side of the campus.

"That there's Faraday Hall," he told her. "Your Chemistry course meets there on Mondays, Wednesdays, and Fridays. Anthropology is there too, and it looks like you'll be attending ESL and History on Tuesdays and Thursday over in Thayer Hall. It's just across the way—the ivy-covered building on the other side of the quad."

"ESL, sir?" Azza asked.

"It's your freshman English class. English as a Second Language. It's required for all foreign students."

"I am not freshman, sir. I am freshwoman."

"Yes, but—"

"And as you can tell, sir, my English is perfectly fine—"

"May-be," he answered, drawing out the syllables, "but it's still your second language, right?"

"In truth, sir, English is my third language. I learned Arabic as a child, French as a teenager in the *banlieues*, and English only after that, when my dear father commanded that I would pursue my studies in America. That I would become a chemical engineer and a citizen of the world."

"Well, that sounds mighty lofty!" said Mr. Skakel, chuckling as he tried in vain to stave off yet another coughing fit. "I'm not sure how Fremont factors into that particular equation, but it's certainly part of the world. There's no denying that."

"Please explain, sir," said Azza, "why I must enroll in this ESL, this Anthropology, and this History when I want to take my baccalaureate degree in chemical engineering."

"Those are your general education courses, Ms. Amari," he replied. "You've got to complete your gen-eds before you can start your major. That's how it works."

"But I want to be chemical engineer," Azza protested, "not anthropologist or historian. Or whatever ESL does for a career."

"You're not the first freshman to complain about gen-eds," said Mr. Skakel, gently laughing to himself. Azza wondered, briefly, if he were poking fun at her expense. "Those courses are part of your common body of knowledge, Ms. Amari. *That's* how you become a genuine citizen of the world," he added. "Now you have a great semester, you hear!"

As Mr. Skakel tipped his felt hat and climbed back into the utility van, Azza loitered near the Registrar's office for a moment, still not convinced about why she needed these gen-ed courses when the only common body of knowledge that she really wanted related directly to graduating and becoming a chemical engineer. But that would have to wait for now.

With a shrug, she began walking across the busy campus in the direction of Faraday Hall. As she lugged her textbooks across the quad, with the stars and stripes of the American flag reigning high atop a silvery pole in a center parklet, Azza studied her classmates as they loped around her. Every last one of them seemed to be white, blond mostly, with a few brunettes thrown in for good measure.

Where is diversity? she wondered to herself as she walked among the indifferent college students. To a person, almost every one of them was busying themselves with a smartphone, their eyes glued intently to the screen as their thumbs beat a staccato drumbeat across the tiny screens, a pair of earbuds invariably nestled among their downy hair.

As she inched ever closer to the stately entrance to Faraday Hall, Azza happened upon an orange wooden kiosk papered with flyers. The kiosk teemed with advertisements, most of them announcing PART

TIME JOBS, GOOD PAY. Or TAILGATE PARTY AT OSU THIS SATURDAY! GET TURNT, Y'ALL! Then there were ads trumpeting ROOMMATE WANTED, M OR F, ALL BILLS PAID, and, even stranger still, 21 PILOTS CONCERT TIX! CLEVELAND ROCKS!

What is "21 pilots"? she wondered to herself as she made her way up the steps to Faraday Hall. And what is this "turnt," and why do you want to get it?

As Azza pushed open the massive metal door to the building, she ran headlong into another student, his earbuds popping out of his ears from the force of the collision. A scraggly kid with matted blond hair, a backpack dangling from his shoulder, and a pink skateboard clutched in his arms, he made a show of looking her up and down.

"Seriously?" he said, with a scowl burrowing across his face.

Azza could only stand there and watch as he walked brusquely away from her in disgust, eventually disappearing into the swarm of students milling about the quad. She stood there, crestfallen and arrayed in her College Girl Look.

As she collected herself in front of Faraday Hall, Azza reflexively tugged at the brilliant folds of cloth billowing beneath her chin. And then, without so much as another thought, she marched into the building in search of her Chemistry classroom.

CHAPTER 6:
BYE BYE BIRDIE

Lost in his annual pre-school year stupor, Kip stared at his breakfast cereal, soggy and besotted with milk. As he desperately attempted to shake the cobwebs of sleeplessness out of his system, he could hear the intermittent sounds of his mother shuffling about upstairs, rushing to get ready for the new academic year at Northwestern Ohio State. A cacophony of drawers, opening and closing, hangers jostling about on closet rods. Meanwhile, Kip's brown-bag lunch already waited for him on the kitchen counter, itself a conspicuous omen for the dawning of his senior year, which, as he knew all too well, was set to begin in a little under 45 minutes. In truth, he was less concerned about navigating yet another year in the doldrums of high school and more anxious about running into Birdie, given their unsettling Friday afternoon encounter at Domino's. And worse yet, the mysterious appearance of her VW outside of Woody's Drive-In. What, pray tell, was she doing there? And who was she there *for*?

For his part, Kip had been explicitly avoiding any Birdie interactions throughout the weekend. She had already texted him numerous times, but those were fairly easy to ignore. The only near miss occurred late Saturday night, when Birdie tried his cell phone, and, chicken that Kip was, he allowed the call to go straight to voicemail. Her message, which he had replayed upwards of a dozen times since she recorded it, was simple and straight to the point: "We need to talk," she said, her acid tone reminding Kip of the inexplicable emotional indifference that had polluted his relationship with her since Friday afternoon. Or, more accurately, the sorry state of Birdie's current feelings about him.

In an effort to banish his wayward girlfriend from his mind, if only temporarily, Kip had spent the better part of Sunday with Fletch rummaging through the Hayes storeroom, a mass of poorly organized physical artifacts and presidential papers. Fletch felt like it was the perfect day for a Marv-less going over of the museum's assorted contents—Sunday being the security guard's day off and all. Together, Kip and Fletch had already given the wares in the exhibit hall a thorough inspection—as if the First Lady's pear had somehow been obscured by the well-preserved fabrics of the First Family Wardrobe exhibit or, more elaborately still, President Hayes's extravagant model train set. Kip even went to the trouble of looking inside each and every one of the miniature buildings on the massive Victorian layout, which featured nine separate trains making a circuit around a small-scale re-creation of downtown Fremont as a tony burg with a bright future.

As Kip made the short drive home on Sunday night, he couldn't help thinking about the disconcerting image of the train set, which had proven to be the most popular exhibit—*by a wide margin*—in the long history of the Hayes. With many of the same buildings still in existence—and having fallen into varying degrees of dilapidation and disrepair—he was struck by the pristine version of the miniature, old-timey Fremont in contrast with its faded, twenty-first-century reality. Was Fletch's presentation of the exhibit somehow feeding into a larger, civic-wide disease of wishful thinking? Did the townspeople really believe that the train set, with its overwrought depiction of Fremont in a decidedly different and much more prosperous era, could somehow make them forget about their collective downtrodden present?

Failing to ferret out the pear among the detritus of the enormous storeroom had left Fletch exhausted and Kip crestfallen. For his part, Fletch was almost surely headed for the unemployment heap. Mel Donahue would see to that. And the pear?—well, the pear was well on its way to being lost to the great dustbin of history. Fletch had no memory of the sculpture other than seeing the thing ensconced in its remote place in the exhibit hall. And Kip couldn't remember ever seeing the pear at the Hayes *at all*. The only concrete evidence of its existence was a single entry in the museum's inventory.

By Monday morning, as Kip hovered precariously over his morning cereal, he had committed the description of the missing artifact to memory. In point of fact, he had recited it to Fletch so many times during their misbegotten Sunday treasure hunt that he knew it cold, word for word. Heck, if the 57-word sketch were included on the SATs, which he was feverishly studying to retake in October, Kip would surely achieve a perfect score. "Goodbye, Northwestern Ohio State. Hello, Princeton," he thought to himself as the familiar words of the description roiled around in his brain:

> 1960.3.91. Plaster of Paris figurine of a European pear with a 24-carat gold stem; a gift to Lucy Hayes from Patrice de MacMahon, President of the Third Republic of France, 1 April 1879; presented to President Rutherford B. Hayes and the First Lady by Ferdinand de Lesseps; "BONHEUR" is carved into the base; W-3.75 D-3.75 H-5.75 in.

"Bonheur," Kip said aloud to himself as his mother hurried into the kitchen. "WTF," he muttered.

"Bonheur?" said Mrs. Beckelhymer. "What does that mean? Is it French?"

"It's nothing," Kip replied. "Just something from the Hayes."

"Fletch Clawson should thank his lucky stars that you joined the museum board. If you didn't have a passing interest in history—"

"It's more than just a passing interest," said Kip, interrupting her. "You make it sound like it's some kind of fad with me."

"You know what I mean," his mom replied. "Let's hurry things up now. I need to get to the Registrar's office as soon as possible. It's the first day of classes, and Dr. Smyth will be pulling out his hair. Or what's left of it. There's nothing like the chaos of a new school year. Speaking of which—"

"I know, Mom," said Kip, standing up from the kitchen table.

"Your senior year, monkey!" Mrs. Beckelhymer exclaimed, as she pulled her son into her warm embrace. For his part, Kip tried to squirm his way out of her arms, grimacing in futility as he attempted to pull away.

"Go ahead," she said. "Frown all you want. But this is a big day for me, too. And I know that your father, if he were here—"

"Not today, okay Mom?" Kip asked, turning to face her. "Let's not go there today."

And with that, he strode out of the kitchen, his mother staring after him, thunderstruck.

• • •

Stepping out of the Powder Puff, Kip studied his classmates as they ambled towards the entrance to Fremont High School, a nondescript cinder-block structure on the northern edge of town. Trudging along like wayward snails, they seemed even less enthused than Kip to start the new school year.

"Dude, this blows," said Ry, sidling up beside him in the parking lot, still wearing the green walking shorts from Friday night.

"Don't you ever do a wash?" Kip asked, staring at his friend in disbelief.

"My mom's out of town," said Ry. "She doesn't get back from Aruba until Thursday."

"DIY, Ry."

"Huh?" he said, turning to face Kip.

"There are YouTube videos that can teach you how to do a wash in, like, three minutes flat. Probably even give you detergent suggestions and everything. The whole nine yards."

"Thanks for the life lesson, dude," Ry said with a smirk. "I'll make a mental note. Squirrel it away in my hope chest."

"Don't be a smartass," said Kip, as they fell into step with the defeated throng heading into school.

"Hold up, bro. Oh, fork me!"

"What?—"

"Birdie at 12 o'clock!"

"At 12 o'clock—*really*? Who even talks that way? You play way too much Call of Duty—"

"Dude, she's, like, 30 yards in front of us!"

"You're delusional. I don't see her—"

"The pigtails, asshat! They're a dead giveaway. And, holy moly—she's not alone!"

"*Holy moly*?"

"Don't shoot the messenger, Beckelhymen!"

"Wait a minute," said Kip, straining his eyes. "I see her now. Dang, that's Birdie all right."

And there she was: Kip's estranged girlfriend walking towards the boring, ho-hum entrance to Fremont High, with nary a care in the world. And hand-in-hand with some other guy, his backpack slung across his shoulder like everybody else.

"Who is—"

"Never seen him before," said Ry, interrupting him. "And I know *everyone* in this Godforsaken school. But hey—"

"But hey, *what*?"

"Now that you've seen the light, you can get your groove on. Start playing the field. Finally have some real fun around here before you go off to Yale or whatever."

"Maybe it's not even her—"

"Now who's being delusional?" said Ry, pulling a crumpled paper out of the pockets of his walking shorts. "What's your first class?"

"Are you serious?" Kip asked.

"I'm moved on. Miss Pigtails bores me. She's ancient history, dude. Yesterday's news. So back to our regularly scheduled programming: What. Is. Your. First. Class?"

"AP English," Kip sighed.

"Swell. Mine's Health and Wellness. See you at lunch!"

And with that, Ry strolled briskly towards the entrance, leaving Kip to contemplate his uncertain future alone.

• • •

As it happened, Kip didn't have to wait very long. When he arrived at Miss Pearson's first period AP English course, Kip made his way to a desk in the far corner of the classroom—and as far away from Miss Pearson, a homely spinster who invariably smelled of mothballs, as possible. This semester, the class would be reading *Who's Afraid of Virginia Woolf?* Knowing Miss Pearson's reputation for spraying spittle on the students in the first few rows as she read from the assigned books, Kip knew better than to make himself an easy target for all that saliva when his teacher inevitably read crazy old Martha's lines aloud for the class. No, he could most certainly do without a spit bath from Miss Mothballs.

Just seconds before the bell rang, Kip observed Birdie as she flew into the classroom, her pigtails dangling to and fro, and took a seat in the first row—the desk closest to the door and well within Miss Pearson's salivary radius. As their teacher delivered a point-by-point enumeration of the syllabus, Kip could only stare in wonder at Birdie who seemed, well, normal. Hunched over her desk and staring intently at the syllabus in front of her, Birdie would pause occasionally to toy with one of her pigtails or scratch the side of her face with the eraser tip of the pencil that she clutched in her left hand. But mostly, she was just being Birdie—no different from the same winsome girl who had cuddled with SpongeBob SquarePants in the front seat of the Powder Puff on a carefree summer's day that now felt like a million years ago.

When the bell rang, Kip leapt up from his desk, intending to corral Birdie on her way to second period. But he never had a chance. Just as quickly, Birdie gathered up her things and bolted for the door as Kip tried to negotiate his way through the mass of other students trying to put Miss Pearson's AP English class behind them.

By the time that Kip alighted in the lunchroom, he had passed through Physics and AP History without any further Birdie sightings, and a quick scan around the cavernous high school cafeteria suggested that nothing was imminent. There were simply no pigtails in evidence.

For a moment, Kip stood below the giant "Welcome back, Little Giants!" banner hanging above the lunchroom, still hoping to catch a glimpse of his wayward girlfriend.

"Dude, you are so pathetic," said Ry, who had quietly pulled up alongside of him. "If you start to cry right here in the cafeteria, we are officially no longer friends. Come on, let's get in line. It's pizza day!"

"I brought my lunch," said Kip, unzipping his backpack and reaching into it, where he found . . . *nothing*. "Oh, man. I must've left it at home—"

"Whatever, Beckelhymen. Pizza's on me," said Ry, holding up his cafeteria card. "How was AP English?" he asked, as they fell into line.

"Birdie was there."

"Oh, dude. Enough already."

"Fine," said Kip. "How was Health and Wellness?"

"Off to a slow start. But I expect a quick turnaround. Rumor has it that we'll be talking about the reproductive system this semester."

"Very nice," said Kip, as a hair-netted cafeteria worker placed a rectangular slice of sausage pizza on his lunch tray.

"That's no Honolulu Hawaiian," said Ry, glaring at the pasty-looking slice of pizza laying placidly on his tray. With its tiny hair-like sausage morsels peeking out of a layer of dried mozzarella cheese, the pizza rested against a fruit cup and a helping of canned green peas.

As they neared the end of the lunch line, Kip and Ry paused to take in the aroma of freshly baked brownies wafting among the stainless-steel chafing dishes.

"Eff the pizza," said Ry, making an exaggerated gesture of inhaling the chocolaty scent that engulfed the room. "It smells like Willy Wonka's dick in here!" he exclaimed, laughing aloud at his own joke.

As they reached the end of the line, the white-coated cashier shook her head in disgust as she swiped his card.

When they finally settled into a table in the corner of the cafeteria, Ry abruptly grabbed his brownie and pushed his tray aside.

"So much for Health and Wellness," said Kip, still looking around the lunchroom in a futile search for Birdie.

"So which is it?" said Ry, dispatching with his brownie in two economical bites. "Do you want to find Miss Pigtails and keep your splendid love connection going? Or are you trying to avoid her altogether?"

"A little bit of both, I guess," Kip replied. "And what do you mean by 'splendid love connection'?"

"I was being sarcastic, dude. You're a freakin' mess, you know. I wasn't going to tell you about it, but given the sorry state you're in—"

"Tell me about *what*?"

"That Nate saw the Birdwoman in AP Physics in third period," said Ry, stealthily reaching for Kip's untouched brownie.

"Nate's a jerk."

"Nate's the jerk who's banged at least two members of the cheerleading squad," said Ry, "which makes him a certified, grade-A playa in my book. Hey, if you don't want my intel—"

"Come on, Ry, you gotta tell me. I didn't qualify for AP Physics."

"Dude, you're, like, in the top 10. How's that even possible?"

"You know I'm not sciency."

"Whatever," said Ry, taking a bite from Kip's brownie. "Anyways, Nate knows this other dude—the one that we saw this morning. Apparently, he lives one street over from me. On Pebble Beach."

"Oh, good God."

"I know, dude. It sounded stupid coming out of my mouth. But anyways, this new kid just moved here from, like, Connecticut or some shit."

"And?"

"That's all I've got," said Ry, neatly finishing off Kip's brownie and wiping his mouth. "Are you gonna eat your pizza?"

• • •

When the long first day of school finally came to its merciful close, Kip and Ry joined the swarm of their classmates heading back to the parking lot.

"Did you ever notice how much faster everyone moves at the end of the school day?" Ry asked.

"I've figured it out," said Kip, ignoring him as they walked in the direction of the Powder Puff. "If I can find a way to avoid Birdie until June, which is only, like, 275 more days, then we can make it through senior year as a couple."

"Dude, that's not how it works," said Ry, as they stepped up to the Subaru.

And that's when they saw her: Birdie, sitting cross-legged on the pavement next to the Powder Puff's rear wheel-well. Her forehead was taut with concentration as she busied herself with her phone, ripping off one text after another as her thumbs danced across the screen.

"Well, if it's not Miss Pigtails," said Ry, holding his chin up high.

"Hey, Ryan," she replied, standing up to join them beside the car. "How's it going?"

"Bitchin'," said Ry.

"Bitchin'?" said Kip, giving him a sidelong glance.

"So I heard you're seeing what's-his-name over on Pebble Beach," said Ry. "Nice area."

"Isn't that your neighborhood, too?" Birdie asked. "And his name is Todd. He just moved here from Boston."

"So is that your problem with me?" said Kip. "Is it 'cause this new guy lives by the country club, and I'm stuck downtown? If you want me to take you to Woody's for cheese fries, I can hook you up. It's not like it's the Four Seasons—"

"As in winter, spring, summer, fall?" Ry asked, with a quizzical look plastered across his face.

"You know I'm on a tight budget," Kip pleaded, as Birdie stared at the pavement. He couldn't help noticing the gold promise ring, which now encircled the ring finger of her right hand.

"You're a pizza delivery boy," she answered, turning the gold band over and over with her free hand.

"My mom's a single parent, for God's sakes. *You know that.* And besides, things aren't so bad. I took you to Six Flags!"

"Dude, don't give her the satisfaction," said Ry. "Wait," he added. "Isn't your dad a cop, Birdie? When did you get all blue-blood and shit?"

Before she could respond, Kip's phone buzzed into life with an incoming text.

"It's my mom," he said, glancing at the screen and then, pointedly, at Birdie. "I gotta go."

"What's up?" Kip asked, climbing out of the Powder Puff in front of the Registrar's office. His mother sat nearby, sipping from a cup of coffee and sitting on a wooden bench with Dr. Smyth, who was rubbing his scalp and squinting his eyes in the afternoon sun.

"Master Beckelhymer," Dr. Smyth cried out, smiling up at Kip.

"Dr. Smyth," said Kip, reaching down to shake hands with the Registrar. "You know I'm not 12 years old anymore, right?"

"Nonsense," the older man answered. "You'll always be Master Beckelhymer to me."

"Thanks for coming over to the campus, Kip," said his mom. "I . . . I'm sorry about what I said this morning. But things are looking up, okay? Dr. Smyth has an opportunity for you."

"Yes, let's get down to business, shall we?" said Dr. Smyth, smiling warmly at Mrs. Beckelhymer. Standing up from the bench, he pointed towards the Powder Puff, its rusted-out carcass lying in wait in front of the Registrar's office. "How well does that thing run?"

"It's no Audi, if that's what you're asking," said Kip. "But it's roadworthy."

"Kip, your mum and I have found ourselves in a bit of a predicament," Dr. Smyth continued. "It seems Mr. Skakel has had a heart attack—"

"The old guy from Admissions?" Kip asked.

"Yes, Master Beckelhymer, Mr. Skakel is the old guy from Admissions," said Dr. Smyth. "And he's in a bad way. It's doubtful that he'll be returning to the college. But you see, he was driving one of our students to school—"

"And we need you to take over for him," Kip's mother interrupted. "Dr. Smyth will pay you."

"Oh, absolutely," said Dr. Smyth. "I'm thinking $250 per week to give the student a lift back and forth from the Holiday Inn out by the Turnpike. What say you, Master Beckelhymer?"

"But we don't have that kind of funding," Kip's mom protested.

"Sure we do," said Dr. Smyth. "I fired Harley Vinson. It will come out of his fee."

"What's a Harley Vinson?" Kip asked.

"The con man who secured an international student for a commuter college without dormitories or meal plans," said Mrs. Beckelhymer.

"That's kinda funny," Kip replied.

"It surely is," said Dr. Smyth, who was pointedly not laughing. "So are you in, Master Beckelhymer?"

As Kip piloted the Powder Puff away from the campus, he was absolutely giddy, smiling from ear to ear at his unexpected good fortune. $250 a week meant no more Domino's. He was in the money now—*take that, Birdie*! But just as suddenly, he realized that, in truth, he had nothing to smile about. After all, Birdie had ditched him back in the school parking lot. In broad daylight, no less—and right in front of Ry.

But then Kip found himself smiling yet again. She hadn't *actually* broken up with him, if you really thought about it. Nobody had said anything about breaking up—and certainly not Kip.

Just 275 more Birdie-free days to go, he thought to himself. Then she can run off with Mr. Pebble Beach all she wants.

CHAPTER 7: DRIVING MISS ISLAM

Come Tuesday morning, as the sunlight cut through the gauzy-thin curtains of room 19 at the Holiday Inn, Azza jerked awake with a start. Her *General Chemistry* book lay splayed open across her chest. Squinting through the semi-darkness, she caught sight of the microwave oven's eerie green display.

6:15 AM. *There was still plenty of time.*

Struggling to free herself from beneath the weight of the massive textbook, Azza tiptoed across the cold linoleum floor to her desk, where the Anova laptop rested in its dormancy. Firing up the old laptop, she logged into Little Tunisia. And—*voilà!*—she had transformed into Anna Karenina yet again. With a few stray keystrokes, she navigated her way back into the "Lifestyle and Tourism" subthread, where the latest message awaited her:

كل شيء على ما يرام

She absolutely beamed at the sight of the words, basking in the comfort of the elegantly arrayed Arabic script. Now it was she—*er, Anna Karenina*—who knew that her correspondent, her dear father, was safe, too. That she—that Azza/Anna—was not the only one who had made it through another day alive in a hostile territory. This time, she selected a very different emoticon to register her feelings. It was the same, lump-in-the-back-of-your-throat emoticon that she had seen on the Facebook pages of the American kids, the most jubilant, the most revered "tears of happiness": :'-)

• • •

With her hijab done up in the style of her College Girl Look, Azza waited at the curb in front of the Holiday Inn, standing vigilantly on the lookout for Mr. Skakel and his white utility van. She scarcely noticed when the rusted-out, powder-blue hatchback made its circuit through the roundabout in front of the hotel and pulled up to the curb. But then the driver opened up his car door with a noisy clunk and leaned over the battered roof in her direction.

"You must be the international student," he said, flashing a faint smile of recognition as he tried to place where he had seen her before. And then, quite suddenly, he got it: she was the girl he had seen in the Registrar's office.

Azza stared at the young man for a moment in a kind of disbelief. Blond and thin, with an unruly lock of hair resting on his unblemished white forehead, he looked, for all the world, what she imagined Middle America to be like.

"I am she, sir," said Azza. "But where is Mr. Skakel?"

"He's out sick."

"May Allah bless Mr. Skakel and his family with renewed health and happiness," she replied, bowing slightly.

"I guess so," he said sheepishly. "My name's Kip. I'm your driver now."

"Very well," she said, reaching out to open the rear door.

"Feel free to ride up front with me," said Kip.

"I do not wish to be in the suicide seat, sir," said Azza, as she settled into the back seat of the Powder Puff.

"The *what*?" said Kip, taking his place behind the wheel.

"The suicide seat. It is the most dangerous place in the automobile, correct?"

"Well, I don't know about that. I mean, I just got my license, but I'm a really safe driver—"

"I have heard that sitting in the passenger's seat is also known as riding shotgun," said Azza, interrupting him.

"That's right!" said Kip.

"Yes, sir. I do not wish to do that either. To ride shotgun. No, thank you."

"Do you know why they call it riding shotgun?" said Kip, as he turned over the ignition and the Powder Puff sputtered back to life.

"No, sir, I do not."

"See, back in the Old West," said Kip, pulling the Subaru away from the curb, "the passenger's seat in a stagecoach was called the groom's seat. And the person in that seat would be looking out for bandits or Indians or whatnot. And they'd be armed with a shotgun to ward off enemies. So they'd be riding shotgun. Get it?"

"You seem to know a lot about history," said Azza. "And firearms."

"I guess," Kip replied, glancing awkwardly into the rearview mirror.

"But I still do not wish to ride in the suicide seat."

"Suit yourself," said Kip, turning his eyes back to the road. "What's your name?"

"Azza Amari, sir."

"Is that right?" said Kip.

"What else would it be?" she replied, quizzically. "Of course, it is right."

"What does Amari mean?" Kip asked.

"It means 'moon' in Arabic," she replied, briefly glancing out of her car window, where she saw a turban-clad Sikh riding a metallic blue motorbike. Head down, eyes glued to the road, he made for a strange sight, by any measure, in rural Fremont.

"*Moon*. I like that," said Kip.

"I have read that it also means 'I am pregnant,'" said Azza.

"That's kinda weird," said Kip.

"It would be very weird, indeed, sir."

"So what is your major over at the college?" Kip asked, glancing up at the rearview mirror.

"Chemical engineering. I am freshwoman, sir. What do you study?"

"Oh, I'm not at Northwestern Ohio State. I'm a senior—"

"But you seem so young, sir."

"Sorry. I meant that I'm in twelfth grade. In high school."

"I see," Azza replied.

"Where are you from?" Kip asked, as he turned onto stately, tree-lined College Avenue.

"Paris, sir."

"French, huh?" said Kip,

"Tunisian, actually," she replied. "My family left Tunis when I was five-years-old. Our life in Bobigny is all I have ever known."

"Until now," said Kip, smiling as he glanced at her reflection in the rearview mirror.

"That is correct, sir," Azza replied. "Now I am international student at Northwestern Ohio State College. I am living my new life in Fremont."

As Azza spoke, Kip stared into the rearview mirror, where he saw a police cruiser make a U-turn. As the squad car fell into line behind the Powder Puff, he could feel his body growing cold with fear. Was he about to be pulled over? And on his very first day as a driver-for-hire?

Staring into the mirror, his brow creased with anxiety, Kip watched as the black-and-white followed him along College Avenue. When the police cruiser pulled within a car length of the Subaru, Kip made out the image of the driver. And he recognized him immediately. Kip had known the man for the balance of his teen years, actually.

It was Birdie's father, Officer Hudgins. He was staring, stone-faced and unflinching. His eyes following the Subaru as if he were tailing Kip.

Was this all about Birdie? Kip wondered to himself. Was it because he wouldn't give in and let her dump him like she wanted? He couldn't help remembering how Officer Hudgins had followed him a few times after he first got together with Birdie, how it made him feel creeped out. Sometimes, Kip would even notice the police cruiser parked nearby after they left the movie theater over in Stony Prairie. Or after a quick bite at Woody's after school. In truth, Kip thought it was kind of endearing the way the guy was looking after his daughter and all. Kip liked to think that, in a way, Officer Hudgins was looking out for him, too. Kip liked the thought of that a lot. But after a while, Officer Hudgins had stopped trailing him, as if he had somehow earned the guy's trust.

But now it was happening all over again, as though Officer Hudgins were trying to figure out what was going on with Kip and his daughter. And now he sees Kip riding around with some new girl in the Powder Puff, Kip thought to himself. Well, I guess I'd be worried, too. On account of Birdie and all.

As Kip pulled the Powder Puff up in front of Faraday Hall, the police cruiser slowed to a crawl as it continued its way along College Avenue. For the briefest of moments, Officer Hudgins turned his head in the direction of the Subaru, his eyes emotionless as he peered into the vehicle as it idled on the edge of the campus.

"Thank you, sir," said Azza, her voice breaking the spell as she began to fumble with the door handle.

"Should I pick you up here around five, I guess?" Kip asked, having regained his composure.

"Very well," she replied, before hastily exiting the Powder Puff.

Kip's eyes followed after Azza, her brightly colored hijab awash in the morning sunlight, as she walked swiftly towards the entrance to Faraday Hall. It was as if she were driven by an energy of her own making. And as Kip observed his passenger from another land making her way through the morning throng, he couldn't help notice the other students, who paused from the doldrums of their morning routine to stare at her in a kind of stunned disbelief.

• • •

As Kip pulled the Powder Puff back into the traffic that crawled along College Avenue, Azza made her way to one of Faraday Hall's ancient, decaying ground-floor classrooms. The old lecture hall, complete with a miniature stage at the front of the room, smelled vaguely of mold. Azza took her seat in the first row of stiff metal desks. A male student slouched beside her. Clad in a tee-shirt, walking shorts, and flip-flops, he rested his head on the battered desktop.

As grey-haired, matronly Dr. Matthews brought the class to order, she began scrawling the day's discussion topic on a timeworn blackboard, its surface mottled by the faint chalky outlines of lessons-gone-by: SCRIPTURAL ANTHROPOLOGY

Pulling a green spiral notebook from her handbag, Azza prepared to take notes, carefully turning to the first blank loose-leaf page. As she dutifully copied Dr. Matthews's words from the blackboard, carefully mimicking her professor's block capital letters, Azza listened intently as the professor launched into her lecture. For Azza, it sounded like a fusillade of almost indecipherable language as Dr. Matthews plowed through her presentation, scarcely bothering to raise her eyes from the yellowed notes on the lectern.

After a few moments, Azza managed to catch up with the swirl of language, her mind locking onto a single, multisyllabic word:

Delectable.

Azza was familiar with the term, of course. But she was jolted just the same. To Azza's ears, Dr. Matthews had used the word in the strangest possible fashion. In a way that felt foreign to her. That felt somehow invasive.

"The young woman, her blouse hanging low across her chest, pried the apple loose from the clutches of the tree. Nestled among the fecund orchard, she ate at the bright red piece of fruit, her mouth moving in a delectable rhythm as she chewed upon the pulp."

For Azza, Dr. Matthews's usage seemed somehow obscene—dirty even. She was so moved that she looked up in the direction of her professor, who held firmly to her place in front of the lectern.

In a single abrupt motion, Azza thrust her hand up in the air, suddenly catching Dr. Matthews's attention, as if she had been startled by the hijab-wearing student's unexpected burst of energy.

"Yes, Ms. Amari?" said Dr. Matthews.

"I am confused, Professor, by your usage in this instance," said Azza. "Is the apple—what is it doing here in our class? I don't understand how this apple, how it matters to my learning of Anthropology? What difference does it make to the history of civilization and our understanding of human history and culture? Professor?"

Dr. Matthews paused for a moment at the front of the classroom, allowing her eyes to drift upward towards the coffee-colored stains on the ceiling tiles overhead.

"Ms. Amari," she finally said, breaking the silence. "The apple is a metaphor for the fall of the whole of civilization. It is the signal religious image of the Judeo-Christian world, is it not? The woman, as she eats the apple in the orchard, is not only a temptress, but she, too, is tempted by the apple, which is both delectable and which is eaten *delectably* by the young woman. Don't you see?"

For a moment, Azza lapsed into silence, as if she were attempting to process—to *decode*—Dr. Matthews's words. As she prepared to answer, she could feel the other students becoming restless, shifting in their seats as the exchange continued.

"This story is Biblical, Professor. Am I correct?"

"Well, isn't it just the same as in your Qur'an, Ms. Amari?" Dr. Matthews replied.

"The woman, she is Eve?"

"In a manner of speaking, Ms. Amari. She is an Eve-like figure, who, in her weakness, succumbs to the entreaties of the serpent and eats from the tree of knowledge. And as the story goes, she will, in turn, tempt Adam to also disobey God, and together they will be expelled from Eden."

"But that is not the parable in the Qur'an," said Azza, her words erupting in a staccato rush.

"It is the narrative of original sin," said Dr. Matthews, her voice unmoved by Azza's wave of emotion. "As the story goes, the descendants of Adam will be punished for their parents' transgression. It is at the heart of the scriptural tradition—"

"But that is not in the Qur'an, Professor," said Azza, interrupting her. "Eve, or Hawwa as we know her in Islam, is no weaker than Adam. They are equally responsible for their actions in the Garden. And Allah, in His infinite wisdom and mercy, forgives them both. He does not punish them across the generations."

"I'm sorry, Dr. Matthews," said the student sitting next to Azza, his voice breaking the silence of the classroom, "but that doesn't make any sense. Everybody knows that in Islam, women are, like, the property of men, right?" As he spoke, the student pulled himself out of his slouch, rubbing the sleep out of his eyes as he gathered his thoughts. "I don't think men and women are equal about anything in the Middle East," he said, turning his head towards Azza, yet still gazing downwards. "Yeah, that doesn't sound right to me."

"That's a very good point, Mr. Jones," said Dr. Matthews, nodding her head. "Not surprisingly, many religious scholars describe Islam as a patriarchal culture in which women hold secondary status."

"But Professor," Azza pleaded, her voice rising in unison with her angst, "in the Qur'an women are seen as the daughters of Lot, as capable of atonement and becoming the pure representation of all that is holy and that must be revered—"

"Whatever," interrupted the student sitting adjacent to Azza. "Next thing you'll be telling us is that Islam is some bogus religion of peace."

Azza would never hear Dr. Matthews scold the student for his derisive tone, nor would she follow the remainder of the lecture on Scriptural Anthropology. She simply closed her spiral notebook and lapsed into a kind of protracted silence that would only be shattered by the commotion of the class breaking up for the day.

As each student left the classroom, Dr. Matthews distributed copies of a slick blue pamphlet with the word ALICE stenciled across the front. Some of the students deposited the pamphlet with a shrug into the trashcan beside the door, while others forced the brochure into the bowels of their backpacks.

Azza was the last student to exit the room, having waited for everyone else to take their leave. As Dr. Matthews handed her a copy of the pamphlet, she gently patted Azza across her robed shoulder blade with her free hand, as if she were engaging the younger woman in some form of unspoken, mysterious solidarity.

But Azza's mind had already gone elsewhere. As she walked slowly along the narrow pathway at the heart of Faraday Hall, she studied the pamphlet's contents:

> In this day and age, you can never be too safe. With ALICE, students, faculty, and staff can be ready if and when an active

> shooter or other hostile presence enters our campus. By learning the five steps of ALICE, you can prepare yourself for handling any emergency associated with a violent intruder. Remember: knowledge is power. Learn ALICE today.

As Azza left the building and ambled across the quad in the direction of her ESL class, she committed the acronym to memory, slowly repeating each of the words aloud to herself, as if they were a mantra:

Alert.
Lockdown.
Inform.
Counter.
Evacuate.

CHAPTER 8:
WITHOUT A TRACE?

"You're kidding me, right?" said Ry from his place in the Powder Puff's passenger's seat. "A pear?"

"It's a plaster of Paris *figurine,*" Kip replied, correcting him.

"I cannot believe you're dragging me to see that creepy dude in that equally creepy museum just so we can look for some crappy old pear."

"Like I said before, Ry, it's a plaster of Paris figurine that happens to be molded in the shape of a pear."

"Dude," said Ry, "this is not how I planned to spend my afternoon. Now that Miss Pigtails is sayonara, we're supposed to be two playas on the loose, remember? Not freakin' fruit detectives."

"Did you know," said Kip, ignoring him as he steered the Subaru onto Hayes Avenue, "that the pear is actually the name of the species of tree that bears the edible fruit that we call a pear?"

"Oh, dude," said Ry, "you are, without a doubt, the single biggest geek I have ever met. No wonder Birdie threw you over for that douche from Boston."

But just as quickly as the words were out of his mouth, Ry realized that he had gone too far. As Kip pulled up behind the museum, he promptly climbed out of the Powder Puff and slammed its rusty driver's side door with a heavy metallic clank.

"I was only kidding, Kip!" said Ry, trailing after him as he made his way towards the grand entrance of the exhibition hall.

As they passed through the vestibule, Kip and Ry were met by Marv, smiling as always as he tipped his blue watchman's cap in their direction.

"Good afternoon, Mr. President!" said Marv. "And this must be

Vice President Wheeler. Greetings, fine gentlemen!"

"Vice President *who*?" Ry asked.

"Just play along, Ry," said Kip. "But if you must know, William A. Wheeler was President Hayes's VP and formerly a Congressman from Malone, New York. Are you gonna go and call me a geek again?" he added, glaring at Ry before turning his attention back towards the man in uniform. "Marv, this is my a-hole friend Ryan."

"Dude, that's not very presidential of you," said Ry, shaking hands with the security guard.

"Have you seen Fletch?" Kip asked, ignoring Ry's last remark.

"Should be back any minute now," said Marv. "He's been over at Donahue Ford since around lunchtime. Chairman Donahue called some kinda emergency meeting."

"Donahue Ford, Driving Fremont Since Y2K!" Ry sang out.

"That's still a heck of a jingle, isn't it, son?" said Marv, laughing uproariously.

"An emergency meeting with Chairman Donahue—that can't be good," said Kip, pursing his lips.

"I reckon not," Marv replied as he nestled his index fingers inside his belt loops. "Old Fletch was pretty stressed out when he left. But like I said, he should be back any time now. Feel free to wait for him in the back if you boys want. The only people in the museum are a group of seniors from the old folk's home over in Sycamore Hills. But don't worry about bothering them none. They can't hear a darned thing!"

And with that, Marv broke into a full-on laughing fit, unhooking his fingers from his belt loops and clapping his hands along with his guffaws.

"So, President Hayes, what are we supposed to do now?" Ry asked as they strode across the main floor of the museum. Off in the distance, the group from the old folk's home were loitering around a giant relief map depicting the earthy contours of the Panama Canal. And from the sounds of things, the museum's visitors were none too happy.

As the voices from the old folks continued to escalate along with their apparent dismay, Kip made his way over to the Panama Canal exhibit to ferret out the problem with Ry reluctantly following along in his wake. Some of the elderly visitors were awkwardly snapping photographs of the exhibit, while others were jabbing their fingers at the museum's glossy brochure and staring in bemusement at the docent, a petite brunette whose badge helpfully identified her as COLBY.

As they inched even closer, Kip couldn't help but admire Colby's pageboy haircut. She wore a thin white blouse accompanied by a smart, well-pressed navy blue skirt. Kip had to admit, if only to himself, that he was impressed with the results of Fletch's latest venture. Most of the other volunteers whom Fletch had recruited into his newly minted Young Docents program were pretty slovenly. Kip sometimes wondered if Fletch had simply wandered into town and handed out dollar bills to lure young-looking guides into the museum so as to make the Hayes seem more relevant to today's youth—just another one of Mel Donahue's suggestions to curb the museum's attendance rates, which had been in a veritable free-fall for the past several years. But Colby was clearly something else altogether.

"What seems to be the problem here?" Kip asked, trying to effect his most customer-friendly voice.

"Who are *you*?" said Colby, looking at him askance as she stood between two elderly women with their brochures clutched tightly in their hands.

"Kip Beckelhymer. I'm a junior member of the museum's board of governors."

"Yeah," said Ry, backing him up. "The board of governors. Take that."

"I don't think we've met," Kip said to Colby. "When did you join the Young Docents team?"

"I'm Colby," she replied. "This is my first day. My family just moved here from Minneapolis."

"Oh, Minneapolis is very nice," said an elderly man with a giant Nikon camera strapped around his neck.

"I'm surprised we haven't seen each other at school," Kip continued. "Especially in AP History."

"That's 'cause I'm not in AP History," Colby replied. "I'm a junior in AP Physics."

"Of course, you haven't met Kip," Ry chimed in, a sardonic smile creeping across his face. "He's not sciency."

"Be that as it may," said Colby. "These two guests are upset about the Panama Canal exhibit."

"Yeah," one of the elderly women piped up. "Says right here in the brochure that there should be a replica of the lease that President Hayes signed for the—what was it, Madge?"

"For the Isthmus of Panama, Helen," said Madge.

"That's it!" said Helen. "The lease for the Isthmus of Panama. We wanna see it."

With that, Kip began searching frantically among the contents of the exhibit for the facsimile. But the only items in evidence were the relief map, a bust of Ferdinand de Lesseps, and an empty space on the wall where the lease should have been mounted.

"I see what you mean, ma'am," said Kip, who was staring at the vacant, discolored spot on the wall of the Hayes. But then he caught sight of Ry, who was propping his elbow on the ivory-tinted bust of de Lesseps.

"What do you think you're doing?" Kip asked.

"Resting my arm," said Ry.

"On Ferdinand de Lesseps?" Kip asked, incredulously.

"How do I know who this dude is?"

"This *dude* was a French diplomat and the engineer behind the first attempt to build the Panama Canal."

"*So*?" said Ry.

"So he's not an armrest," said Kip.

"Whatever," said Colby. "The man was pretty corrupt."

"The man was a pioneer," said Kip, correcting her.

"Not hardly," Colby replied, her pageboy bouncing in unison with her retort. "De Lesseps caused quite a scandal in his day. He even riled up President Hayes, who couldn't afford much in the way of distractions."

"Why's that?" asked Ry.

"Yeah, why's that?" asked Helen, still clutching her brochure.

"'Cause of the election of 1876," said Kip. "Probably the most contentious presidential election of all time."

"Well, until recently perhaps," Colby interjected.

"No," said Kip, flatly. "*Of all time*. On the first count, Hayes, the Republican candidate, actually had fewer electoral votes than Tilden, the Democrat, losing 184 to 165 with 20 electoral votes unresolved in Florida, Louisiana, South Carolina, and Oregon."

"That seems like a lot of electoral votes," said Madge.

"Yes, ma'am, it was. In fact, it was the *most* electoral votes ever overcome in a disputed election," said Kip. "The crisis wouldn't even be resolved until five months after election day, when the Democrats agreed to throw all 20 of the electoral votes to Hayes if the Republicans withdrew federal troops from the South, bringing an end to Reconstruction."

"Well, isn't that nifty?" said Ry.

"You're dang right it is," said Kip, staring intently at Colby. "The final negotiated tally had Hayes winning 185 to 184, even though Tilden had bested him by 200,000 in the popular vote."

Colby began slowly clapping her hands. But just as suddenly, she abruptly stopped, letting her hands fall to her hips. "You forgot just one thing."

"What's that?" said Kip, crossing his arms in front of his chest.

"1960," Colby replied.

"Oh, man," said Ry, his eyes shining brightly in anticipation. "This is some kinda geek standoff."

"Kennedy Nixon?" Kip asked as he allowed himself a tiny chuckle. "Check your facts. JFK beat Tricky Dick by 84 electoral votes. That's a landslide compared to Hayes Tilden."

"That's one way of looking at it," said Colby, as a tiny smile crept across her face. "But here's another: the electoral result may seem robust, but Kennedy took the election by .2 percent of the popular vote. And there are historians who contend that JFK didn't even win by that much—that LBJ swooped in and worked his backroom magic in places like Texas and Illinois, throwing the election to the Democrats."

"But Hayes Tilden went by three percent of the popular vote. *In the other direction!* You're comparing apples to oranges!"

"Agree to disagree," said Colby, her arms folded resolutely in front of her gleaming white blouse.

"Heck, even Bush Gore went .5 percent of the popular vote against the eventual victor! Kennedy Nixon doesn't even compare—"

"Agree to disagree," Colby repeated, her pageboy bobbing up and down with her words.

"Yeah, dude," said Ry, barely containing his glee. "Agree to disagree!"

"This is all very informative," said Madge, staring up at Kip with a blank look on her face, "but what about the lease?"

"I really don't know, ma'am," said Kip. "I'll be sure to take it up with Mr. Clawson, the museum's director, as soon as he returns. You have my word."

"Something tells me you won't have to wait very long," said Ry, nodding in the direction of the entryway. As they observed from their vantage point across the museum, Fletch was racing across the main floor. The portly director must have sensed trouble in the unusual gathering around the Panama Canal exhibit, having broken into an awkward gallop, his arms flailing about his hefty sides.

Kip and Ry met the older man by the Rutherford B. Hayes, American Statesman exhibit, a life-sized wax figure of the 19th President dressed in his reverential finery.

"What's the ruckus, Kip?" said Fletch, panting beside the waxy approximation of the former president, who was staring off in the distance, wearing a bowler hat, with a gleaming silver sword by his side. "Don't tell me someone damaged the de Lesseps bust. It's one of our most valuable holdings."

"De Lesseps is just fine," said Kip, taking a sideways glance at Ry, who was staring in bewilderment at Hayes's mannequin. "But the Isthmus of Panama lease is nowhere to be found."

"The replica's gone, too?" cried out Fletch. "As if this couldn't get any worse."

"Hey, what happened over at Donahue Ford today?" Kip asked.

"Oh, it's bad, Kippers. Donahue has moved up the audit. That awful car salesman is demanding that an inventory be completed by October 1st. If Emily still had an ounce of affection for me, she would forestall my doom—I just know she would. But there's more: Somebody leaked Donahue a copy of the original museum catalogue. All he has to do is collate the new inventory against the old catalogue, and it's . . . it's—"

"I know," said Kip, interrupting him. "It's curtains for you."

"For the *museum*," said Fletch, correcting him. "And if somebody leaked the catalogue, then it means there's a traitor in our midst." In that same moment, Kip and Fletch glanced at each other, then turned their attention towards Ry, who was wearing the President's bowler hat.

"Well, don't look at me," said Ry, staring back at them. "You two are the resident museum geeks. I'm just visiting."

"I don't think I trust him," said Fletch, gesturing at Ry.

"That's okay," said Kip. "Nobody does."

"But what does it really matter," Fletch continued. "First the pear, now the replica. How shoddy has the Hayes organization become under my watch? Speaking of which," said Fletch, "put that bowler back on the President right now, Mr. Langham!"

"Sorry, dude," said Ry, awkwardly placing the felt hat atop Hayes's waxy head. "But you're wrong, you know."

"Oh, really now," said Fletch. "Wrong about *what*?"

"The pear and that replica thingy," said Ry. "They haven't gone missing. Somebody probably lifted that stuff."

"I should think not," said Fletch. "The Hayes doesn't cater to that kind of clientele."

"If you ask me," said Ry, "I don't know why anybody in their right mind would steal those things. I mean, I'd definitely lift that cool hat. Or that sword over there," he said, gesturing towards the President's Union Army rapier. "I don't get in any swordfights to speak of, but that would be cool to have around. But a *pear*—who wants to steal something like that? It's kinda goofy."

"Okay," said Kip. "I'll play along. Why does anybody steal anything?"

"Because of a perception of value," said Fletch, nodding his head as he tapped his fingers rhythmically across his ample chin.

"Yeah," said Ry, "but who in their right mind would see anything of value in the First Lady's crappy old pear?"

"Did somebody mention Lucy Hayes?" Colby asked, having strolled over from her place by the Panama Canal exhibit. In the distance, her gaggle of old folks was heading towards the exit.

"I trust that you've met Colby here," said Fletch, his spirits buoyed by her appearance. "She's the great shining light of my Young Docents program!"

"Yeah, she's a shining light all right, huh Kip?" said Ry, elbowing his friend in the ribs.

"Did you know that Mrs. Hayes was the first First Lady to hold a college degree?" Colby asked.

"No kidding," said Kip. "Fun fact: she was also the very first First Lady. That stuff is Hayes 101."

"Fine," said Colby. "Then let's amp things up a bit. Follow me."

With Colby leading the way, Kip, Ry and Fletch trailed the docent into a nearby anteroom, where a full-length portrait of the First Lady hung in quiet repose. With her jet black hair framing her delicate features, Mrs. Hayes stood before a parkside scene wearing a burgundy gown and holding a clutch of yellow carnations.

"She's pretty hot," said Ry, chuckling to himself.

"Classy," said Colby, frowning at him. "If you want a closer look, the family tomb's out back."

"Pass," Ry deadpanned.

"This is a copy of Mrs. Hayes's official portrait, which hangs in the White House," said Colby. "So whaddya say, Kip? Who painted it?"

"Nice try," said Kip with a note of triumph in his voice. "It was Daniel Huntington, the very same artist who created portraits for Abraham Lincoln and Martin Van Buren."

"Well done," said Colby. "You clearly have a knack for trivia. But how's your sense of irony?"

"My *what*?"

"Sure, Daniel Huntington painted the First Lady's portrait," said

Colby, "but who paid his commission?"

For a moment, Kip seemed positively stunned. As if it had never occurred to him to engage in such subterranean levels of Hayesian research. Then he glanced over at Fletch, as if he were hoping the director would come to his aid. But for Kip, there would be no such luck.

"You're on your own there, Kippers," said Fletch. "Looks like she's stumped you, kid."

"Give up?" Colby asked, with a twinkle in her eye.

"Fine," said Kip. "You got me."

"Alrighty then," she replied. "It was the Women's Temperance Union."

For his part, Kip could only hang his head in shame.

"Of course!" Fletch boomed. "There's your irony. Who else would fund the portrait of the most famous teetotaler in American presidential history but the greatest anti-alcohol crusaders of all time!"

"It's ironic all right," said Kip, still reeling after being bested by Colby. "But it gets even stranger still. She refused to take any alcohol herself, yet she actually opposed prohibition."

"If you think about it," said Colby, "it's hardly surprising. She was a strong and confident person, ripe for being torn down by society. Truth is, she was a most unusual woman for her time and place. People didn't know how to take her."

And that's when it hit him, as Kip turned away from the portrait of Lemonade Lucy with a start.

"Oh, shoot," he said, looking towards Ry, his eyes now wide with alarm. "We're late!"

As Kip steered the Powder Puff, its tires squealing as he made the wide turn back onto Hayes Avenue, Ry braced himself in the passenger's seat, holding on for dear life. The green-tinted LED clock on the Subaru's dashboard flashed the awful truth. It was 5:14 PM.

"I can't believe I screwed this up already," said Kip, rapping his hands on the steering wheel as he piloted the hatchback towards the Northwestern Ohio State campus. "Dr. Smyth is paying me $250 a week just to drive a student back and forth to the Holiday Inn, and I blow it on the very first day!"

"Dude, you need to slow the eff down," said Ry.

"What happened to being a playa on the loose?" Kip laughed.

"A playa on the loose is one thing," said Ry. "A dead playa is another."

"It must get exhausting being such a cool guy all the time, Ry."

"You have no idea," he replied. "Being the life of the party is, like, a full-time job."

"Wait," said Kip, "if you're Mr. Cool, what does that make me?"

"You're, like, my entourage, dude," Ry replied. "My sidekick!"

As Kip turned onto College Avenue, with the leafy-green campus coming into view just ahead, he slowed down the Powder Puff to a crawl.

"What are we looking for?" Ry asked.

"She should be around here someplace," said Kip, glancing at the sidewalks for any signs of life, although there were very few students in evidence given the lateness of the hour. Northwestern Ohio State was a commuter school, after all.

"*She*?" Ry asked. "Dude, when did you start holding out on me?"

And that's when Kip spotted Azza, sitting in front of Faraday Hall on a park bench, her arms folded in front of her as she clutched her books to her chest.

As Kip pulled the Powder Puff beside the curb, Azza stood up, the brilliant folds of her hijab swirling about her olive face. And suddenly, Ry looked up and saw her, too, and the ashen look that washed across his own face spoke volumes.

"Whoa, dude," said Ry. "What the eff is this?"

CHAPTER 9:
PDA

As Azza settled into the back seat, the ALICE pamphlet clutched tightly in her hands, Kip pulled the Powder Puff away from the curb. As he piloted the hatchback along College Avenue in the direction of the Holiday Inn, Azza sat in silence and stared at the backs of the two boys' heads—the blond All American behind the wheel and the one with the jet-black scraggly hair in the suicide seat.

Why would anyone in their right mind sit there? she wondered to herself. And she certainly didn't want to ride shotgun. She knew that with absolute certainty.

As the tree-lined avenue faded into the industrial buildings and strip malls that dotted the outskirts of town, the black-haired kid suddenly turned to face her, his lanky arm flopping across the headrest.

"So what's with the getup?" he asked, staring blankly at her from his place in the front seat.

"Jesus, Ry," said Kip, jabbing him sharply with his right hand. "Where do you get off?"

For a moment, Azza was stunned, although in truth it was hardly the first time that anyone had accosted her about her headwear. In fact, truth be told, it was actually one of the least offensive displays that she'd experienced. As she stared back at the kid in front of her, she quickly marked him as non-threatening. No, this kid wasn't dangerous in the slightest. He was just ignorant.

And then, just as suddenly, Ry broke Azza's stare and turned to face the driver, a scowl gripping his face.

"Whaddya mean, 'where do I get off'?" he said. "You know how well I play with the ladies. I get off everywhere—and plenty!"

This kid is not just ignorant, Azza thought to herself. He's egomaniacal.

And Kip—he seemed nice enough. But how reliable could he be if he's already showing up late—and with this Ry kid as some kind of irreverent sidekick?

As it turned out, Kip and Ry were the furthest things from her mind. As Kip pulled the hatchback up to the Holiday Inn, she girded her courage and blurted it out.

"I have a request, sir," said Azza, her voice broken and tentative.

"I know, I know," said Kip. "I promise to be on time in the future. I will never be late to pick you up again. You have my word."

"Thank you for your promise," Azza replied. "But this is not my request. My request is that I be able to do the ALICE."

"Whoa, whoa, whoa," Ry interrupted. "How do you do *who*?"

"She is not a who, sir," said Azza. "She is a what."

"Right," said Ry, "but—"

"But what, sir?" said Azza. "The ALICE is alert, lockdown, inform, counter, evacuate."

"Oh, I get it," said Kip. "ALICE is an acronym."

"That is she!" said Azza. "And how can I be doing the ALICE if I cannot even drive a car?"

"What the eff?" said Ry.

"I do not know what is F," said Azza, "but the E in the ALICE is evacuate. And I cannot evacuate properly if I cannot drive a car."

"You could evacuate on foot, you know," said Kip.

"Yes, sir," said Azza. "I have been evacuating on foot my entire life. Now I am ready to roll, as you say here in America."

"Do we actually say that?" Ry asked.

"Sometimes we do," Kip replied. "Try using it in a sentence."

"Okay," Ry answered. "How about this? Whaddya say we roll over to Woody's?"

"Woody's, sir?" Azza asked. "What is a Woody's?"

"Woody's is a restaurant," said Kip.

"Well, more of a diner, really," Ry interjected.

"But what about my meal plan?" Azza asked, her voice rising in intensity.

"Woody's *is* Ry's meal plan," said Kip. "That and Domino's pizza."

"At my house, the Honolulu Hawaiian is a delicacy," said Ry, "but I'm in the mood for Woody's."

"The Honolulu Hawaiian is patently disgusting," Kip replied, "and Woody's is only slightly better. The last time I ate there with my mom I smelled like hot wings for a week—"

"But, sirs," Azza protested, her voice growing even louder still, "*what about my meal plan*?"

Now it was Kip and Ry who looked stunned. The two boys stared back at her from the front seat, their mouths agape in confusion.

For a moment, Azza thought one of them might even cry.

"If you don't mind," said Kip, glancing across the front seat at his friend, "we could be your meal plan tonight."

"Yeah," said Ry. "It's the least we could do after being late and all. Besides, how good could the food be at the Holiday Inn anyway?"

Azza had no argument there. The food at Holiday Inn was—wait, how did the blond boy say it?—patently disgusting.

"All right," said Azza resolutely. "I will go with you to the Woody's."

• • •

By the time that Kip pulled the Powder Puff up in front of Woody's Drive-In, the dinner rush was in full swing—or at least what counted as a dinner rush on a weekday evening in Fremont.

The three friends sat in a booth in the far corner of the restaurant. Above them hung an old fishing net and a wooden fishing rod. As they scanned their Woody's menus, Ry suddenly looked up in Azza's direction.

"Do you have any, like, food issues?" he asked. For her part, Azza looked downward in response.

"What Ry is trying to ask," said Kip, "is do you have any dietary restrictions?"

"I try to eat halal whenever I can," Azza replied.

"Halal?" said Ry. "What is that? Some kinda rice?"

"No, sir. Halal refers to food that is permissible in my culture. I try to avoid eating meat that has not been slaughtered under the supervision of a mullah. And I never eat pork. But really, that is the extent of it," said Azza.

"Huh," said Ry. "How about that."

Then Azza began laughing uncontrollably.

"What's so funny?" Ry asked.

"I do have one additional constraint, sir," she replied, still chuckling to herself. "I like to restrict myself, whenever possible, from eating bad food."

"Yeah, I prefer the good stuff, too," said Ry, laughing along with her.

"So what about this?" Kip asked, pointing to the calamari appetizer on the menu.

"I will not eat the octopus, sir," she replied.

"Why not?" said Kip. "Is it not halal?"

"I will not eat the octopus for ethical reasons. Octopi are very smart, sir. They are thinkers, capable of deception."

"No way," said Ry. "How could they possibly be deceptive?"

"They can play games with you, sir. Pretend that they are one thing when they are really another. I learned in my Anthropology class that they are tricksters, too, and that they can even devise tools that they fashion out of coconut shells from the ocean floor."

"No kidding?" said Ry.

"No, sir," Azza replied. "I never kid about the octopi."

"Okay, so then what if something's not halal?" Kip asked. "What is that called?"

"Then it is haram, sir," said Azza. "Something that is haram is forbidden by Islamic law."

"That seems kinda bad," said Ry.

"Oh, it is worse than bad," said Azza. "It is an abomination. Something that is haram is strictly prohibited no matter what. Even if the offender has good intentions, even if he has an honorable purpose, Islamic law cannot be broken."

"So what happens if you break it?" said Ry.

"But you cannot break Islamic law, sir. It is not an option."

"Okay," Kip interjected. "but let's say someone does break it. So what happens then? People do bad things all the time."

"Allah says that you will enter the fire," said Azza.

"That sounds like hell," said Ry.

"That is exactly what it will be," Azza replied. "Allah's mandate is clear: 'Thou makest enter the fire, him Thou hast indeed brought to disgrace, and there shall be no helpers for the unjust.'"

• • •

As Kip and Ry devoured their Woody's triple cheeseburgers with Cholula sauce, Azza picked at her order of house pancakes and syrup, with a quartet of plump red strawberries on the side.

"So whaddya think?" Ry asked. "Does that count as the good stuff?"

"It is very sweet, sir. But it is certainly not bad. And it is halal."

"And not haram?" Kip asked.

"Definitely not haram," said Azza. "Now, sirs, if I may ask you about something."

Kip and Ry looked at each other with deep concern, as if Azza were about to consign them to enter the fire right then and there at Woody's.

"I would like to discuss my request," Azza continued. "Will you teach me how to drive?"

"You mean drive the Powder Puff?" Ry asked.

"The Powder Puff, sir?"

"That's what Ry calls my car," Kip replied, glaring at him. "But sure, I guess I can teach you how to drive. We could practice at the museum. There's a huge parking lot behind the exhibit hall."

"What is this museum?" Azza asked.

"It's the Rutherford B. Hayes Presidential Library and Museums," Kip replied, beaming as he dispatched with the last bite of his cheeseburger. "Hayes served as the 19th President of the United States from 1877 to 1881."

"Oh, Jesus," said Ry, "nerd alert."

"The museum includes Spiegel Grove, the President's estate," said Kip, ignoring him, "along with the exhibition facilities, which were established on Memorial Day in 1916."

"I would like to see this museum," said Azza. "It sounds like an important part of American history. And I am an American student now. It is my duty, right?"

"If you think that your duty is to be bored out of your freakin' mind," said Ry.

"Don't listen to him," said Kip. "Learning about history is everyone's duty. And what better place to start than the Hayes, which was the first presidential library."

"The only thing interesting about that cruddy museum is the fruit mystery," said Ry.

"What mystery is that, sir? Is there something wrong with American fruit?" said Azza, looking back and forth at her new American friends and down at the half-eaten berries on her plate. "I don't understand."

"He's talking about the First Lady's pear," said Kip.

"Her pear?" Azza asked. "Won't it be spoilt by now?"

"First of all, it's a *figurine,*" said Ry, giving Kip a sidelong glance. "It's made out of plaster or some shit." As he finished his sentence, Ry caught Azza wincing and looking away from the table.

"And it's gone," said Kip. "But we're going to find it."

"We can try," said Ry. "But like I told you before, somebody didn't just randomly lift that thing. You have to wanna steal something like that, right?"

"I would think so," said Azza, turning her attention back to the table. "It sounds very valuable, sir. I will help you to find this figurine and bring it back to this museum."

"Why the hell would you wanna do something like that?" Ry asked. "If it weren't for Mr. Heartbreak here, I wouldn't touch this thing with a 10-foot pole."

"Mr. Heartbreak?" said Azza, as Kip turned away sheepishly.

"Oh, you didn't know?" Ry asked. "Kip here's in mourning for

Miss Pigtails, his girl-toy."

"Please don't talk about my girlfriend that way," said Kip.

"Dude, she's a stone-cold bitch," said Ry, "and we both know it."

"Here, dumbass," said Kip, foisting a menu in Ry's direction. "How about some dessert? You've never met a meal you didn't like."

"I've clearly hit a nerve!" said Ry, flipping open his menu.

"You should try the blueberry ice cream," said Kip, looking up from his dessert menu. "It's the house specialty."

"No way, no how," Ry replied.

"What gives? It's delicious," said Kip.

"I don't eat purple food."

"Come on," said Kip.

"No, seriously," said Ry. "I have a rule about never eating anything purple."

"That's food racism," said Kip.

"Food can't be racist, sir," said Azza. "Only people."

"Right," said Kip. "People like Ry, apparently."

"Oh, crap," said Ry, conspiratorially ducking below his menu. "Don't look over there."

"Over where?" Kip asked, scanning across the restaurant floor. And that's when he saw her. And following the direction of Kip's gaze, Azza saw her, too.

"Is that she? Is that Miss Pigtails?" Azza asked.

"Oh, dude, I am so sorry I said all those things," Ry whispered, trying to divert his friend, who was staring, open-mouthed, across the room at Birdie. As they watched, Kip's wayward girlfriend stood up to greet a lanky boy who had ambled into Woody's.

"If she is your girl-toy, sir," Azza asked, "then why is she over there with that other boy?"

"That's not just any other boy," said Ry. "That's him—that's Todd from Boston."

"I see," Azza replied. "Then why is Todd from Boston sitting over there with Kip's girl-toy, sir?"

"Because Kip's girl-toy is no longer Kip's girlfriend," said Ry. "She doesn't want to date a pizza delivery boy."

"I don't do that anymore," Kip protested.

"What do you do now, sir?" asked Azza.

"He's your driver. That's what he does now," Ry replied, still hunkering below his menu.

"What should we be doing, sirs?" Azza asked, as Kip and Ry attempted to obscure themselves behind their dessert menus. "Are we in trouble?"

"We're not in any kinda trouble," Ry replied. "But don't make any sudden moves. We don't wanna call attention to ourselves."

As Azza observed from her place in the far corner of the restaurant, the lanky boy began holding hands with Kip's estranged girlfriend.

"The girl-toy and Todd from Boston are now holding each other's hands, sirs," said Azza. "Should we do something?"

"OMG," said Kip. "This play-by-play is *not* helping."

"Dude, dude, dude," said Ry, "holding hands is one thing. In some cultures, friends hold hands, right? Wait, what do they do in—where are you from again?" he asked Azza.

"She's from Paris by way of Tunisia," Kip interjected.

"Fine," said Ry. "Do friends hold hands in Tunisia?"

"Actually, they do," said Azza. "It is a chaste and right thing for friends and relations to do."

"Okay," said Ry, pointing in the direction of Birdie and Todd from Boston, "but do they do *that*?"

Taking their cue, Kip and Azza stared across the dining room towards Birdie and Todd, who were vigorously kissing above their tabletop as Birdie's braided locks moved back and forth in time with their exertions.

"Jesus, Birdie," said Kip, holding his head in his hands.

"What a funny name," said Azza.

"Yeah," said Ry. "That's why I call her Miss Pigtails."

"That is an even funnier name, sir," said Azza.

"So where does Allah stand on PDA?" Ry asked.

"On *what*, sir?" Azza replied.

"Public displays of affection," said Ry.

"Allah is very clear on such matters," said Azza. "Even between spouses, outward signs of affection and mercy are to be conducted in privacy and repose."

"See, Kip?" said Ry. "I always knew that Miss Pigtails was trouble. She doesn't even know only to show affection in privacy and repose."

"I believe that your friend is right, sir," Azza said to Kip. "The girl with the funny name is best to be avoided. Allah is all-knowing and all-wise. We were not born onto this earth to be slave-boys and slave-girls to our desires. It is a sin to attend upon each other in public as those two are doing."

"Oh, they're doing it all right," said Ry.

"Oh, verily," said Azza. "What they are doing over there—that is not affection and mercy. It is—*how do you say it?*—cheap."

"Oh, it's cheap for sure," said Ry.

"Can you two stop already?" Kip asked, still holding his head in his hands.

"Sorry, dude," said Ry. "It's just hard to concentrate with those guys munching on each other right here in Woody's. I mean, let's be honest: that's some heavy-duty tongue-kissing shit. Sorry, I mean, heavy-duty tongue-kissing *stuff.*"

"You're going to start cleaning up your act *now*?" Kip asked Ry.

As Kip stared at his friend with disgust, Ry looked over at Azza with puppy-dog eyes as if he were seeking her forgiveness. Not knowing what to do, Azza stared down at her lap in embarrassment.

"Good God," said Kip. "You're worse than Birdie and Todd."

"Dude, that's sweet," Ry replied. "You're already referring to them as a couple. Pretty soon we'll be talking about their song. See how this just gets easier and easier?"

"What is their song, sir?" Azza asked.

"They probably don't have one yet. I bet they choose something by Justin Bieber. Probably some sugary piece of garbage like 'As Long as You Love Me.'"

"Ry, will you shut up already?" Kip asked.

"Oh, yes!" said Azza. "I know that one, sir. 'We could be starving, we could be homeless, we could be broke / As long as you love me.'"

"That's right," said Ry, playing along. "'I'll be your platinum, I'll be your silver, I'll be your gold / As long as you love me.' Sure, nice tune. Plastic pop garbage. Definitely Birdie's speed."

"Stop it, Ry," said Kip. "You never know when to quit."

"Believe what you want, Kip," Ry continued, "but I'd have to say that you and Birdie are Donesville as far as making it through senior year as a couple. But hey, I like her chances with this new guy."

"That's it," said Kip. "Let's get out of here." As he stood up, he pulled a wad of dollar bills from his pocket and tossed it on the table. Taking one last look across the room at Birdie, he watched her kissing Todd with what seemed like even greater abandon than before.

But just as Kip began to make his way towards the exit, with Ry and Azza hurrying to join him, he could see Birdie clearly open her eyes and glance in his direction. As if to ensure that he had been watching her the entire time.

CHAPTER 10:
ALL MY FRIENDS ARE HEATHENS

"What a night!" Ry cried out, as Kip steered the Powder Puff across the quiet Fremont streets.

"For *who*?" said Kip, shaking his head. "You have got to be kidding."

"For all of us!" Ry replied. "I told you senior year was gonna be great!"

"Let me know when it starts getting great, then," said Kip.

"I bet you never thought it would be like this when you left Paris, right?" said Ry, turning to face Azza in the back seat.

"No, sir," Azza replied. "My new life in America has been very adventurous so far. And soon I will be looking for a figurine and learning how to drive at your museum."

"That's right," said Ry, glancing across the front seat at Kip. "Just stick with us and you'll be golden."

"I would like to be golden, sir," Azza replied.

As she watched from her perch in the back seat, Kip craned his neck to look into the rearview mirror. And for the longest time, he held his gaze in the reflection of the night. As Kip drove the Subaru in the direction of the Holiday Inn, Azza turned around to see what was preoccupying her driver.

And there, only a few car-lengths back, was a police cruiser tooling along at a discreet distance behind the Powder Puff, but following them nonetheless.

Turning back to face the roadway ahead, Azza trained her gaze into the rearview mirror, where she could see the fear in Kip's eyes. And that was an emotion that she could definitely recognize, that she could always understand.

• • •

Much later that night—long after he had left Ry and Azza for the evening—Kip drove the Powder Puff over to Ballville on a reconnaissance mission. It was a risky mission, to be sure, but he needed information, he reassured himself, and he needed it now.

As he pulled the Powder Puff onto Japack Avenue, Kip eased the car into a parking space near a tiny parklet well away from the house that had been like a second home to him—well, not quite as much of a second home as the Langhams' place over on Augusta, but a pretty close second. Japack Avenue, he thought to himself. Sounds kind of racist. Kip had never considered that before.

As he shut the driver's side door as quietly as he could muster, Kip glanced over at the rope swings where he used to secretly meet Birdie when they were still dating. Which was only last week, he thought to himself with an ironic chuckle. Back in those days, Birdie would slide out of her bedroom window, and the two of them would sneak over to the park, swing back and forth on the rope swings, and talk for hours. Mostly, they would talk about how Kip wanted to get the hell out of Fremont, but at least they were talking.

In a matter of minutes, Kip had sidled up to the Hudgins' house. The cruiser was parked out front right next to Birdie's VW. Right where it belonged—just like always. Kip strolled alongside the ranch home until he found Birdie's first-floor bedroom window. Inside, the room was dark behind her gauzy curtains. As he searched for a pebble among the mulch-riven flower beds beside the house, he wondered to himself if this mission was a good idea. Sure, he wanted to see Birdie outside of Ry's earshot—and certainly nowhere in the vicinity of Todd from Boston. *Hell, no,* he thought to himself.

Wait, what if Todd was in there right now? he wondered. Could that even be possible? Birdie's dad was pretty strict, but things change pretty quickly. Just last week it would have been Kip scarfing down hot wings with Birdie at Woody's, and that already seemed like a thousand years ago.

Worse yet, Kip didn't want to attract any undue attention from Officer Hudgins, whom he was already seeing plenty enough during daylight hours. Throwing caution to the wind, he picked up a pebble and tossed it at Birdie's window, which the tiny stone deflected off of with a muted "plink." And a few moments later, Kip could see the gauzy curtains ruffle slightly, followed by Birdie's appearance, pigtails and all, above the ledge.

"Kip?" she said, rubbing the sleep out of her eyes. Behind her, he could see the giant SpongeBob SquarePants stuffy staring back at him like an apparition.

"Yeah," he said, as she slinked up next to him beside the flower bed.

Lifting her index finger up to her lips, Birdie signaled for him to be quiet. Taking him by the hand, she led him back down Japack Avenue towards the parklet.

"What are you doing here, Kip?" she asked, as they strolled up towards the swings. Her voice was calm, not at all like he expected it would be. Certainly nothing like the confrontational tone she effected in front of Domino's. Or in the school parking lot.

"Why are you doing this to me, B? I don't understand?"

"Do you mean Todd?" she asked in the same tone, tranquil and unflustered. He was already starting to find her nonchalance infuriating.

"Yeah," he replied, "Todd from Boston."

"I like him. That's all," she said. Kip watched as she absentmindedly twirled his gold promise ring about her finger. "I told you that I wanted to see other people."

"Well, you're certainly doing that," he answered.

"It's just that he gives me things, Kip—"

"Are you talking about that again? I'm done with Domino's—"

"It's more than that," she said, searching for her words. "He gives me much more than that. He gives me adult things. *Everything*—"

"*Everything*? Oh, come on, Birdie—"

"I didn't want you to find out this way," she said, staring at the mossy ground of the parklet.

"You wanted to break up, then fine," said Kip, struggling to knock back the tears. To stop the very same waterworks that threatened to derail him back at Domino's. "We're broken up. Just like you want," he continued, having girded his courage. "Have a great life."

As Kip began to leave the parklet, Birdie's voice stopped him dead in his tracks.

"So who's the girl?" she asked, her tone suddenly sharper.

"What are you talking about?" said Kip, turning back to face her. Her lips were pursed ever so slightly. He could just make out the beginnings of a sneer creeping across her mouth.

"The girl with you and Ryan at Woody's tonight—who is she?" Birdie asked.

"She's an international student from the college. She's nobody."

"That's not what I heard," said Birdie.

"Huh?" Kip asked.

"Word is that she's some rich heiress who came over from Paris with a bagful of money," said Birdie. "That nobody knows what she's really up to."

"What she's up to is chemical engineering. I don't know anything about the rest."

"Chemical engineering?" said Birdie. "Don't you think that's kinda suspicious?"

"Oh, like she's some sort of terrorist?" he asked. "What are you going to tell me next—that she's studying chemical engineering so she can build some kind of bomb or something?"

"You've seen how she dresses, Kip," said Birdie. "You tell me."

"Fu—," said Kip, stammering in his anger. "Fuck you."

"I can't believe you said that to me," Birdie screamed. "I don't think I've ever heard you say that to anyone. What the fuck!"

But Kip was already walking away. Hurrying towards the Powder Puff with his anger in full bloom. Without bothering to look back at the parklet, he climbed into the Subaru, revved it back into life, and made his way back down Japack Avenue.

Yeah, he thought to himself, looking up at the greenish-hued street sign as he sped past. Definitely racist.

• • •

When Kip finally made his way home, he was surprised to find his mom sitting in the kitchen, a cup of coffee and a half-eaten sandwich spread out before her on the breakfast table. It had been a long time since she had waited up for him, he thought to himself.

"Did you see her?" Mrs. Beckelhymer asked, as Kip sat down across from her at the table.

"Yeah, just now," said Kip.

"This late?" said Mrs. Beckelhymer, reflexively glancing down at her watch.

"Yeah," he said. "What's with the interrogation? I stopped over in Ballville—"

"I'm sorry, monkey," she said, smiling warmly at her son, "but I didn't mean Birdie—"

"I really wish you wouldn't call me that," said Kip, interrupting her.

"I was talking about Ms. Amari," his mom continued.

"Oh, right, Azza. Yeah, I dropped her off at the Holiday Inn a few hours ago."

"That's good to hear, monkey."

"Seriously, mom. You've got to cut that out. You called me monkey in front of Ry last year, and I've never heard the end of it."

"Look, Kip, Dr. Smyth and I may have gotten you into something with her."

"No, mom. It's nothing. She's all right. Besides, I can use the money. If I had to go back to Domino's now, I would probably, you know, vaporize out of pure shame."

"It's just that there's been a lot of talk about her on campus," said Mrs. Beckelhymer. "I'm sure she has her own problems. I want to help her—I really do, but some of the faculty, even the students, are a little spooked by her right now."

"Azza?" said Kip. "I don't get that, mom. She's kind of quiet, actually. Ry and I took her to dinner at Woody's—"

"Woody's, huh?" she said. "It's probably all over town by now. Did she do anything unusual?"

"Well, she had the pancakes," said Kip. "That's pretty unusual for

Woody's. It's a hot wings and cheeseburger kinda joint. But listen, Birdie was there, too. It got pretty bad. I need to talk to you about something—"

"Did Ms. Amari do anything—did she do anything *untoward*?"

"What do you mean by untoward? She ate the pancakes if that's what you're asking. She said that they were halal, which is supposed to be good, and not haram, which is forbidden. Oh, and Ry was a total pig, but that's nothing new."

"Look, honey, if you don't want to drive her to school anymore that's fine with me. Dr. Smyth will understand."

"Are you kidding?" Kip asked. "Of course, I want to drive her. It's easy money, mom. There's no way I'm going back to Domino's now. I'm tired of smelling like greasy pepperoni and cheese all the time—"

"It's just that people are unsettled these days. You know how things are."

"Is it 'cause of the outfit?" he asked.

"The *hijab*," said Mrs. Beckelhymer, correcting him. "It's probably just that. But it's different, you know. People aren't used to that around here. With everything going on in the Middle East—"

"She moved here from Paris, *mom*," said Kip.

"Right," she replied. "But nobody in Fremont knows that. They'll jump to conclusions—they're *already* jumping to conclusions. They'll think she's a terrorist or something, and I can't have anything happen—"

"Oh, mom," said Kip, standing up from the table.

"I can't have anything happen to you," she said, choking back tears, her lips beginning to tremble and quake. "You're all I've got, you know?"

"Hey, you're all I've got, too," said Kip, standing behind her and hugging her about the shoulders. "But I'll be careful. I always am. Besides, it's just a silly outfit. People will get over it."

"It's a hijab," she said.

"Right, a hijab," said Kip. "And we don't have to go to Woody's. That place is a slimy rattrap anyway."

"It's not Woody's I'm worried about," she said.

"Then what is it, mom?" he asked. "What are you afraid of?"

"I guess I don't really know," she said. "But it has something to do with how we suddenly went from talking about the new school year, like always, to nonstop chatter about this person."

"She's just some girl, mom," said Kip, as he turned to make his way upstairs to his bedroom—and a hasty end to his umpteenth awkward conversation of the day. "Besides," he added. "Ry and I kind of like her. She's sort of—I don't know—quirky, I guess."

"Ms. Amari's not a girl," said Mrs. Beckelhymer, calling after him.

"*Azza*," said Kip, turning to face his mom. "Her name is Azza."

"Point taken," said Mrs. Beckelhymer. "But remember, Kip: Azza's not a girl, she's a woman. And you've lived in Fremont your entire life," she said. "If you're not worried about what could happen, you've forgotten about how people think around here."

• • •

Even later still, when Kip finally settled in for the night, he couldn't help thinking about that police cruiser. About how he'd seen Officer Hudgins following him twice in one day. Perhaps his mom was right about things in Fremont, Kip thought, as he set his well-thumbed biography of President Hayes on the nightstand. Maybe, just maybe, Officer Hudgins's rolling stakeout had a lot less to do with Birdie than he had previously thought.

CHAPTER 11:
BEEP-BEEP, BEEP-BEEP, YEAH!

As Kip waited in the passenger's seat of the Powder Puff, bracing himself against the glove compartment in nervous anticipation, Azza stared straight ahead, her eyes unblinking, her tiny frame planted firmly in the driver's seat. With the Subaru's engine running, a steady stream of exhaust emitting from the ancient car as it sat in idle, Azza gripped the steering wheel with all of her might.

"Whenever you're ready," said Kip, still bracing himself for impact.

"I don't think I can do this, sir," Azza whispered, her eyes staring straight ahead across the sprawling museum parking lot. Except for a few random cars parked near the exhibit hall, the lot was empty.

"When I give the word," said Kip, "try shifting from P into D."

"What is P again, sir?" Azza asked

"P is for Park, and D is for Drive," said Kip.

"No, sir," said Azza, shaking her head vigorously back and forth. "I cannot do this today. I cannot shift into D. Maybe another time."

"I thought you wanted to learn how to drive," said Kip.

"That is true, sir," she replied. "I must be able to do the ALICE. But right now, I am very afraid for my life."

"I'm sorry," Kip said, "but that doesn't make any sense. For one thing, we're not even in gear. So nobody's going anywhere. And second, even if we were in gear, you're not the one sitting in the suicide seat, are you?"

"Very good point, sir," said Azza, still staring dead ahead in the direction of the exhibit hall. "You are right that you should be the one who is afraid. You are riding with the shotgun in the suicide seat, not me."

"Then let's do this!" said Kip, girding up his courage. "Put this thing in gear."

"I am sorry, sir, but I will not be putting this thing in gear," said Azza. "This is enough driving for me today."

"Whatever you say," said Kip. "Just turn the key to kill the ignition."

"I am very sorry, sir," said Azza, her knuckles growing red from exertion, "but I cannot take my hands off of the steering wheel."

With his left hand, Kip reached over to the steering column, turned the key, and shut off the Powder Puff's sputtering engine.

"Should I drive you back to the Holiday Inn now?" Kip asked.

"No, sir, you may not," said Azza, finally lowering her hands from the steering wheel. "Yesterday, I made a solemn bargain with you. That is the museum, is it not?" she added, nodding in the direction of the Hayes. "I will help you to find the figurine and return it to its rightful place."

"Sure," said Kip, "but our bargain was made with the proviso that you would know how to drive. And your driving lessons haven't really started."

"I do not know what is proviso, sir," said Azza, "but I do know that you have begun to teach me in good faith to drive and, ultimately, to do the ALICE. As I have no reason not to trust you implicitly, let us proceed with our search for the figurine at once."

• • •

As Kip and Azza made their way through the vestibule, Marv hurried to meet them, just like clockwork, at the entrance to the exhibit hall.

"Well, if it's not President Rutherford B. Hayes, Junior!" he sang out, his voice echoing off of the marble entryway. "And you must be Lucy Hayes, the First Lady of these United States!" he said to Azza, who stared back at the security guard with a look of profound confusion.

"Don't worry about old Marv," whispered Kip, striding into the exhibit hall with Azza by his side. "I know it's kind of silly."

"It is not silly, sir," Azza replied. "You and Mr. Marv are just male pair-bonding. I learned about such activities in Anthropology. It is a simple masculine ritual that you and Mr. Marv are enacting together. Dr. Matthews says that you are compelled to do so by your race and gender."

"Well, Marv maybe," said Kip. "It's his thing, mostly."

As Kip and Azza made their way into the main exhibit hall, she began to scan the various exhibits, looking up and down as if she might find the figurine lodged behind one of the busts of President Hayes.

"What are you doing?" Kip asked, as Azza began to rummage among the contents of the Domestic Life in the Hayes Administration exhibit, finally settling upon a stray pewter decanter, which she lifted up and began peering inside.

"I am searching for a figurine in the shape of a pear, sir," Azza replied, "to fulfill my part of the bargain."

"You know that it probably wouldn't fit in there, right?" Kip asked, gesturing at the decanter. "The opening's too narrow."

"Oh," said Azza, quickly returning the decanter to the display table. "What are the figurine's dimensions?"

"It's 3 and ¾ inches wide and 5 and ¾ inches high," said Kip.

"And how will I recognize it when I see it? Is it like a pear that you would find in a produce stand, sir—or, how do you say it—in a supermarket?"

"Not exactly. To be honest, I've never actually *seen* the thing. I only know it from the description in the museum's inventory. I've sort of committed it to memory, if you want to know the truth."

"Then tell me your memory, sir, and I will listen," said Azza, waiting patiently beside the Domestic Life in the Hayes Administration exhibit.

"Okay," said Kip. "But just remember that you asked for it."

"Yes, sir," said Azza. "I asked for it."

"Well, here goes nothing," said Kip, taking in a deep breath. "The missing item's inventory number is 1960.3.91. It's a plaster of Paris figurine of a European pear with a 24-carat gold stem. It was a gift to Lucy Hayes from Patrice de MacMahon, President of the Third Republic of France on April 1st, 1879. And it was presented to President Hayes and the First Lady by Ferdinand de Lesseps. The word 'Bonheur' is carved into the base."

"Very good, sir," said Azza. "Your memory has a lot of information stored within it. You must be the envy of your peer group."

"Envy might be the wrong way to put it, actually," said Kip. "I tend to get a lot of eye-rolls when I rattle off something like that."

"Oh, then your peer group is very wrong, sir. Very wrong indeed. Allah has graced you with this extraordinary gift. You should be very proud and use it often."

"Huh," said Kip. "Most people don't see it that way in my experience."

"Those people are mistaken, sir. They should venerate you for this level of detail and knowledge," Azza replied, delivering her words, machine-gun like, with great enthusiasm. "As for me, I now know exactly what the figurine looks like. I will recognize it the instant that I see it. Our investigation has suddenly become much easier thanks to your gift. Our bargain shall soon be fulfilled, Allah be praised."

"But I've already scoured the museum from top to bottom," said Kip, as he gently shifted the decanter back to its original position on the Domestic Life in the Hayes Administration display. "I don't think it's in the building anymore," he added, laughing quietly to himself.

"I don't get it," said Azza. "Why is that humorous, sir?"

"'Cause Ry thinks somebody stole it, along with a replica of the lease that President Hayes signed to take possession of the Isthmus of Panama."

"Why is that humorous?" she asked.

"'Cause you'd have to be pretty lame to steal those things—that's why. I mean, somebody like me would want them. Or Fletch, the museum director. Or maybe that new girl Colby, I guess. But for most people, they're just junk. Besides, they're pretty random, if you think about it."

"Where is this replica, sir?" Azza asked.

"That's just it," Kip replied. "It's missing, too. Like the figurine. It used to be over there near the Panama Canal exhibit," he added, pointing across the main floor of the museum. "But it's even lamer that somebody would steal the replica, assuming anybody stole anything from the Hayes in the first place. I mean, it's not even authentic. It's a facsimile of the real thing, while the pear actually has *some* value, I guess. It's one-of-a-kind, right?"

"I would think so," said Azza. "It must have been the only figurine of its type to be selected for such a special purpose by the President of France. It must be very special indeed. Like your memory, sir."

"Yeah, I guess," said Kip.

"But what does the replica look like?" Azza asked. "Have you memorized its description, too, sir? I must be able to recognize it. Finding this replica might very well lead us to our missing figurine, correct?"

"Oh, I don't have to memorize the replica," said Kip. "That one's easy. I've actually seen the thing, like, a billion times. It's on fake gold parchment with the great seal of the United States of America stamped in a waxy substance that looks like purple gummy stuff. There's a ginormous signature by President Hayes scrawled across the bottom. It's as big as life—bigger than John Hancock's signature on the Declaration of Independence, even!"

"That is very big, sir! I have seen pictures of the Declaration of Independence in school. So very very big!"

"We have a copy of the Declaration of Independence in the archives room if you want to take a look," said Colby, strolling up from the direction of the vestibule.

"It's like you just materialize out of thin air," said Kip, startled by her sudden appearance.

"I'm Colby," she said to Azza, ignoring Kip. "I'm with the Young Docents program."

"I am Azza Amari, Ms. Colby," Azza replied, bowing and shaking the younger woman warmly by the hand.

"Oh, sorry!" said Colby. "My full name's Colby Applegate, but you can just call me Colby. Everybody else does."

"Applegate?" said Kip.

"Colby is a kind of cheese, is it not?" Azza asked.

"Which makes you—*what*—a cheese apple?" Kip said to Colby.

"Very clever," Colby replied, rolling her eyes at Kip. "If you'd like, Marv can open up the archives room for you."

"He is the gentleman who called me First Lady when we entered the museum, correct?" said Azza.

"That's just Marv being Marv," said Colby.

"Huh," said Kip. "I wonder if he has a nickname for you?"

"Not that I know of," Colby replied, shrugging her shoulders. "I guess I'm not that special."

"Guess not," said Kip, smiling and shrugging his shoulders in reply.

"That's high praise around these parts if Marv has taken to calling you Lucy Hayes," Colby said to Azza, who looked away in embarrassment. "Heck, she's the reason I'm into history in the first place."

"Who?" Kip asked. "Lemonade Lucy?"

"Lemonade *what*?" Azza asked.

"That's her nickname all right," Colby replied. "Journalists took to mocking the First Lady as Lemonade Lucy. But that was long after she was dead and gone."

"But you said that Lucy Hayes was a good person, did you not?" Azza asked, clasping her hands close to her chest. "That it was praiseworthy of Mr. Marv to call me by this most exalted name?"

"Oh, she's pretty awesome as historical figures go," said Colby. "She was tough as nails. Had to be, after the contested election of 1876."

"Did she only drink the lemonade?" Azza asked, shifting her gaze back and forth from Colby to Kip and back again.

"Yeah, she was pretty temperate," said Colby, "but it was President Hayes who banned alcohol from the White House during his administration, not the First Lady."

"Oh, I like her then!" said Azza. "I like her very much. She sounds very halal!"

"Maybe so," said Kip, glancing in Colby's direction, "although I doubt that Lucy Hayes ate much meat in her day that had been slaughtered under the supervision of a mullah. She might have even partaken of a little pork now and then, too."

"I don't care, sir!" said Azza, smiling broadly from ear to ear. "She is a woman—how do you say it, Mr. Kip?—who is after my own heart!"

CHAPTER 12: YOU'RE A SKY FULL OF STARS

As Kip drove the Powder Puff along Hayes Avenue, Azza sighed loudly from her place in the back seat.

"What's up?" said Kip, stealing a quick glance into the rearview mirror.

"We are no closer to fulfilling our bargain," she replied.

"Well," said Kip, "we can be reasonably sure that the figurine is not in the museum. Like I said, Fletch and I scoured the place. That only leaves—*what?*—the whole of the rest of the United States, I guess."

As Kip concentrated on the roadway, Azza emitted yet another sigh from the direction of the back seat.

"What? Is it something I said?" he asked, glancing into the rearview mirror yet again.

"You are not very good at the game of flirting, sir," said Azza.

"Huh?" Kip asked.

"That girl—the cheese apple—she is smitten with you, I believe," said Azza.

"Smitten?"

"She likes you. She would like you to woo her, sir. That is what I believe."

"Oh, I don't think so," said Kip. "No, I don't think that's true at all."

"Remember, I am older than you, sir," Azza replied. "I can tell these things."

"Not that much older," said Kip, shaking his head. "Hey, do you want to get something to eat?"

"I know what you are doing, sir," said Azza. "You are attempting to change the subject, correct?"

"Well, yeah," Kip replied. "But I'm also pretty hungry."

As he continued along tree-lined Hayes Avenue, Kip glanced into the rearview mirror for any signs of the telltale police cruiser, which was nowhere in sight. All he could see was a blond kid, his locks flowing in the wind, rolling along on a skateboard. So far, so good, Kip thought to himself.

"Very well," said Azza, "then I will change the subject back to that girl. I am of the belief that she likes you."

"That girl can barely *stand* me," said Kip. "And I can barely stomach her. She's a know-it-all."

"I don't know what is to stomach or to be a know-it-all," said Azza, "but yes, I will dine with you, sir, if it means not exercising my regular meal plan at the Holiday Inn."

• • •

"I have read that this place is not very halal," said Azza, shaking her head as she followed Kip into the McDonald's entryway. "Perhaps we should go back to the Woody's? I could eat the pancakes, which are permissible, and," she added, searching for her words, "they were very delectable, sir. Yes, that's it," she continued, smiling quietly to herself. "They were very delectable indeed."

As Kip and Azza made their way up to the counter, the other patrons trained their collective gaze on the unusual couple strolling into the restaurant. To Kip, it was as if the colorful hijab adorned about Azza's head and shoulders was some kind of tractor beam—like the one in *Star Wars* that, the Rebellion be damned, drew the *Millennium Falcon* into the bowels of the Death Star. Like Han Solo and Chewy, the other diners were incapable of breaking the tractor beam's devastating pull. With their Big Macs and their french fries waiting half-eaten in front of them, they could only sit by and stare, dumbstruck as the Muslim girl walked among them, unfettered and free.

"I don't think Mickey D's is serving breakfast right now," said Kip, trying his best to ignore the gawking patrons. Even the cashier behind the counter seemed to be captivated by the sight of Azza and her ever-present hijab, its billowing folds of colorful fabric rendered even brighter still by the restaurant's fluorescent lighting.

"I'll have a Quarter Pounder with cheese, fries, and a large chocolate shake," said Kip, scanning the menu above the counter. "How about you?" he asked Azza.

"I will have a water, sir."

"Come on," he said, taking a long look at the menu overhead. "You're in America now. You gotta eat like an American. How about the Filet-o-Fish?"

"Fine, sir, I will have this fish. But mostly, I will have the water."

• • •

As Kip began to devour his hamburger, which he supplemented with occasional and very fulsome gulps from his shake, Azza observed in a kind of awe from her place in the booth.

"You must have been very hungry indeed, sir," she said, as she picked at her sandwich, deftly removing the patty from the bun, scraping off the gritty tartar sauce, and skewering a tiny sliver of fish with her plastic fork.

Kip nodded as he took another drag from his chocolate shake, emptying the remainder of its contents with a final, noisy swig.

"Where is Mr. Ry today, sir?"

"I don't know, actually," said Kip, reflexively pulling his phone out of his jeans pocket to check for any stray texts.

"Now, sir, let us return to this girl Colby," said Azza, pushing the rest of her sandwich aside, "I have not forgotten her."

"I was kinda hoping you would," said Kip, setting his phone on the tabletop.

"Do you like her, sir?"

"I have seen her exactly twice in my entire life."

"Then it is not love at first sight?"

"Are you kidding? It's more like annoyance at first sight."

"As I said, sir, I believe that she would like you to woo her."

"I just got done wooing Birdie pretty badly," he replied. "I don't want to get tangled up with Miss Know-It-All."

"Miss Pigtails, Lemonade Lucy, and now Miss Know-It-All," said Azza, raising her hand in a show of surrender. "I give up, sir. There are too many nicknames to carry on a decent conversation."

"Colby may be nice and all," said Kip, "but she's annoying as all get-out. Besides, my only goal is to find the pear, graduate, and get the heck outta Dodge."

"And to teach me how to drive," said Azza, correcting him.

"Yeah, that too," said Kip, as he dispatched the rest of his quarter pounder in a single humongous bite.

"But what is Dodge, sir?"

"Just a saying," said Kip. "Kinda like riding shotgun. Getting out of Dodge means, you know, making a break for it. It refers to Dodge City, Kansas, back in the days of the Old West. You herd the cattle from the trail into the stockyards, get paid, and get out of town with your earnings. And after graduation, I intend to do just that: get out of town and never look back."

"That sounds like you are running away from something, sir. But you have everything here: your family, your Ry, your museum with all of the history that you adore, a college that you can attend."

"Well, life with my Ry gets pretty stale, actually. And there are other colleges in other towns that are far more interesting than Fremont, I assure you."

And that's when Azza saw her—none other than Birdie herself, pigtails and all. She was huddled up in a booth across the restaurant with another girl, their heads bouncing up and down in intense conversation.

And then, as if on cue, the tractor beam returned to the restaurant.

As if she had been disturbed by a sudden moment of quietude in the otherwise noisy malaise of McDonald's, Birdie's friend—her yellow hair, like some kind of golden straw, hanging loosely about her face—stared straight ahead. And her gaze locked directly onto Azza and her otherworldly hijab. Spying the Muslim woman across the way with Kip, Birdie's friend thrust her index finger in front of her, jabbing in the air in Azza's direction. And although she was no lip-reader by any measure, Azza could plainly make out the blonde-haired girl's words as she mouthed them from across the restaurant:

"That's her!"

As Azza watched from her place in the booth, Birdie's straw-haired friend grabbed Miss Pigtails by the arm and pulled her across the restaurant. Within a matter of seconds, they had closed the space between them and were standing directly in front of Kip and Azza's booth.

For his part, Kip was startled by their sudden manifestation at McDonald's. For a moment, he could scarcely breathe. Azza was struck by the smell of lilacs, some kind of perfume she imagined, that accompanied the girl's arrival.

"Sheryl Ann?" he asked, confused by the spectacle appearing so unexpectedly before him at Mickey D's.

"Birdie doesn't give a fuck about you!" said Sheryl Ann, gesturing towards him with one hand, while holding her pigtailed-friend behind her with the other, as if she were protecting Birdie from some sort of imminent danger right there in McDonald's. "And she doesn't give a fuck about *you* either!" she shrieked at Azza, who winced in response.

"That's right!" said Birdie, peering over Sheryl Ann's shoulder. "Zero fucks!"

And then, almost as suddenly as they had appeared, Sheryl Ann and Birdie tromped out of the restaurant, leaving Kip and Azza alone to ponder the maelstrom that they had left in their wake.

"Well, that was pretty awful," said Kip, staring down at the remains of his fries.

After a moment, Azza regained her composure, with the scent of lilacs finally receding from the vicinity. As they sat there alone in their silence, Kip's phone buzzed into life with an incoming text. It was from Birdie, no less.

"ZERO FUCKS!" screamed her disembodied voice across the ether.

"Did you love her, sir?" Azza asked. "Did she give you a sky full of stars?"

"That's just a song," said Kip.

"But it is love, is it not? That feeling?"

"It is," said Kip. "At least I hope it is, I guess. But I don't think Birdie and I have that anymore. She certainly doesn't have it for me."

"No, sir, I do not think she does," Azza replied. "That did not seem like the feeling of love in her voice."

CHAPTER 13: POBODY'S NERFECT

Kip sat alone in his bedroom, working by the lamplight on his desk as he scrolled through an SAT practice guide on his laptop:

> Which of the following statements best represents a nativist attitude toward the influx of immigrants around 1900?
>
> (A) Slavs and Italians will be assimilated as easily into the American way of life as were earlier immigrant groups.
> (B) Ellis Island should be enlarged to accommodate the huge influx of immigrants.
> (C) Immigrants will work for low wages and break strikes, thereby hurting all American workers.
> (D) Native-born Americans should organize to help find jobs and homes for new immigrants so that they can become citizens as quickly as possible.
> (E) Political machines in the large cities should be responsible for providing immigrants with food, shelter, and jobs in return for their votes.

"That's easy," Kip thought to himself. "It's gotta be C. Americans have always felt threatened by outsiders." He clicked the icon next to option C, and a new prompt appeared on his screen:

> Nativism in the United States, consisting of anti-immigrant sentiment and fear of foreign influence, was a major presence in

> politics in the 19th and early 20th centuries. Thus, a nativist attitude would be one that reflects a bias against new immigrants. This points most clearly to the anti-immigrant attitude in answer choice C, which describes immigrants as a threat to American workers—an accurate description of an attitude held by many nativists around 1900.

"Bingo!" said Kip aloud, as his mom inched his bedroom door open.

"Whatcha working on?" she asked, peering her head through the doorway.

"SATs," Kip replied.

"Oh, monkey. I don't know why you're taking them again. Your first score was plenty good enough."

"*Mom,*" he said, glaring at her from across the room.

"Sorry," she replied. "I promised to stop calling you monkey, didn't I?"

"If I don't get a higher score," he continued, "there's no way I'm going to Case Western in the fall, much less anywhere else."

"You're more intelligent than anyone I know—definitely as smart as any of the kids who roll through our office on campus. Smarter, even."

"Maybe so," Kip replied, "but that doesn't get me much further than Northwestern Ohio State. Certainly not to Case Western or, if I win the brainiac lottery, Georgetown. And no matter what, I'm going to need a scholarship."

"Oh, honey, Northwestern Ohio State isn't so bad. It'd be fun to see you around the campus. You could get a couple of years under your belt with our tuition discount and then transfer—"

"I don't want to be a transfer student, mom. I've told you that, like, a thousand times already."

"I'm sorry, Kip. I'd just hate to see you get hurt is all."

"As soon as I finish this history module, I'm heading over to Ry's," he said, ignoring her last remark as he glanced back towards his screen.

"Don't stay out too late, monkey," she said.

Kip looked up from his laptop, glaring at her yet again.

"I'm so sorry," she said. "No more monkey, monkey. I promise!"

• • •

The Powder Puff sputtered and coughed as Kip pulled up in front of 2234 Augusta. He lumbered up the Tudor home's elegant front walkway, and just as he was about to press the buzzer, the massive oaken door flung open, and there was Ry, big as life, wearing a pink terrycloth bathrobe, and sporting a dazed and confused look upon his face.

"Beckelhymen?" he asked, stepping past Kip onto the porch and awkwardly craning his neck as he looked up and down Augusta Drive, which was empty, save for the Subaru parked out front.

"Expecting someone?" Kip asked.

"Dude, I wasn't even expecting *you*," said Ry, as he waved his friend inside. Before closing the door, Ry took one last look around for good measure.

• • •

Kip followed Ry into the Langhams' basement, a ridiculous affair that spanned the length of the house, which was saying something, given the home's sizable footprint. At the far end of the basement was a vintage full-length bar, complete with antique glass mirrors, a gleaming countertop fashioned out of pure Vermont maple, and an iron foot rail.

Needless to say, the bar was in pristine condition, given Mr. Langham's protracted absences as he trolled across the country on what seemed like the world's longest, never-ending business trip. Although he rarely actually saw his father, Ry was regularly besieged by random gifts that would arrive in the mail, a miniature wooden carving of the Alamo, a stainless-steel model of the Space Needle, a plastic rendering of the Gateway Arch, to name but a few of the kitschy souvenirs that pocked the nooks and crannies of the Langham household.

"Shall we retire to the saloon?" Ry asked, effecting his voice in a crude hillbilly accent. After the two friends took up their positions on a pair of polished wooden stools. Kip watched as Ry threw open his robe and pulled a massive reefer from somewhere in its plushy pink nether regions.

"Of course!" said Kip, clapping his hands together. "I should have seen the signs, right? The paranoia, the darting eyes, the whole shebang. You're stoned!"

"It's no biggie, dude," said Ry, taking a long pull off of the gigantic joint.

"It would be quite the biggie if your parents came home, though, right?"

"Dude, dude, dude, it's no big deal," Ry replied. "I do what I want, man. You know that."

"Yeah," said Kip. "Beer in the mailbox, weed in the basement. I see how you roll."

"Just chill out is what I say," Ry answered, as he took another lengthy drag from the reefer.

"Is there any substance that you don't abuse?" Kip asked, wincing as the skunky odor from the weed began to coalesce in the basement.

"Heroin," Ry somberly answered. "I draw the line at heroin."

"How mature," said Kip, waving his hand in front of him in a crude attempt to clear the air. "So where are your parents anyway?"

"Mom's still in Aruba. Dad's in—actually, I don't have the first clue where he's at. Alaska, maybe?" said Ry. "Dude, *relax*. Have a beer, why doncha?" Standing up in front of the bar, Ry stretched his frame over the maple countertop, reached over the bar, and produced a chilled bottle of Stella.

"Fine," said Kip, taking the beer from his hand. "Do you have an opener?"

"Check over there," he replied, gesturing towards the far end of the bar. "I think I left it near the Astrodome."

Doing as Ry had instructed, Kip made his way to the far end of the bar. And sure enough, there it was: an old-timey wooden bottle opener lying next to a scale model of Houston's domed stadium, yet another reminder of the furtive meanderings of Ry's father.

"It's startin' to get around the peeps, you know," said Ry, contemplating the smoldering joint in his hand and still speaking in his countrified voice.

"Dear Jesus," Kip sighed, "*what's* starting to get around?"

"The story about you and Miss Pigtails," he answered, his accent shifting, inexplicably, into a kind of bizarre Southern California drawl. "That you're Donesville and all. It's tough times, my brotha. I feel you."

"Who the eff am I talking to?" Kip asked. "You've been telling me to break up with Birdie since . . . since I first started dating her, come to think of it. 'We're gonna be two playas on the loose,' you said. So what gives? When am I gonna get mine?"

"Oh, so that's what this is about," said Ry, nodding to himself as he took another pull from the joint.

"*What are you talking about*?" Kip asked, setting the Stella down on the bar top with a thud.

"We both know what I'm talkin' about, my brotha," said Ry. "If you and the Birdwoman had gone all the way, we wouldn't be havin' this conversation, you feel me?"

"Right," said Kip, "like you've ever gotten laid."

"I told you about Cheyenne."

"Here we go again," said Kip, shaking his head.

"Chey was hot, dude. And she was hot for *me*," said Ry, his California drawl having suddenly disappeared as he set the smoldering reefer on the bar.

"Right, and she had that tattoo or whatever on her shoulder blade that said—"

"'I love my daddy.'"

"I thought it was 'I heart my daddy?'"

"Same difference," said Ry. "And it was on her *left* shoulder blade. And every time I was, like, pumping her—"

"I know, I know," said Kip. "It was creepy because all you could think was—"

"That I am pumping away at daddy's little girl. Wait, have I told you this before?" Ry asked, his drug-induced haze having all but dissipated.

"Dear Lord, yes," said Kip. "Yes, you have, Ry. Possibly a hundred times. But you haven't told it since that July 4th cookout at your cousin's house, so, really, it hasn't gotten old in the slightest."

"Man, I'd like to see Chey again," said Ry, wistfully shaking his head back and forth.

"Yeah, I'd like to see her, too," said Kip. "Because we both know she doesn't really exist."

"But I told you, dude, about the tattoo—"

"You always do, Ry. It's the little details that make the story seem more believable."

"But it's the God's-honest-truth, Beckelhymen. I'm not shitting you."

"Show me Cheyenne, and then maybe I'll believe you.

"*Maybe*?" Ry snorted. "All you have to do is look at her right shoulder blade, and then you'll know it's the righteous truth."

"You said it was her left shoulder blade, like, five seconds ago!"

"I can't believe you're doubting me—"

"Okay, let's assume for a minute that you and Chey actually got it on," said Kip. "How do I know you didn't give her some knockout drug like ketamine or GHB?"

"Like I'd even have access to that kinda stuff—"

"Ry, your dad's in pharmaceuticals! I've seen his stash upstairs in his study. You show it to anyone who will so much as give you the time of day. You have ready access to everything under the sun!"

"Dude, that's foul!" said Ry, staring down at the maple bar top. "Besides, I don't need drugs to bring the ladies to their knees. It just happens naturally. They can't help themselves around me."

As Ry contemplated his reflection in the finely polished wood, Kip began to snicker. "Dude," said Ry, "what's so fuckin' funny?"

"You are, Ry. That's what's funny. Sometimes, I think you're all talk. What's that expression?—'all hat and no cattle.' That's you, man."

"Oh, that's not fair, dude," said Ry. "You know I'm not like the rest of those asshats at school. I may mouth off a lot, but I'm cool with anything. Take Azza, for one thing. You don't hear me calling her a raghead like everyone else, do ya?"

"They call her a raghead, Ry?" said Kip. "What is this—Operation Desert Storm?"

"That's my point, Beckelhymen. I'm totally cool with her. She's just another kid to me. I'm color-blind, you know? Like, she's just a real person to me."

"A real person like Cheyenne?"

"Dude, that's not funny. I'm being serious here. Azza's an awesome chick, man. And that girl—what's her name from the museum? Was it Colby? She's awesome, too. Kinda geeky for my taste, but you know, whatevs. Which reminds me—"

"Dear Jesus, what now?" Kip asked, taking a swig from his beer.

"Do you think she'd go for me?"

"Who? *Colby*?"

"No, Azza!" said Ry.

Without warning, Kip started snickering yet again, this time breaking into full-on laughter. Setting his beer down on the bar top, he fell into a coughing fit, sputtering stray bits of Stella as he attempted to regain his composure.

"Somehow, I don't think your lifestyle's very halal, if you know what I mean," said Kip, still chuckling quietly to himself.

"Dude, I would change for her," said Ry. "Seriously, I could be all pious and shit for the right girl."

"Ry, she moved all the way out here to study chemical engineering, not to get wrapped up in your hot mess."

"That's uncool, dude," said Ry. "A brotha doesn't talk about another brotha that way."

"Next, you're gonna say 'bro's before ho's,' right?"

But before Ry could answer, they heard the massive oaken door slam shut upstairs.

"Is your mom back from Aruba?" Kip asked.

"Oh, fuck," said Ry. "This can't be happening."

"*What* can't be happening?"

"My fuckin' dad is back."

"From Alaska?"

"No, dude. I mean, it could be Alaska. Who the fuck can say? All I know is that we gotta clean all this shit up pronto."

"What happened to 'it's no big deal, man. I do what I want'?" Kip replied.

"That went out the window when my dad got home," said Ry, who pulled off his bathrobe, rolled it up into a ball, and tossed it on top of the bar.

"Like I told you before, 'all hat and no cattle,'" Kip said, as he drained his Stella in a final swig.

"Dude, help me clean this shit up before he comes down!"

As Kip watched, Ry pulled a billowing black garbage bag from behind the bar and began flinging the detritus of the evening inside. First, Ry dispatched with Kip's beer bottle, followed by the reefer, which he snuffed out in the folds of his bathrobe, before cinching up the bag and tossing the whole lot, the disheveled pink robe and all, behind the bar.

Leaping over the maple countertop, Ry reappeared with a can of deodorizer, which he began to spray liberally around the basement in a desperate attempt to quell the residual odor of the weed.

"That'll never work, man. It smells like pure skunk in here."

"You could try helping for a change, Kip," said Ry, tossing the can of deodorizer back behind the bar.

And that's when Mr. Langham clunked down the basement stairs and made his appearance.

"I thought I heard you boys down here," he said, as he strode across the room and took a spot on one of the bar stools. "Mind pouring me a cognac, son?" he asked Ry.

"A *what*?" Ry asked, still attempting to shake the cobwebs out of his weed-addled mind.

"Cognac is a brandy, son," said Mr. Langham, straightening the lapels of his lime green blazer. "It's the Rémy Martin bottle right there behind the bar. You can't miss it."

"Oh, don't be so sure about that, Mr. Langham," said Kip. "If anyone can find a way to miss something, it would be your son."

As Ry pulled a shot glass out from behind the bar, he banged the side of his head with his hand, still trying to rouse himself from the effects of the reefer.

"Do you have a headache, Ryan?" Mr. Langham asked.

"He probably does now," said Kip.

"Son, one simply doesn't pour cognac in a shot glass. You need to use a snifter for brandy," said Mr. Langham, chuckling to himself. "You can't take him anywhere, can you?" he asked, turning to face Kip.

"No, sir," Kip replied, beaming from ear to ear, "you certainly can't."

As Ry poured the cognac into the smooth, balloon-shaped glass on the bar top, Mr. Langham held the snifter up to the light for closer inspection. Meanwhile, Kip winced as the skunky smell began to reassert itself yet again in the vicinity of the bar.

"Will you look at that, fellas?" he asked. "You really know you're onto something special when brandy takes on this rich shade of brown. It's exquisite," he added as he twirled the russet-colored liquid around in the snifter before taking his first nip.

"How did your trip go, Mr. Langham?" Kip asked.

"These business jaunts start to run together after a while," he replied, "but this one was different. I felt like a chemist again for the first time in—I don't know—*years*. Even got to work in the lab for a bit."

"Kip can't help you there, Pop," said Ry. "He's not sciency."

"*Au contraire,* son. Anyone can comport themselves like a scientist if they want to. You simply need to be willing to perceive the world through the lens of the scientific method. You can solve virtually any problem in that fashion," said Mr. Langham, taking another nip from his brandy.

"*Any* problem?" Kip asked.

"Surely," Mr. Langham replied. "You begin by making an observation, then you ask a question, formulate a hypothesis, make a prediction based upon that hypothesis, and then test it. The answer to the question will then be reached through logical deduction and evidence."

"So," said Kip, "let's say you worked in a museum, and one of the artifacts has gone missing—"

"That would be your observation," said Mr. Langham. "Go on."

"And you want to know what happened to it—"

"There's your question," said Mr. Langham. "Next."

"Ry here thinks it was stolen," Kip continued.

"That's a reasonable hypothesis," Mr. Langham replied.

"Right," said Kip, "but how do we make a prediction based upon that hypothesis?"

"You consider the possibilities," said Mr. Langham. "What would be the motive for stealing the artifact? Was it a painting or some kind of precious jewel?"

"Hell, no," Ry interjected. "It wasn't even remotely that cool. It's a lame old paperweight in the shape of a pear—"

"Actually, it's a plaster of Paris figurine that belonged to First Lady Lucy Hayes," said Kip, interrupting him.

"Then you have to assume that somebody would try to fence it," said Mr. Langham. "How else could you accrue any value from the theft? Unless, that is, the thief simply had to have the thing in their possession for its historical import or some such reason."

"But that would be a different prediction, right?" Kip asked.

"Sure would," said Mr. Langham, taking another nip of brandy. "But if you went with the original prediction, you'd have to assume the thief will be trying to fence it."

"Fine," said Ry, his wits clearly having finally returned to him, "then what's our logical deduction? Where do we find the evidence to test out the hypothesis?"

"If I were the culprit," said Mr. Langham, "I'd try to turn the artifact over for some quick cash, say, from a pawn shop. They'll supposedly buy anything, right?"

"Even here in Fremont?" Kip asked.

"Sure," Mr. Langham replied. "I bet there are a few dozen pawn shops between here and the lakefront alone. Many more as you skirt closer to the big cities."

"Pawn shops, huh?" said Kip, lost in thought as he tapped his fingers rhythmically upon his chin.

"And now for the big unveil," said Mr. Langham, who produced a copper molding of the space shuttle from the pocket of his blazer.

"That's right!" said Ry, taking the miniature spacecraft into the palm of his hand. "Now, I remember. You went to Florida!"

CHAPTER 14: FML

Azza sat alone in Faraday Hall's first-floor computer lab. An enormous bay window offered a picturesque view of College Avenue, bright and floral in the late afternoon sun. Only Azza wasn't using one of Northwestern Ohio State's PC stations. Instead, she wrestled with her old Anova laptop, which she balanced precariously on her knees. With no time to lose, she logged into Little Tunisia for the first time since that morning. She desperately needed to know if her father was safe and sound. As it happened, the alarm bells had gone off during her predawn visit to Little Tunisia, when his regular morning message had failed to materialize.

With a few taps on the keyboard, her alter-ego Anna Karenina meandered her way into the "Lifestyle and Tourism" subthread, but to her dismay, there was nothing there to see. Only the very same blank silence that she had registered earlier that morning. Her father, for all intents and purposes, was incommunicado. And Azza, for her part, could feel the fear washing over her as she pondered the uncertainty of his fate in a distant, far-flung hemisphere.

Glancing up from her laptop, Azza spotted the Subaru parked out front, with Kip sitting in the driver's seat, staring straight ahead and tapping his fingers impatiently on the steering wheel. Meanwhile, the back-seat windows were rolled down, with a pair of bare feet dangling outside. It must be Ry, she thought to herself. Who else, really, could it be?

Sitting there in the computer lab after her visit to Little Tunisia, Azza could feel her sense of fear transform into a darker, malingering feeling of dread. Allah be praised, her dear father would make his presence known soon enough, and only then would her waking nightmare be ended.

But at the same time, Azza realized that she had little choice but to get on with it. If her experience in her adopted homeland had taught her nothing else, she had learned how to take the blows associated with living each new, uncertain day in a foreign land. And so, with her pulse returning to a degree of normalcy, she stowed away her laptop in the valise.

And when Azza looked up again, she found herself eye-to-eye with Kip, the All American one. The other guy—the gross one—must still be back in the car, she reasoned, bare feet and all. For a moment, she searched Kip's face for any sign of irritation—as if he'd had to trouble himself to climb out of his car, walk over to Faraday Hall, and rescue the pathetic, helpless foreign student. But she didn't need a rescuer, Azza thought to herself. If her adopted American compatriots didn't know she could take care of herself, they'd all figure that out soon enough. That they would.

But Kip wasn't irritated in the slightest. He just smiled at her for a moment, then gave a little wave and pointed in the direction of the hatchback. After she nodded and smiled in return, he gave her a thumbs up as if to say, "No hurry, Ms. Amari. Your driver patiently awaits." She had to admit that she liked the sound of that—especially about patience, which, Allah be praised, was always a virtue in her book.

By the time that Azza strolled over to the Subaru, Kip was back behind the wheel. She could see Ry napping in the back seat, his feet still hanging out of the window. After a few seconds, he cracked his eyelids open, and, seeing her standing there, motioned for her to take the front seat. But Azza wasn't having it. She shook her head back and forth, and, getting the hint, Ry flopped his gangly body over the armrest into the front, where he landed with a thud. Seizing the moment, she opened the door and climbed into the back seat.

"Azza, dude, you seem kinda bummed today," said Ry, who was resting his head against the passenger's side window.

"I am not a dude," she replied. "This is America. I am a chick."

"Okay, but what's up, A?" Ry asked. "You don't seem like yourself."

"What do you mean, sir?" Azza asked. "I am always myself. I am always she."

"But you seem like you're in kind of a bad mood," said Kip.

"I am, sir," she replied, fussing with the unruly folds of her headscarf. "I am having a bad hijab day."

"Is that really a thing?" Kip asked, glancing at Azza's reflection in the rearview mirror.

"Most definitely, sir," said Azza. "A bad hijab day takes on many forms."

"Like what?" said Ry, repositioning his head against the window.

"Like when you laugh really hard and feel your hijab beginning to unravel," she answered. "When that happens, I am LMHO."

"As in Laughing My Hijab Off?" Kip asked.

"That is correct, sir," said Azza. "Then there are the stupid people of the world with their stupid questions like 'Do you shower in it?' or 'Do you sleep in it?'"

"I get the shower thing," said Ry from his place in the front seat, "but I figured you wore the thing to bed. Isn't that, like, the devout thing to do?"

"Don't be a retard, Ry," said Kip. "Of course, she doesn't wear her hijab when she sleeps. What's wrong with you?"

"I don't know, Beckelhymen," Ry replied. "I guess I'm just one of the many stupid people who roam the earth."

And that's when the hatchback slammed into a pothole on College Avenue. The ensuing collision jarred Ry's head against the passenger's side window.

"FML!" Ry screamed, as Kip struggled to right the Powder Puff.

"What is FML, sir?" Azza asked.

"Means 'Fuck My Life,'" Kip replied. "Seems that Ry's having a bad hijab day, too. Only in his case, it's a weedover."

"A weedover, sir?" Azza asked.

"Yeah," said Kip. "It's kind of like a hangover, where you have to weather the effects after a night of heavy drinking. Only for Ry, it's the express result of smoking way too much reefer for his own good."

"Shut the eff up, dude," said Ry. "My head is pounding."

"Try hydrating," said Kip.

"Water sucks," Ry replied. "I don't like how it tastes."

"It is written, sir," said Azza, "that Allah created the water first above all things—even before creating the light, the darkness, the earth, and the heavens."

"Maybe so," said Ry, "but water still tastes like nothing, and I drink for taste."

"Sounds like we've got a stalemate on our hands," said Kip, as he turned into the parking lot behind the Hayes. "Personally, I'd go with Allah over Ry."

"I would, too, sir," said Azza. "Allah is all-knowing and all-wise."

"Yeah, and Ry is all-grungy and all-toked-out," said Kip, as he climbed out of the car, which was sitting in idle in the parking lot. For her part, Azza sat stone-faced in the back seat, staring straight ahead as if in a trance.

"It's time," said Kip, drumming the palms of his hand on the Subaru's dilapidated roof. After emitting an elongated sigh, Azza opened the door and joined him beside the Powder Puff.

"Ry, clear out," Kip instructed, clapping his hands together. As if performing some kind of Pavlovian response, Ry flopped over the armrest yet again, landing in the back seat of the car in a clump.

"You got this," said Kip, holding open the driver's side door for Azza.

"I am doing it for the ALICE," said Azza resolutely, as she climbed in behind the wheel. Meanwhile, Kip walked around the front of the car and took up his place in the passenger's seat.

"All you've got to do is put it into D," he said, "and we're off."

"I don't think I can do it, sir," said Azza. "I thought that I could, but it feels different in this seat."

"Sure you can," said Kip. "It's as easy as pie."

"I believe that I would rather eat the pie, sir."

"Let's take your mind off of things, then," said Kip. "What'd you do in school today? Learn anything new?"

"Most of my time is spent studying for Dr. Matthews's Anthropology class, sir," said Azza.

"Dr. Matthews? My mom says she's great," Kip replied.

"She is not great," said Azza. "Only Allah is great. But especially not Dr. Matthews. I hate her."

"Whoa there, A," said Ry. "Why do you hate her? That sounds kinda extreme."

"Dr. Matthews is very disrespectful. And she is cruel and unknowing," said Azza. "I hope that she enters the fire."

"Aren't you supposed to avoid saying mean stuff like that?" Kip asked.

"Yeah," said Ry, "what's so awful about her dumb class anyway?"

"Dr. Matthews is requiring every student to learn how to tell a joke," she replied, gripping the steering wheel with all of her might. "It's an in-class assignment for our Studies in American humor unit."

"Sounds interesting," said Kip.

"No, sir. It is not very interesting," she said through gritted teeth. "I have been practicing in my hotel room all week."

"By yourself?" Kip asked. "How can you practice a joke without an audience?"

"Yeah," said Ry. "Try it out on us."

"No, sirs," said Azza. "That would be very embarrassing."

"If you gotta tell it in front of your whole class, then you can test it out on us!" Ry protested.

"I'm with Ry," said Kip. "Tell the joke or put this thing in D."

"Very well, sir," said Azza, her knuckles transforming into even deeper shades of red. "Two cannibals are eating a clown. One cannibal says to the other, 'Does this guy taste funny to you?'"

"*And*?" Ry asked.

"That was it, sir," Azza replied. "That was the joke."

"Oh, I get it," said Kip. "That was pretty good."

"No, it was not, sir," said Azza. "It was not good, and it was not funny."

"She's right," said Ry. "It wasn't very funny. When you gotta tell a joke, you can't force it. Being funny is a gift."

"Please show me how to tell a joke, sir," said Azza. "I would like to be funny and receive credit for my in-class assignment."

"Alrighty then," said Ry, sitting up and resting his hands on the armrest, "let the joke master take over!"

"This is probably not a good idea," said Kip. "For all of our sakes, Azza, please—*please!*—put this thing in D."

"I would like to hear the joke, sir," Azza replied.

"Here goes!" said Ry, smiling with unchecked glee. "Do you know what the ideal woman looks like?"

"No, sir," said Azza. "What does she look like?"

"She's three-feet tall with a flat head and no teeth," said Ry.

"Okay," said Azza, "why is she three-feet tall with a flat head and no teeth?"

"So you have somewhere to set your drink while she's sucking you off!" said Ry, who began laughing uproariously from the back seat.

"Dude, that's awful," said Kip.

"It is not so abhorrent, sir," said Azza. "The man is slaking his lust, right?"

"I guess," said Kip, staring at her from across the front seat. "But it's not very twenty-first century."

"A man's lust doesn't know any time or place," said Azza, her hands beginning to loosen on the steering wheel.

"You realize you're defending the objectification of womankind, right?" Kip asked. "And what is this 'slaking his lust' bit? Sounds like a romance novel."

"That is what I read, sir. In the Barbara Cartland. "

"In Tunisia?" Kip asked.

"No, in Paris, sir," said Azza. "It was in Arabic translation."

"All I am saying is that it's not very feminist of you to defend Ry's nasty joke," said Kip.

"I *am* a feminist, sir," said Azza.

"Hold up a sec," said Ry, "how can you be a feminist and wear that getup at the same time?"

"Don't you understand, sir? It is my face, and I am free to cover or uncover it. In this country, no one will make me take it off unless I want to. Is that correct?"

"Yeah," said Kip. "I mean, it's supposed to be."

"Then I will continue to wear it to honor my beliefs," she said. "And my father's beliefs, too."

"But don't you want to fit in?" Ry asked.

"I want to be me. And right now, I want to wear the hijab, sir. If I decide to no longer wear it, then I will take it off. But it will be up to me. I will be the one who decides."

"I don't know," said Ry. "We may have to agree to disagree on this one, A."

"Of course, she can be a feminist," said Kip. "You're being ridiculous."

"Fuck you, dude!" said Ry. "You're the one who's being ridiculous!"

"Whatever, asshat!" said Kip. "It's hard to take anyone seriously who's stuck in a weedover!"

"You are both ridiculous, sirs!" Azza shrieked, as she arched back her elbow and slid the gearshift from P into D.

And with that, the Powder Puff lunged across the parking lot, with Azza gripping the steering wheel even more tightly than before. The sudden surge of forward momentum tossed Ry to and fro about the back seat, and he began shouting "FUUUUCK! MYYYY! LIIIIFE!" as the vehicle hurtled in the direction of the museum. Meanwhile, Kip fought to right himself in the passenger's seat as the Powder Puff sprang closer and closer to the building. At the last possible moment, Kip reached over with his left leg and plunged his foot onto the brake, bringing the car to a wrenching stop just short of the concrete curb that ran alongside the Hayes.

With the force of the vehicle coming to a sudden halt, Azza thrust her hands out in front of her, jamming them against the horn in the same instant. After a moment, Kip reached over and eased her palms off of the blaring horn, and for the next several seconds, the three friends sat quietly inside the Subaru as they struggled to regain their senses.

It was Kip who spoke up first.

"Azza," he said as gently as he possibly could, "you didn't have your foot on the brake."

"What brake, sir?" she replied. "All you told me about driving was to put the car in D, so I put it in D."

"Way to go, dumbass," said Ry. "You shoulda told her about the brake."

Before Kip could so much as answer, Marv appeared by the open driver's side window, summoned no doubt by the sound of the car horn blaring from the parking lot.

"Whoa, there, Lemonade Lucy!" said the security guard, panting heavily as he propped himself up on the frame of the vehicle.

For a moment, Azza still seemed caught up in the daze associated with the Powder Puff's near-demise in the Hayes parking lot. But just as suddenly, she had righted herself.

"Why did you call me by that nickname, sir?" she asked, staring up at Marv from her place in the Subaru's driver's seat. "Do I remind you of the First Lady?"

"Sorry, ma'am," said Marv, still convulsing after making his mad dash from the museum to the parking lot. "I didn't mean anything by it."

"It kind of makes sense," said Kip. "Mrs. Hayes was a teetotaler, you're halal, right?"

"I don't really know what teetotaler means," said Azza.

"I know this, actually," said Kip.

"Sure you do!" said Ry, laughing from the back seat.

"Teetotaler comes from England, mid-nineteenth-century," said Kip. "A guy named Richard Turner, who was a temperance society member, had a speech impediment. He was trying to advocate for total abstinence from liquor, but when he said 'total abstinence,' it came out as 'tee-tee total abstinence.' So to be free from drink is to be a teetotaler, get it?"

"So the dude was a stutterer *and* a lightweight?" Ry asked.

"Your memory for facts is very strong," Azza said to Kip. "Does this make you Mr. Know-It-All, I wonder?"

"*President* Know-It-All, I should think!" said Marv, doffing his cap before making his way back towards the museum.

"I believe that is enough driving for me today," said Azza, climbing out of the Powder Puff and returning to her place in the back seat.

"All right!" said Ry, flopping his body over the armrest into the passenger's seat yet again.

"Next time, try using the car door," said Kip, as he buckled himself behind the wheel. "Where to?"

"Woody's would sure hit the spot about now," said Ry.

"The munchies, huh?" Kip asked, as he turned over the ignition and began driving across the parking lot towards Hayes Avenue.

"I would like to resume our search for the figurine," said Azza. "We must keep our bargain, sir."

"The pawn shops it is!" said Kip.

"What is pawn shops, sir?" Azza asked.

"And why are we going there?" Ry asked, glaring at Kip from across the front seat.

"Am I dreaming," said Kip, "or were you sitting right next to me last night when your dad suggested we look for the pear in area resale shops?"

"Oh, right," said Ry. "It's kinda hazy, but yeah, it's coming back to me now!"

As Kip prepared to make the wide turn onto Hayes Avenue, he caught sight of a familiar figure walking towards the Powder Puff from the direction of the museum. And Kip recognized her even before he saw her telltale pageboy haircut flopping in rhythm with her footsteps. But before he could so much as utter a single word, Azza beat him to the punch.

"Is that her, sir?" Azza asked. "Is that Miss Know-It-All?"

CHAPTER 15:
THE RYANOCEROUS AND THE BALLBUSTER

With big rigs and SUVs scudding past the Powder Puff along Old Highway 20, Kip piloted the aging hatchback towards the outskirts of Stony Prairie. Ry sat up front, a slight drool trickling down his chin as he napped against the passenger's side window. Meanwhile, Azza sat in the back with Colby, who periodically poked Ry with a pencil through the tiny crevice between the seatback and the door.

"Dude, enough already!" said Ry, wiping the drool off of his chin as he resettled himself against the car window.

"What's with your friend?" said Colby, smiling from her place in the back seat.

"Mr. Ry is suffering from a weedover," said Azza.

"I thought it smelled like skunk in here. Stay classy there, Ry," she said, poking him again with the pencil.

"You can drop her off anytime," said Ry, still nestled against the window. "Anywhere along the highway would be just fine by me."

"I may have to ditch you both if you don't cut it out," said Kip.

"No way, José," said Colby. "You won't be getting rid of me so easily."

"All right," said Kip, staring into the rearview mirror. "But remember: you're the one who decided you wanted to hang with us. And us includes Ry."

"Seems to," said Colby, staring at the prairie as it careened past the window. "Where are we going anyway?"

"To the pawnbroker," said Azza. "We are searching for the figurine. If we find it, Mr. Ry tells me that I will be golden."

"You're already golden in my book, A!" sang out Ry from his place in the front.

"Thank you, sir," said Azza. "I am very proud to be golden. Soon, I will learn how to drive so that I may do the ALICE."

"Gonna have to master the brake first, A," said Ry.

"What's the ALICE?" Colby asked, turning to face Azza in the back seat.

"It is a procedure for eluding a violent intruder in an emergency situation," said Azza. "I would try to outrun the intruder, but alas, I am not very fast. But if I can drive a car, I will be able to get away."

"So it's an acronym?" Colby asked. "Does E stand for escape, then?"

"No, E is for evacuate," said Azza.

"What about R and T?" said Ry, chuckling to himself up front.

"I have forgotten those letters, sir," said Azza, looking down at her lap. "I will need to study the ALICE some more and commit it to memory."

"So you're doing all of this to outsmart a violent intruder at Fremont High?" Colby asked.

"You're kidding, right?" said Kip, staring at Colby's reflection in the rearview mirror. "Azza doesn't go to high school. She's a freshman at Northwestern Ohio State."

"Freshwoman, sir," said Azza.

"But she looks so young!" said Colby.

"Thank you," said Azza. "I use moisturizer."

"Oh my God, I almost forgot!" said Colby, producing a rectangular box that she had secreted away in her handbag. "I got this for you!"

Colby thrust the package, which was swathed in burgundy wrapping paper, into Azza's lap. For her part, Azza could hardly believe her eyes. In truth, she had rarely ever received a gift of any kind, the poverty of the *banlieues* being what it was.

"I don't know what to say," Azza whispered.

"Open it!" said Colby.

Carefully unwrapping the box, Azza removed a pristine hardcover book with the words *First Lady: The Life of Lucy Webb Hayes* emblazoned in brilliant gold lettering across its spine. As she gazed at the gilded volume, she began to weep.

"Nobody has ever given me a book before," Azza whispered, her eyes filling up with tears.

"Then I am proud to be the first!" said Colby, turning her attention back to the passenger's seat. "So, Ry," said Colby, banging the back of his headrest with her open palm, "are you high right now?"

"Kip," said Ry, ignoring her, "please ask our unwanted guest to kindly refrain from hitting the back of my seat. Or talking. Or breathing—"

"Who's the unwanted guest here?" said Colby, rapping the back of his seat again for good measure. "I'm not the one suffering from a weedover."

"Speaking of weed," said Kip, "is marijuana halal or haram?"

"Wait," said Ry, sitting upright and staring at Azza across the armrest. "I know this! I've watched, like, a thousand movies where some old Arab dude is smoking a hookah and looking all solemn and shit. Pot's gotta be halal in Islam, right?"

"It is most definitely haram, sir."

"No way!" said Ry, banging his fist on top of the armrest. "I've seen some serious smoking in *Raiders of the Lost Ark* and *Alice in Wonderland*."

"*Alice in Wonderland*?" Kip asked. "Are you mental?"

"That one's the best, Beckelhymen!" said Ry. "The old dude is high as a kite and blowing multicolored smoke rings!"

"For one thing," said Kip, "that old dude isn't a dude at all. He's a caterpillar."

"And his name is Absolem," Colby added, "and he's definitely ancient—a million years old, I think."

"How could you possibly know that?" Kip asked, smirking as he stared at her reflection in the rearview mirror.

"I took a lot of AP English back in Minneapolis," Colby replied.

"Whatever," said Ry. "The point is that the caterpillar—excuse me, *Absolem*—is a Middle Eastern pothead bonging his ass off all the livelong day, ya feel me?"

"How do you profess to know anything about my culture, Mr. Ry?" Azza asked, quickly raising her voice to a shout. "The Qur'an is very clear about narcotics: 'O you who believe! Truly, intoxicants and gambling and divination by arrows are an abomination of Satan's doing: avoid it in order that you may be successful.'"

For a moment, the friends sat in awkward silence as the Powder Puff rolled across the highway.

It was Ry, predictably, who finally broke the ice.

"Well, that doesn't sound like AP English to me," he said.

"I am being very serious here, sir," said Azza. "I don't know about you, but I would like to be successful."

"Okay, fine," said Ry. "But getting high is fun. Is the Qur'an against having fun?"

"Marijuana contains THC, does it not, sir?" said Azza. "THC is bad for the brain. Do you want bad brain, Mr. Ry?"

"Too late," said Colby, laughing as she rapped the back of Ry's headrest yet again.

"There it is!" said Kip, pulling the Powder Puff off of the highway and into a gravel parking lot. As he eased the hatchback in front of a light blue mobile home, rusty and bedraggled from untold years on the windswept plains, a cloud of dust wafted around the vehicle. A huge billboard beside the trailer identified it as STONY PRAIRIE PAWNS. And just below that, a pair of signs proclaimed QUICK AND EASY MONEY! and GOT GOLD? WE PAY CASH!

"Dude, that shack is the same color as your car," said Ry, chuckling as he climbed out of the hatchback.

"It's a mobile home," Kip replied.

As Ry and Colby made their way into Stony Prairie Pawns, Kip and Azza trailed behind.

"Allah be willing," said Azza, "we will find the figurine in this place. Will that not please you, sir?"

"If it's part of history," Kip asked, "isn't it worth saving? That would be reason enough for me."

"History is important, sir, but we must be cautious about allotting too much value to worldly attachments," Azza replied. "The Qur'an tells us that it is a foolhardy imagination that measures itself based upon the accumulation of baubles and trinkets."

"Well, it may be a bauble," said Kip, "but the figurine might even help a friend of mine keep his job."

"And in so doing, we would fulfill half of our bargain," Azza added, as they stepped over the threshold.

• • •

Stony Prairie Pawns was mostly empty, save for an elderly woman standing next to a cash register. By her feet lay an old hound dog, dead to the world and lost in sleep. The shelves were loosely stocked, save for an array of outdoor goods including tents, sleeping bags, and canteens, along with an impressive inventory of survival gear.

"Pass," said Kip, as he studied the camping equipment.

"Not into roughing it, huh?" Colby asked.

"Not in this lifetime," he replied. "I'm kind of an indoor guy."

"Check it out!" said Ry, spotting a firearms display on the far wall of the pawn shop. "This thing is ginormous."

As Ry loped across the store to get a better look, Azza followed closely in his wake. Meanwhile, Kip and Colby began skimming through the store's inventory for any signs of the figurine.

For his part, Kip began leafing through sheaf after sheaf of old magazines.

"You really think somebody hid a plaster of Paris pear inside a discarded copy of *Field & Stream*?" Colby asked.

"Don't forget about the replica," Kip replied. "It may not be as valuable as the pear, but it might lead us to the culprit."

As he turned his attention to a pile of *National Geographic* magazines, Colby crept up beside him.

"I like Azza," said Colby, looking back over her shoulder in the direction of the firearms display. "She's kind of spunky."

"Me, too," said Kip, as he continued scanning the shelves of Stony Prairie Pawns.

"But I don't get that ALICE business, do you?" Colby asked.

"What do you mean by that?" said Kip, glancing back at her.

"I guess I don't really mean anything by it," Colby replied. "But why would you need to know how to drive to be able to elude an active shooter? Northwestern Ohio State is mostly a pedestrian campus, isn't it? I don't know what the ALICE acronym stands for, but the letter D as in Drive is nowhere to be found, right? I mean, doesn't that concern you just a little bit?"

"I hadn't really thought about it," said Kip, turning to face her in the middle of the aisle. "But you gotta admit that Azza seems like a really sincere person. If she says she wants to learn how to drive on the off-chance that it might help her get away from some maniac, then I pretty much believe her. I mean, imagine wearing that outfit every day in the middle of Ohio."

"Kip! Dude!" screamed Ry from across the store.

"Where's the fire?" Kip asked, as he and Colby rushed to join him.

"We found it, sir!" said Azza, slowly opening up the palms of her hands to reveal a wooden carving of a pear.

"Very funny," said Kip. "It's nice to see you two getting along so famously."

"Yeah, weren't you locked up in some kinda culture war, like, five minutes ago?" Colby asked.

"We're just fine, aren't we, A?" Ry replied, as Azza nodded solemnly beside him. "We bonded over that sweet arsenal," he added, gesturing at the veritable wall of weaponry that towered over them.

"There's nothing like a bunch of guns to bring folks together," said Colby.

"Seriously, dude, have you ever seen so much firepower in your life?" Ry asked, with a giddy smile plastered across his face.

"Speaking of weaponry, did you know that President Hayes was wounded during the Civil War?" Kip asked. "He was in the 23rd Regiment of the Ohio Volunteer Infantry. In September 1862, Lieutenant Colonel Hayes and his troops rendezvoused with the Army of the Potomac after the Battle of Bull Run—"

"Snore, dude, snore," said Ry, interrupting him. "I don't hear any guns in this story."

"It was after the Battle of Bull Run," Kip continued, glaring at his friend in front of the firearms display, "when the future President

Hayes was *shot* through his left arm while leading his troops against General Lee's Army of Northern Virginia. Things got pretty scary, too, when the wounded Lieutenant Colonel Hayes was briefly felled behind enemy lines. But he was back in action by the time his brigade made Antietam."

"Thanks for the mansplaining there, Kip," said Colby. "But Hayes never made it to Antietam."

"Sure he did," said Kip. "Antietam was the bloodiest single day in American history, with some 23,000 casualties. Hayes was there, I promise you."

"Sorry, slick," said Colby. "You're overreaching. Hayes sat out the rest of the Maryland campaign. He didn't see action again for nearly two years until he led his troops at the Battle of Buffington Island in July 1863."

"Huh," said Kip, staring away in confusion. "I didn't know—"

"Do you ever get tired of busting my boy Beckelhymer's balls?" Ry asked Colby.

"Isn't this usually when you refer to me as Beckelhymen?" said Kip.

"Pipe down, dude," said Ry. "I'm trying to make a point here."

"Actually, the only thing better than busting Kip's balls is busting *your* balls," said Colby.

"Oh, it's on!" said Ry.

"What is on, sir?" Azza asked, looking back and forth between Ry and Colby. "Do we need to turn it off?"

"Consider yourself warned!" said Ry. "Once you unleash the Ryanocerous, you better start watching your back!"

"The Ryanocerous?" Colby asked. "I'm not sure what I should be more worried about—the fact that you call yourself the 'Ryanocerous' or that you're referring to yourself in the third person."

As it happened, none of the friends had noticed the grey-haired cashier who had ambled up beside them near the gun display.

"Can I help you kids?" she asked.

"Sure," said Kip, shrugging his shoulders. "We're looking for a plaster of Paris pear figurine. It's almost six inches tall, and—"

"I don't know nothing about no pear," the woman replied. "Unless you're buying or selling something, you best move on."

"Hold up a sec," said Colby, stepping out in front of the others. "If you don't have anything like that in stock, well that's cool and all. But is there anywhere else we might try?"

"You might shoot on down to the one in Ballville," the old lady replied with a sneer. "They call themselves B&C Super Pawns. It's over on 536. Big yellow sign and a whole lotta junk out front. You can't miss it."

CHAPTER 16:
CLEARING YOUR GARAGE, CROWDING YOUR WALLET!

"You sure you're okay with heading down to Birdie's neck of the woods?" Ry asked, as they made their way back to the Powder Puff.

"Birdie's out of the picture," said Kip. "She's the last thing on my mind. What really bothers me, though," he continued, looking over his shoulder to see if the others were in earshot, "is Colby. She was right, you know. I *was* overreaching."

"What? *No!*" Ry replied.

"I'm serious," said Kip. "Antietam was a rookie mistake. I was trying to make the story sound better than it actually was. Why do I do that?"

"Dude, maybe you like her?"

"Hardly," said Kip.

"What's so bad about digging another chick, monkey?" Ry asked. "Anything's better than Miss Pigtails."

"I plead the fifth," Kip replied. "And don't call me monkey. You know how much that pisses me off."

"Jesus," said Ry, "I can just see it now: you and Colby are gonna get married and have these, like, super geek babies. And they're gonna grow up and bore everyone to tears with their constant geek arguments about Lemonade Lucy's dress size and whether or not President Hayes preferred boxers or briefs."

"Oh, man," said Kip, "has it gotten that bad?"

"It's actually much worse," said Ry, "but I've been holding back 'cause you're down in the dumps and all."

While the store may have been situated in a strip mall instead of a mobile home, there was very little to differentiate B&C Super Pawns from Stony Prairie Pawns. For one thing, the parking lot in front of B&C Super Pawns was empty, save for a rusted-out pickup truck parked beneath a faded sign that promised, as with Stony Prairie Pawns, to fill its patrons' pockets with cold hard cash: CLEARING YOUR GARAGE, CROWDING YOUR WALLET!

As the friends made their way towards the store's entrance, Ry held out his arm and gestured in the direction of the coffee shop next door. Clearly visible in the window overlooking the parking lot were Birdie and Todd from Boston. They were holding hands, with big goofy smiled on their faces, as they waited in line for their coffee drinks.

"Dude, she's like a bad penny," said Ry, shaking his head back and forth.

"What does that mean, sir?" asked Azza.

"I don't actually know," Ry replied, "but my mom says it all the time."

"So that's the famous Birdie, huh?" said Colby. "Those pigtails are kinda passé."

"I'd say that Birdie and Todd from Boston were stalking us," Kip answered, "but there are only, like, five places to go after school in the whole area."

"Keep telling yourself that, dude," said Ry.

"You know, Kip," said Colby, stroking the strands of pageboy, "you could do a whole lot better than her."

"That's what I've been saying all along!" Ry added. "The Birdwoman is bad news!"

"I believe the cheese apple," said Azza, nodding vigorously in Kip's direction. "You should trust her intuition, sir."

• • •

As with Stony Prairie Pawns, B&C Super Pawns was heavily stocked with survival gear and a gun display that easily rivaled its competition across town. A white-smocked clerk stood by a cash register near the entrance, his scraggly beard and bleached apron giving him the appearance of some kind of wayward butcher who had wandered into the pawnbrokers instead of a grocery store. His appearance was rendered even stranger by the patch, complete with a yellow smiley face, that he wore over his right eye.

And if B&C Super Pawns had a specialty, it was clearly camouflage wear. A huge display offered everything from a three-piece camo suit to a camo baby bib. At one point, Colby happened upon a pair of camo stiletto heels, smirking as she held them up for Kip's inspection.

"Maybe there's a camo hijab in there somewhere," Ry joked. "That would really help you do the ALICE, right, A?"

For her part, Azza could only stand and stare at Ry, stone-faced with her arms crossed in front of her.

"Not cool, Ry," said Kip, as he tossed a camo-colored bong in his friend's direction. "This looks more like your speed."

As Ry executed a clean two-handed catch right there in B&C Super Pawns, the bearded clerk bounded over from his station by the entrance.

"Be careful now," he said, panting as he caught up with the kids by the camo display. "Just remember: you break it, you buy it."

"Have you seen anything that looks like a plaster of Paris pear?" Colby asked.

"Can't say that I have," the bearded clerk replied, catching his breath. "That'd be kinda weird, right?"

• • •

For a while, Ry busied himself by a rack of used electric guitars, most of them devoid of strings. Every now and then, Colby would glance over and see Ry playing air guitar in time with the fuzzy in-store music being piped in from some mysterious corner of the pawn shop.

Later, as Kip and Azza browsed the shelves in a vain attempt to happen upon the pear, Colby noticed a stocky man loping into the pawn shop, nodding politely at the clerk as he passed the cash register, and making a beeline for the gun racks. He caught Azza's eye, too, giving her a protracted stare as he began fumbling with the handgun display.

"You know, it's funny how you wanted to know about the pear thingy," said the clerk, turning to face the kids from his place by the door. "Nobody asks me much about anything except guns and guitars, and here you are, coming in and asking me about something out of the blue."

"Yeah," said Colby, "I guess it's sort of funny."

"Only you're the second person in as many days to do that, you see?" said the clerk. "The other guy came in just yesterday with a funny question about some kinda rare document. He asked me if I knew any collectors or some shit like that."

"Well, do you?" Colby asked as she took a step back into the store.

"Do I what?" asked the clerk

"Do you know any collectors?"

"Sure shootin' I do!" the clerk replied. "I sent the fella over to Turley's down in Fort Seneca. Only you can't go there today."

"Why's that?" Kip asked, stepping up to join Colby by the cash register.

"'Cause they're closed. It's past six. Business hours is over for the day. About to close up myself."

"Did he show you the document?" Kip asked.

"See, that's when things got a little weird," the clerk replied. "I asked him if I could see the thing—you know, to determine its value and whatnot—and he got all paranoid. Said I was trying to rip him off. Said I was trying to steal his inheritance. I mean, what's that about anyway?"

"Turley's, huh?" said Colby.

"Yeah, they're over on Main Street," the clerk replied. "You should ask for Liam. Tell him Randy from B&C sent you his way."

"Liam? *Really*?" Kip asked. "In Fort Seneca?"

"Yeah, he's Irish, I think," said the clerk. "But don't let that worry you none. He's the real deal."

As Kip turned to leave the store, he noticed that the stocky customer had caught Azza's eye yet again. And for her part, Colby noticed, too. Ry might have seen what happened next had he not been wind-milling a beat-up old Les Paul in time with a Muzak version of "Pinball Wizard."

And that's when Kip saw the stocky man lock eyes with Azza, make a gun sign with his fingers, and take a shot at the woman in the hijab. Feigning the act of blowing away the ensuing smoke from the barrel of his pretend gun, he smiled broadly at Azza from his place across the store.

"Holy crap," said Kip. "That's unacceptable, right? You can't do that kind of stuff in real life, can you?"

Instinctively, Colby moved in front of Azza, as if shielding her from a marauder.

"FML," said Azza, her eyes still locked on her aggressor, who had gone back to browsing the wares of the firearms display.

As Azza watched, Kip began moving in the direction of the gun exhibit. By this point, Ry had put down the beat-up guitar, confused by the inexplicable scene unfolding across the shop.

"No, sir," said Azza, placing her arm across Kip's midsection. "Only violence begets more violence. Allah tells us that we must say 'salām' to this man and go on our way."

"That may be your religion," said Kip, "but that doesn't make it mine."

"We go now," said Azza, her voice even more firm than before. As her friends looked on, she placed her hands together as if in prayer and bowed in the direction of the stocky man, who was still busying himself with the handgun display.

"Oh, Allah!" said Azza. "You are peace and from You is peace. Blessed be You, most holy possessor of glory and honor."

And with that, the Middle Easterner turned on her heel and walked straight out of the store, followed closely by her trio of American friends, thunderstruck by what they had just witnessed. As if they had never seen anything like it in all their lives.

CHAPTER 17:
WE'RE AN AMERICAN BAND

Dr. Matthews stood at the front of the bus, gripping the steel support beam with all of her might as she labored to deliver her lecture. With each bump in the road, she would glance up towards the heavens, as if willing some creator up above to protect her on her journey—a journey rendered even more perilous by her stubborn desire to remain current with the course syllabus even as she commandeered her students on a field trip to visit the home of the once proud and noble Shawnee Nation in Bellefontaine, about 90 miles south of Fremont. And for most of those miles, the hired bus driver had regularly interrupted Dr. Matthews's lecture in a desperate attempt to get her to take her seat.

From her vantage point in the extreme rear of the bus, Azza observed her professor's behavior with mild amusement as Dr. Matthews steadied herself against the relentless sway of the bus as it veered along the highway. Azza had ceased taking notes not long after the class had departed from the Northwestern Ohio State campus after she realized that Dr. Matthews could barely speak in complete sentences from her makeshift lectern at the front of the bus. And besides, Azza was forced to divide her attention between her socially awkward professor and the student slouching in the seat just across the aisle from her. It was the very same kid who had chided Azza about Islam during the first week of school. He was still clad in a tee-shirt, walking shorts, and flip-flops. That must be his uniform, Azza thought to herself.

"Ma'am, I know I'm starting to sound like a broken record here," said the bus driver, pawing at his scalp in deep frustration, "but you've really gotta sit down. I don't have the foggiest idea what your college policies are in regards to field trips and all, but at Buckeye Express, our rules are pretty clear. Sit down and buckle up. No exceptions."

"Just a few more minutes please," Mrs. Matthews pleaded, her eyelids fluttering as she stared up at the bus's pea-green ceiling panels. "I'm about to conclude my remarks on the . . . on the Toba catastrophe."

"The Toba *what*?" the bus driver asked.

"Oh, it's really quite fascinating," Dr. Matthews replied, her matronly grey hairdo bouncing in rhythm with the bus's galloping forward momentum along the highway. "The Toba supervolcanic eruption occurred some 75,000 years ago in present-day Indonesia. Scientists describe it as a near-global extinction event that threatened the survival of our species."

"Ma'am, I'm afraid you're gonna have your own extinction event if you don't take your seat," said the driver, who pointedly slowed the vehicle down as he piloted the bus onto the Bellefontaine off-ramp.

"Some scientists estimate that the Toba catastrophe reduced the earth's human population to a small parcel of survivors—perhaps as few as 3,000 people—and that this relatively homogeneous group repopulated the world as we know it today," said Dr. Matthews.

Azza thrust her hand up in the air with such force that Dr. Matthews, even with the relentless sway of the bus, couldn't possibly miss.

"Yes, Ms. Amari?" said Dr. Matthews.

"I am confused, Professor, by your timeline. How do you reconcile the scientist's revelations about a 75,000-year-old event with the teachings of Allah—of even your own Bible—that date the creation of the earth to only a few thousand years ago?"

"Oh, Jesus," said the sloucher, throwing up his arms and scowling at Azza from his place across the aisle. "Not this garbage again."

"I'm afraid you are missing the point, Ms. Amari," said Dr. Matthews. "You are confusing your own spiritual beliefs with the larger issue of racial difference. Don't you see? If we are all descendants from such a small group of survivors, then why is the human race so irretrievably bent on destroying one another when we are made from the very same stuff?"

"But Professor—"

"Ms. Amari," said Dr. Matthews, interrupting her. "I must remind you of one of the most important aphorisms related to the conundrum of learning: 'When you hear hoofbeats, don't think of zebras.'"

"What do you mean by that, Professor?" Azza asked, standing up abruptly from her seat. "I must know!"

But Azza's efforts would be in vain, as the driver had somehow managed to bring the bus to a halt without sending Dr. Matthews tumbling down the aisle in some kind of absurd professorial gymnastics. Looming alongside the vehicle was the Logan County History Center, an exquisite post-bellum mansion in the heart of Bellefontaine. As Azza watched from her place in the back of the bus, the other students had already begun gathering up their belongings and filling up the aisles as they piled off of the vehicle.

Azza followed the swarm of students into the mansion's towering foyer, where they began pairing off with their interview subjects. One by one, they began trudging off to the far corners of the center, finding a reasonably private nook to conduct their interviews, and working their way through the prewritten spate of questions.

Azza stood by as her classmates met up with their Native American subjects and descended into the mansion. Feeling a panic growing inside of her, she traipsed through the parlor to the living room, eventually making her way through the dining room to the mansion's massive eat-in kitchen. All the while, she periodically studied the mysterious typewritten name that she had received from Dr. Matthews back in Fremont: METHOATASKE. Azza had no idea what it meant, much less how to pronounce the most unusual name.

As Azza made her way to the veranda at the back of the home, she eventually passed Dr. Matthews herself, who was reclining on a divan with a newspaper held aloft in front of her. Every now and again, Dr. Matthews would gaze skyward, her eyes fluttering in that odd trance of hers, as if she were looking for God.

As Azza stood on the veranda, not quite certain about what to do next, a gold-coated representative from the Logan County History

Center caught up with her.

"There's one more back there," he announced, gesturing towards a grove of trees behind the mansion.

Azza wordlessly held up the typewritten name for his inspection.

"I'm afraid so," he said, his eyes glazing over with empathy. "If you need anything, just give a holler. Now go on," he added, wiping a bead of sweat from his brow. "She's waiting for you out in the gazebo."

As she passed from the tree line into a clearing, Azza could detect the scent of the old Shawnee woman before she actually saw her—or to be more accurate, she could smell the odor of the woman's pipe long before she glimpsed Methoataske in the flesh. It was the scent of finely honed tobacco, of honeysuckle and rose petals. Of molasses and smoldering ash. In truth, Azza couldn't entirely place it, but she smelled it just the same.

"Thanks for coming all this way," said Methoataske, sitting in a lawn chair in the center of a white gazebo. "They won't let me come indoors no more." A second empty lawn chair rested nearby.

Azza had no doubt that Methoataske's words were the stuff of literal truth. The frail-looking Shawnee seemed to be somewhere in the vicinity of 100 years old, periodically parting her lips to take a lengthy drag on her wooden pipe. The only thing she was wearing was an old leathery loincloth. And she was topless, Azza was loath to discover, with her wrinkled brown dugs hanging right out in the open for anyone to see. After a single quick glance at Methoataske's exposed chest, Azza averted her eyes in embarrassment. She wouldn't risk looking at the old woman's distended breasts again. No, she most certainly wouldn't be doing that, she promised herself.

"So you're doing some kinda report, huh?" said Methoataske. A toy tomahawk sat on a small table in front of her, along with several others in various stages of production. As Azza looked on from her place at the edge of the gazebo, Methoataske grabbed a fresh piece of varnished wood, inserted a rubber knife blade into a pre-cut groove, and then pasted a clutch of colorful feathers onto the end of the handle. "Dr. Matthews, she hasn't sent any students my way in a long time. Even when she does, I'm never quite sure how I can help, but I don't mind none. Come on up and sit with me."

Stepping into the gazebo, Azza took her place in the lawn chair beside Methoataske, briefly pausing to retrieve a notepad from her valise. Not knowing how else to proceed, Azza posed the first of the prewritten oral history questions:

"What is your full name, and why were you named this?" Azza asked, holding her pencil aloft above her notepad. She may have been nervous as all get-out about interviewing the old, half-naked Shawnee, but Azza was bound and determined to ace Anthropology. She had meant what she said to Ry about being a success. America was hard work, Azza had long ago decided, but she was dead-set on prospering in her new life in this strange land. She would be a chemical engineer or die trying.

"Child, I don't even know *your* name," said Methoataske, taking another drag from her pipe. "Why should we be talking about mine?"

"I am Azza Amari," she replied.

"I've never heard no name like that," Methoataske replied. "What does it mean?"

"It means 'moon,'" said Azza.

"Huh," said Methoataske, with a sigh. "You already know my name on account of that paper in your hand," she added, gesturing in Azza's direction with her pipe. "Methoataske means 'turtle laying its eggs.'"

"Why did your parents name you that way?"

"Beats me," said Methoataske. "Why is anybody named anything?" As she took another drag from her pipe, Methoataske started laughing uproariously.

"What is so funny?"

"I just remembered an Algonquin squaw I met once. She was called Makkitotosimew. Means 'she who has large breasts.'"

"That cannot be true," said Azza.

"Oh, it's a fact," said Methoataske. "That was her name. But it sorta proves my point. Makkitotosimew had the prettiest face I ever seen, but she had itty bitty titties. Kinda like these," she said, staring down at her own sagging areolas.

Azza looked away in embarrassment, as she began scrawling a rapid-fire series of notes on her pad.

"What is the date and place of your birth?" Azza asked, consulting the next question on her list.

"Born in 1923, but I don't know the date—don't even know the month," Methoataske replied. "Took my first breath right here in Ohio. Never left this territory—not even for a day. Do you know what Ohio means?"

"No, I do not," said Azza, setting down her pencil.

"It's not Shawnee, I can tell you that much," she said. "It's Iroquois. Means 'great river.' Now, I like that, see? I like the notion that this whole journey we're on is some kind of big old river of life."

"Do you remember hearing your grandparents describe their lives?" said Azza, reading the next question. "What did they say?"

"You're all business, ain't you?" said Methoataske. "Serious as a heart attack, I'd say. Well, all right. If that's how you wanna be, I'll play along. My grandparents didn't say nothing about their lives, if you wanna know the truth. But if you asked 'em straight out, they'd tell it like it was whether we liked it or not. And most of the time, we didn't like it none. Truth is, we've seen a lot in our time. Trail of Tears, Wounded Knee. Shitshows, one and all."

"What is a Wounded Knee?" Azza asked.

"Long ugly road to today is what it is," said Methoataske. "To this day right here. Now, Wounded Knee, *the massacre,* happened in 1890. That was when the cavalry went into the reservation in South Dakota to disarm the Lakota, and all they ended up doing was wiping out a bunch of men, women, and children. Proud people who did no wrong, except be Indians. Which brings us to Wounded Knee, *the incident,* which happened way back in '73. I was much younger then. Just turned 50," she said, laughing and taking another pull from her pipe. "Thought I knew everything there was to know in this world. Wounded Knee—now that was a standoff between the American Indian Movement and the government. There weren't many of us killed, as those sorta things go, and the sight of our people standing up for the suffering of our ancestors gave you a lump in the throat, a new sense of purpose or whatever you wanna call it. But then it ended in a stalemate, which is really a kinda surrender. And since then, it's been nothing but booze and casinos—and kitsch," she said, tossing the toy tomahawk aside. "Since the white man came, it's been one long slow march to death. That's what happens when majority becomes minority. Homeland don't matter no more. Might makes right. You know what I mean?"

"I think so," Azza replied. "How is the world different now from when you were a child?" she said, reading the next question.

"You just don't quit, do ya, darlin'?" Methoataske asked.

"I am sorry," said Azza, staring up at her from her notepad. "Did I do something wrong?"

"No, no, no. You don't need to worry none," said Methoataske. "But this world is plenty different now, and it's getting worse every day on account of we have diversity now, ya hear? Used to be that Indians was Indians, and that was fine. But now, we're all Native Americans and whatnot. Now everything's gotta mean something. It can't just be. Take that headscarf you're wearing. People think it represents your faith or whatever. Or worse, they think you're a terrorist or oppressed, right? But either way, it stands for something other than yourself. That's what they think when they see you out here in the so-called Heartland. You know that, don't ya?"

"I suppose," said Azza.

"So what do you think they see when they get a look at me?" she asked.

"You would seem very different to them," said Azza. "Just like me. That is what they would be thinking."

"We may be different looking," said Methoataske, "but there ain't nothing the same about you and me—other than we're outsiders in a place where the insiders stand tall. When it comes to me, people most likely be saying to themselves, 'why is that wrinkled old topless lady smoking a pipe in broad daylight?' But I hear you, darlin'. I get what you mean. You gettin' all this down?"

"I am, yes," said Azza, as she filled up her pad with notes.

"Did you know that the Shawnee are not recognized by the Federal

Government?" said Methoataske. "This ain't Oklahoma where there are reservations on every corner. No way, no how. This is Ohio, where we are the United Remnant Band of the Shawnee Nations. Sounds like we're some branch of the Elks Club or the American Legion."

"If you could be any historical figure, who would you be?" Azza asked, shifting to the next question.

"That's easy," Methoataske replied. "I'd be Chief Tecumseh. He once said, 'Live your life that the fear of death can never enter your heart.' Now I like that. 'Course, I know that it's bullshit, but I like it just the same. Everybody I know is afraid of something. Chief Tecumseh was the great and honorable leader of the Shawnee nation, led a confederacy of warriors that numbered in the thousands. Born in Ohio country, like me. A hero on the battlefield, noble among his kin. Shot dead, through and through, by a white man at the Battle of the Thames, but lives on as a bona fide American folk hero. You could call him an Indian or a Native American, but I say he's an American—he belongs to all of us now, whether we like it or not. That's the only way this here country's ever gonna move forward, ya know? When somebody finally says 'we gotta *do*.' Do you understand what I mean by that?"

"Are you saying that we need to accept each other for who we are?" said Azza, setting her pencil down on her notepad.

"Yeah, but it's more than that. 'We gotta *do'* means that we gotta stop it with all of the talking around each other, trying to define what each other's words mean, and pigeon-holing each other and whatnot. 'We gotta *do'* means we gotta agree on how to move this whole thing forward and then do it. No more talking, only doing in everybody's best interest. There's so much talking now, but not enough doing. I'm sick of all the talking, aren't you?"

"Oh, yes," said Azza. "I, too, am sick of all of the talking. Americans talk very very much, don't they?"

"They do, they do!" said Methoataske. "And I'm the worst. I never shut up. I gotta start doing more and talking less. But anyways, 'We gotta *do'* means living. Like old Tecumseh said, you gotta live your life without fear. Means going forward no matter what. People are always looking for angles and trying to get their little bit. But they gotta *do,* too.

They gotta get over themselves and start living their own lives and stop trying to live ours for us, right?"

"You are correct, Methoataske," said Azza. "Did I pronounce your name correctly?"

"Not even close," said Methoataske. "But who gives a shit? It's just a name. Everybody's too . . . too *fixated,* that's the word—they're so fixated on *what I am* that they don't have a clue about *who I am.* That's the problem with living in the here and now. There's no place to be somebody. But that's why 'we gotta *do,*' see?"

"So what are you going to do?" Azza asked.

"Well, I can tell you what I'm not gonna do. For me, 'we gotta *do*' means I sure ain't putting my shirt back on unless I damned well feel like it. Shit, I like how these little titties look," she said, jutting her chin out and holding her head up high. "And you wear that scarf of yours whenever and wherever you like, ya hear?"

Azza couldn't help smiling at this last remark. And for a moment, she mimicked Methoataske and held her head up high, too, her hijab sparkling as it caught the light of the midday sun.

And that's when Azza saw him out of the corner of her eye—the gold-coated representative from the Logan County History Center. He was glaring at Azza from the edge of the clearing and feverishly tapping the face of his wristwatch.

Azza stood up from her lawn chair, and, as she turned to face Methoataske, bowed in the old Shawnee's direction.

"Don't take any shit out there, ya hear?" said Methoataske. "Show respect for all men, but grovel to none."

For a moment, Azza allowed herself to ponder the old woman's words. "Show respect for all men, but grovel to none," she whispered aloud to herself. She liked that sentiment a lot, she truly did.

"Goodbye," said Azza, as she stepped down from the gazebo.

"I prefer 'salanoki,'" said Methoataske.

"What does it mean?" Azza asked.

"Oh, Salanoki—now that's an old one. Means 'until we meet again.'"

"Until we meet again," said Azza, smiling as she caught up with the gold-coated man at the edge of the clearing.

"I was just about to go out there and rescue you," he said, as he walked briskly back towards the mansion. "She's a handful, that one. Never know what she'll say. A real loose cannon in my book."

As Azza followed him along the path back to the main house, she suddenly broke into a panic. "I didn't get to ask all of my questions," she said. "Dr. Matthews will be very disappointed."

"I wouldn't worry about Dr. Matthews," he said. "She's been coming out here every semester for years. Besides, the other students are already back on the bus. You gotta get a move-on."

As Azza arrived back on the veranda, she hoped that what Methoataske said would come true—that they would meet again someday.

CHAPTER 18:
YOU MUST REMEMBER THIS

Kip leaned against the Powder Puff, staring in the direction of Fremont High. Or, to be more precise, he was staring off in the distance at Colby, who was sitting cross-legged on the campus lawn, where she was studying with a group of other Fremont students.

"This may be the saddest thing I've ever seen," said Ry, ambling up to join him next to the Subaru.

"Why's that?" Kip asked.

"Senior year is in full swing, and you could be one of Fremont High's greatest playas. Instead, you're a freakin' stalker."

"What are you going on about *now*?"

"You heard me," said Ry. "You're checking out Miss Know-It-All from afar. I get it, dude. All you need is some binoculars—maybe hide in the bushes behind the band hall. Take a good long look."

"You're ridiculous."

"And you're an asshat."

"That's it," said Kip, reaching for the car door.

"*What's* it?" Ry replied.

"Why are we even friends, Ry?" said Kip, turning to face him. "What do we remotely have in common?"

"Whoa," Ry replied, taking a step back. "Chill out. What's gotten into you?"

"I'm being serious here," said Kip. "Our friendship doesn't make a lick of sense."

"Sure it does, dude. Remember how we had homeroom together back in fifth grade?"

"I remember homeroom," said Kip, "but I don't remember us

hanging out all that much."

"Sorry you have a shitty memory and all," said Ry, "but we were, like, the dynamic duo of Fremont Elementary. What's all this about anyway?"

"I guess if you really knew me," said Kip, "if we really were best friends, you'd know that I'm never going to be some kind of playa. I mean, let's be honest, I spend most of my free time in a museum. If that doesn't make me a geek, then—"

"Hey, if you wanna go after Colby, be my guest. But just remember: she busts your balls, like, every possible chance she can get. If that's what you're looking for in a best friend, then have at it."

"You're not hearing me, Ry," said Kip, throwing his hands up in the air. "Just forget it, okay. Let me give you a lift home."

"Peace out, Kip," he replied. "I can find my own ride."

Kip watched as Ry began making his way towards the bus stop. But then just as suddenly, Ry turned around and traced his steps back, coming face-to-face with Kip right there in the school parking lot.

"You and me are friends because your mom asked my mom if I would hang out with you," said Ry, poking Kip in the chest with his index finger. "She said you were lonely. On account of your dad being gone and all. So there you have it—now you know everything."

"Now I know everything," said Kip, folding his arms in front of his chest.

And with that, Ry stomped away to find his bus.

• • •

After hastily parking the Powder Puff along Main Street in Fort Seneca, Kip caught up with Fletch outside of Turley's Collectibles, where he was pacing back and forth on the sidewalk.

"Oh, I thought you'd never come!" said Fletch, grabbing Kip by the shoulders.

"I got out here as fast as I could," said Kip. "It's not like I drive out to Fort Seneca every day, you know."

"I'm sorry, Kippers," said Fletch. "I'm on edge is all. The audit's coming down in a matter of days."

"Relax, Fletch. We've got a line on the replica now, and if we can retrieve the document, then the figurine can't be far behind."

"Oh, I'm afraid it's worse than that," said Fletch.

"Look, Fletch, I've been thinking about this," Kip replied, "and if push comes to shove, we can make our own figurine. We get some plaster of Paris from the hobby store, and we're good to go—"

"No, Kippers," said Fletch. "What I mean is that things have gotten worse. It's not just the pear and the replica anymore. Colby and I conducted a second inventory, and there are several additional pieces that are not unaccounted for: one of President Hayes's prized pocket watches is gone, and so is one of the First Lady's diamond brooches. And at least another half-dozen state documents are missing from the President's papers."

"Wait, that's impossible!" Kip protested. "We ran our own inventory, and we accounted for every last artifact—"

"No, we didn't, Kip," Fletch replied with a sigh. "I combed through everything I possibly could, but half the time, you were on your phone, trying to get that girlfriend of yours to give you the time of day—"

"*Ex*-girlfriend," said Kip, correcting him.

"It doesn't matter anymore, Kip. I'm ready to take my medicine. The car salesman's gonna finish me off as director of the Hayes. There's no turning back now. I just know it."

• • •

As Kip took his first step inside Turley's Collectibles, he nearly doubled over in shock. Where Stony Prairie Pawns and B&C Super Pawns had been veritable dumping grounds for useless odds-and-ends, Turley's Collectibles was all spick-and-span professional. There were a few glass cases situated up front. On display were an array of rare items—several of which sported the great seal of Ohio. But the prize exhibit was a signed proclamation with an august signature that Kip knew on sight.

For a moment, he stared at the document in awe, as Fletch

nervously hovered over his shoulder.

"Like that one, do ya?" Standing in front of Kip and Fletch was a red-haired man in a smart three-piece suit. His accent was unmistakably Irish.

Still mesmerized by the sight of the document splayed out before him, Kip could only nod in response.

"It was penned by none other than President Jefferson. He was writing to congratulate Acting Governor Charles Willing Byrd on the Congressional acceptance of Ohio's constitution and the granting of its statehood in February 1803."

"It's incredible!" said Kip.

"If you were to, say, inform me that you were in the market for rare documents, I'd probably tell you that it's one of a kind," the man continued, "but that wouldn't be entirely true. There were numerous copies made at the time, and this is one of them. But it's still a beaut, right?"

"It sure is!" Kip replied.

"I'm Liam," he said, shaking Kip warmly by the hand. "How can I assist you and your dad here? I do most of my business with other brokers over the internet, but I don't mind a walk-in now and again."

"Oh, he's not my dad," said Kip, laughing awkwardly at the suggestion. For his part, Fletch could only look on in shock. It was as if the whole awful business—the morass of disappearing artifacts from the Hayes, the impending loss of his directorship—had finally gotten the best of him.

"We're looking for something a little out of the ordinary," said Kip, as Fletch, still rendered mute, vigorously nodded his head in affirmation.

"A little out of the ordinary, huh?" Liam asked.

"Yeah," Kip replied. "Randy from B&C Super Pawns said that he sent a customer your way who was trying to sell him some rare documents. Randy said he thought the guy was kinda weird."

"That's funny," Liam replied. "I mean, Randy's sort of weird, right?"

"I guess you could say that," Kip answered. "The eyepatch with the smiley face is pretty bizarre."

"Listen," said Liam, "I'd like to help you out, mate, but customer information is privileged. I'm sure you understand—"

Without warning, Fletch broke his self-imposed radio silence, exploding in a fusillade of words.

"Listen yourself, *Liam*," he shrieked. "There's nothing privileged about it! Are you a lawyer, sir? A man of the cloth? A therapist?"

Liam stared back, incredulous as the rotund man with the oversized horn-rimmed glasses had an honest-to-goodness tantrum right there beside the display case. For his part, Kip was thunderstruck as he watched the typically meek-mannered Fletch become positively unglued, his spittle flying in rhythm with his rant.

"I didn't think so!" said Fletch, answering his own question. By this point—as Kip himself was loath to discover—Fletch was quite literally frothing at the mouth. "So here's how it's gonna be, *Liam*. You're gonna tell young Kippers and me what happened with this weirdo, and then we're gonna be on our way!"

For a moment, Liam simply stared back at Fletch, awestruck in the wake of the older man's outburst.

"I don't really know what to say," Liam replied, shaking his head back and forth. "This guy called me up, really paranoid on the phone. He said that he had a document of extraordinary value. So I, uh, invited him to come on down to the shop and show it to me."

"Is that when he mentioned something about trying to steal his inheritance?" Kip asked, glancing at Fletch, who was trying to catch his breath after his spontaneous eruption.

"Yeah, that's exactly what happened," said Liam. "So Randy told you about that, huh? Anyway, I was about to say something to the effect of '*what inheritance*?' when the guy abruptly hung up."

"And that was the long and the short of it?" Fletch asked, his arms folded across his ample chest.

"No, that's the craziest part," Liam replied. "I thought it was over, too. I never expected to hear from the guy again. But the next thing you know, this emaciated woman—I mean, thin as hell, just wasted away—shows up at the door like you two did just now, only without all the theatrics," he added, glaring in Fletch's direction.

"And let me guess," said Kip, "she was holding a replica of President Hayes's lease for the Isthmus of Panama."

"That's right!" said Liam, punching his fist in the air. "I knew it was a fake right off. And I told her so, too. And no sooner had I delivered the bad news than she just about wilted right in front of me. Seriously, I thought she was gonna pass out from distress—as if cashing in on that document was her last, best hope for survival."

"So what happened next?" Kip asked.

"She walked right out the door," said Liam, gesturing towards the entrance to Turley's. "I gave her a head-start before going outside. I was hoping to catch a glimpse of the paranoid freak from the phone, but no such luck. I arrived just in time to see her hop in the back of a yellow cab and head back up Main Street. And just like that, she was gone."

"That's bizarre," said Kip.

"No doubt," Liam replied. "The only thing weirder was you two showing up this afternoon. There's no way I'll be sharing anything with dimwitted Randy anymore, I can promise you that. It's kind of funny, though."

"How so?" Fletch asked.

"I feel sort of sorry for you guys—especially *you*, mate," said Liam, glaring at Fletch. "You came all this way for nothing."

"I don't think so," said Kip.

"Why's that?" Fletch asked.

"We simply need to apply the Scientific Method is all," said Kip.

"Okay," said Fletch. "I'll play along with you, Kippers. What's your hypothesis?"

"That the cab driver and the paranoid dude on the phone are one and the same," said Kip.

"I get it," said Liam. "Why else would the taxi be waiting for the emaciated bird right outside on Main Street?"

"So following your logic," said Fletch, "how do we test that hypothesis?"

"We hail a cab, I guess," said Kip, shrugging his shoulders.

Later that afternoon, Kip hovered above a plate of hot wings at Woody's as Colby looked on from her place across the table.

"Sure you don't want any?" he asked, his face growing red from the spicy concoction.

"Oh, no thank you," she replied, shaking her head back and forth. "I'm getting a contact high just sitting here with you."

"That's cool," said Kip, wiping his brow with his napkin. "I'm just glad you could meet up on such short notice."

"About that," said Colby, leaning towards him. "Where's your sidekick? Aren't you two usually joined at the hip?"

"No," said Kip, setting his napkin on the table. "It's not like that at all."

"Maybe I'm just curious about why you called me instead of him. Or Azza," said Colby.

"It's just that you seem to be almost as knowledgeable about President Hayes as I am. I mean, you're really into history, right?"

"*Almost as knowledgeable*?" she asked, smirking at him from across the table.

"Hey, I've been meaning to ask," said Kip, "what brought you out to Fremont anyway? Must be hard to leave the big city behind."

"It was hard all right," Colby replied, absentmindedly toying with the salt and pepper shakers. "But mostly because of my parents and their, uh, problems. My dad's problem, actually."

"What kind of problem did he have?"

"The availability of other women besides my mom, mostly," said Colby. "Which drove her to move us someplace more affordable—and just about as far away from my dad as she could possibly get. And while I understand that he's, you know, a major dick and all, I still miss him, you know? I mean, he's my dad."

For a moment, Kip looked away, uncertain about how to act or even what to say—*what, really, could he say*? He knew almost exactly how she felt. But then, when he heard the sound of Colby sniffling quietly to herself, he carefully eased his hand up from his lap, reached across the table, and clasped her own. Her hand felt smooth and warm to the touch. Just like he had imagined it would be.

"So here's the thing," said Kip, smiling at her from across the table. "I want to test out a pet theory of mine that a cab driver over in Fort Seneca may be involved in lifting those objects from the Hayes."

"Well, that's easy," said Colby, removing her phone from the pocket of her jeans. "There can't be that many taxi services in this area. It's not like I'm in Minneapolis anymore, right?"

As Kip looked on, Colby began tapping feverishly on the screen of her phone.

"Just as I thought," she said. "There are only two cab companies around here, and neither of them is in Fort Seneca—no surprise there. Both services have addresses in good old Fremont."

Colby dialed the first company, only to receive a blaring busy signal.

"Must not be them," she said.

"That's not very scientific."

"But it's a method," she replied, winking at him from across the table. With a few stray clicks of her fingers, she dialed the second cab company.

"It's ringing!" she announced. "Yeah, can you pick me up outside of Woody's Drive-In?" she remarked into her phone. "That's right—it's the place downtown by the river. No, 10 minutes would be just fine."

And with that, Colby set her phone down on the table and smiled in Kip's direction.

"I guess that's one way to do it," he said.

• • •

As late afternoon turned into dusk, Kip and Colby stood alongside the curb in front of Woody's. The street was mostly empty, save for an occasional vehicle ferrying its driver home from work.

"So about Antietam," said Kip.

"Are you still on that?" Colby replied, turning to face him under a streetlight.

"I guess, technically, Hayes was absent from the battle," Kip continued, "but those were his troops. I mean, *he* trained them, right?"

"Yeah, I don't want to play that game anymore," said Colby. "I'm ready to move on to something else." As Kip watched, Colby quickly closed the gap between them, pressing her lips lightly against his own.

After a few moments, she pulled away, smiling up at him as the lights from the taxicab illuminated their bodies, silhouette-like, in front of Woody's.

Together, they walked towards the cab. As they neared the vehicle, the driver leaned towards the open passenger's side window.

"Are you my fare?" he asked. Wearing a bulky canvas jacket, the driver was reed-thin and clean-shaven. His pale skin glistened in the nighttime air.

"We sure are!" Colby sang out, opening the back-seat door and motioning for Kip to join her inside.

As he pulled the door shut behind him, Kip heard the sound of an electronic click.

"Can't be too safe around these parts," said the driver, patting at a conspicuous bulge on the side of his jacket. "Where can I take you kids?" he asked, glancing at their reflection in the rearview mirror.

For a moment, Kip and Colby stared at each other uncertainly in the back seat. But then suddenly, Colby had it.

"How about the Presidential Library over on Hayes Avenue?" she asked, smiling confidently at Kip from across the back seat.

"That's only, like, a couple a miles away?" the driver asked. "Whatever," he added, shrugging his shoulders. "It's your money."

As the cab pulled away from Woody's Drive-In, Kip glanced back at the restaurant, and, parked right out in front, the Powder Puff. Turning his attention back to the interior of the taxi, he began scanning the contents of the vehicle. In truth, he had no idea what he was looking for, but he knew that they had fewer than five minutes to test out his hypothesis.

And that's when he saw it: the cabbie's state license displayed in a grimy plastic frame attached to the passenger's seat sun visor. In almost the same instant, Colby saw it, too. As the driver made the wide turn onto Hayes Avenue for the last few moments of their trip, she began fishing her phone out of her purse. Working as quietly as possible, she began positioning the lens to capture a photo of the cabbie's license. Glancing over at the driver, she prepared to take the shot, confident that he was concentrating on the roadway in front of him.

Only Colby had forgotten about the flash.

As the cabbie made the final turn into the driveway in front of Spiegel Grove, with its ochre-colored brick façade illuminated by the eerie spotlights that Kip knew so well from his nighttime excursions to the museum, Colby pressed the button on her camera app.

For a microsecond, the flash filled the interior of the taxicab with a blinding light. And just as suddenly, the vehicle was plunged into darkness yet again.

"What the fuck is wrong with you kids?" the driver sneered, wildly blinking his eyes as he tried to regain his vision in the wake of the flash. In the process, he slammed the car into a trio of metal garbage cans near the entrance to the building.

As he brought the taxi to a screeching halt in front of the exhibition hall, Colby began yanking forcefully at the door handle, but to no avail.

"What are you doing?" the cabbie shrieked. "You gotta pay the fare, goddammit!"

As Colby desperately tugged at the door handle, Kip glanced at the meter on the dashboard. $2.59.

Pulling open his wallet, he grabbed a ten-dollar bill and flung it across the armrest. As the cabbie pocketed the cash, he released the electronic lock. Within seconds, Kip and Colby had leapt from the vehicle and started running towards the Hayes.

Meanwhile, ever-faithful Marv was already bounding in their direction from his station in the exhibition hall. Seeing the elderly security guard running across the lawn, the cabbie thrust the car into gear and sped back across the parking lot towards Hayes Avenue.

"Good Lord, Kip, are you kids okay?" Marv asked, catching his breath beside them in front of the exhibition hall.

"I think this may be the first time you haven't greeted me as President Hayes, Junior," Kip observed, his limbs still shaking from their experience back in the cab.

"Now, I'm serious, son!" said Marv. "Who was that fella anyway?"

"Well, let me see," said Colby, fumbling with the camera on her phone. After quickly resizing the picture and homing in on the license, she had their answer.

"Edgar Ray Ahrens," said Colby, squinting as she held up the grainy photo for their inspection.

CHAPTER 19:
TIME TO PRETEND

The next morning, Kip picked up Azza at her usual curbside spot in front of the Holiday Inn. Driving away in the Powder Puff, Kip was positively ecstatic about the previous evening's exploits.

"But who is Edgar Ray Ahrens, sir?" Azza asked.

"That's where the trail runs cold," said Kip. "I tried googling him, but nothing came up. Well, almost nothing. There were a few random obituaries. But I figure that we can disregard those. The guy's definitely not dead. I mean, we rode in his taxicab and all."

"Were you and the cheese apple afraid, sir?" said Azza. "I cannot believe you got in the car with that man."

"To tell you the truth," said Kip, "it was Colby's idea. I don't think I would have had the guts otherwise—"

Glancing into the rearview mirror, Kip saw the police cruiser tooling along at a discreet distance behind the Subaru. His old friend Officer Hudgins was back on the case. As Kip made the final turn onto College Avenue, the cruiser peeled away and headed in the direction of the river. Meanwhile, a feeling of relief set in as Kip watched the familiar image of Faraday Hall looming just up ahead.

After bringing the Powder Puff to a gentle halt alongside the curb, Kip watched as Azza climbed out of the vehicle and began making her way towards the leafy green quad. Dozens of students were hurrying off to class as a lonely skateboarder caught Kip's eye as he cut across the quad and made a beeline in the direction of College Avenue, pitting him on a collision course with the young woman in the hijab.

Kip watched the events unfold from his vantage point in the front seat of the Subaru, as if the whole thing were some YouTube prank video that had been transformed into a bizarre slow-motion sequence. As for the Skateboard Kid: to Kip's eyes, he seemed like an odd rush of energy and derision, taking on the form of a yellow haze of human motion with his scraggly blond hair whipping behind him in his wake. In the last possible moment before he collided with Azza, he knelt down upon the board, arched his back, and grabbed the hijab, unraveling it with his hands as he sped past his victim.

With the window rolled down on the Powder Puff, Kip heard the Skateboard Kid's cry of war as plain as day. "Allahu Akbar!" he screamed in the very same instant in which Azza turned to confront her pursuer, only to find herself face-to-face with the empty space he had occupied only a microsecond before, having already sped beyond her into the quad. As the Skateboard Kid rode off towards some far-flung area of the campus, the purple and pink folds of Azza's hijab fluttered behind him like the colorful tail of a kite. As the kid propelled the skateboard even faster still, the hijab streamed ever higher into the clear blue sky before disappearing out of sight altogether.

For her part, Azza remained firmly planted where her attacker had left her. She had a vacant look in her eyes, and she was silent in contrast with the hoots and hollers emanating from some of the other students. At one point, Kip distinctly heard somebody scream "Go back to ISIS!" But by that time it no longer mattered, as Azza had fallen into a lifeless daze and become oblivious to her surroundings.

As Kip gazed at Azza from his place in the Powder Puff, she looked suddenly beautiful to him, as if he had never seen her before that moment. To his eyes, she took on the look of some tragic runway model, with her long black hair unfurling about her in exquisite layers, framing her exquisite oval face, which had been abruptly revealed for all the world to see without benefit of the hijab.

Azza's piercing green eyes darted about, looking for the missing appendage of her hijab as if she were some kind of insensate body roaming in search of the decapitated head that, only moments before, had been a central part of its being. But what Kip saw in her eyes was a far cry from the sultry beauty found in the perfumed pages of some high-concept magazine ad. No, what he saw in them wasn't the least bit erotic. What Kip glimpsed in Azza's eyes was the look of pure terror.

And that's when he was able, finally, to rouse himself from his state of temporary bewilderment and escape the clutches of the Subaru. Breaking into a full gallop, he began running after the Skateboard Kid, like some kind of one-man posse in bloody pursuit. As he ran past Azza, standing forlorn and confused at her place in the quad, his feelings became even more visceral, as he wanted to rescue her from the awfulness that he had just witnessed, to avenge the pain that he could see written across her face. But mostly, he just wanted to *get even*. To catch up with her attacker and do God-knows-what—anything to make his blood stop boiling and quell the unbridled fury that he felt pounding deep within his heart.

As it happened, Kip only managed to catch up with the Skateboard Kid after he had looped around the tiny building that housed the Registrar's office. With the hijab still flying high in his wake, the Skateboard Kid seemed bent on making a second pass through the quad when he ran—*smack!*—into the full force of Kip's body. Positioning himself like a linebacker, Kip executed a clean hit that halted the kid in midflight. As the riderless skateboard continued on its lonely path towards the orange wooden kiosk outside of Faraday Hall, the blond kid lay prone on the sidewalk as Kip pummeled him mercilessly with both fists, his knees grappled about the student's torso as the esteemed junior member of the board of governors of the Rutherford B. Hayes Presidential Library did his worst.

• • •

The next few hours elapsed for Kip in a kind of slow-motion haze. For the longest time, he waited in an anteroom near the Dean's office, watching as an endless parade of students and faculty crossed in front of his sightline. Eventually, one of those people happened to be his mother, the Assistant Registrar herself, who came to sit with him as he lingered there awaiting his fate. Only it turned out that it was all a matter of jurisdiction, with Kip being a high school student and all. The Dean had little choice but to hand him over to the Fremont High Vice

Principal, Hurley Meriwether, whom the student unrelentingly derided as "Burly Barrelhead" because of his world-class obesity, which was rendered even more remarkable by his incredible, oversized head. As Kip and his mom awaited Burly Barrelhead's arrival, they observed as the Skateboard Kid limped into the Dean's office to take his medicine. Other than a few bandages on his face, he didn't look that much worse for wear. Clearly, the folks in the college health center had been at the top of their game that morning.

A few minutes later, Burly Barrelhead ambled into the anteroom to take custody of Kip. As they drove across town in the Vice Principal's brick-red station wagon, Kip and his mom sat in the back seat as if they were heading off to county lockup in a squad car. But in truth, it was much ado about nothing. As he explained during the drive over to Fremont High, Burly Barrelhead wasn't allowed to even punish Kip, much less scold him—given that the incident had occurred off-campus. The most that he could do was recommend that Kip enroll in behavioral counseling. And who didn't need a little of that now and again? Burley Barrelhead asked.

As they climbed out of the station wagon in the traffic circle of Fremont High, Mrs. Beckelhymer assured the Vice Principal that Kip would sign up for counseling at once. As Kip went off in search of his third-period class—AP history, as it turned out—Burly Barrelhead suddenly realized that he had driven Mrs. Beckelhymer all the way out to Fremont High without a means of returning to the Northwestern Ohio State campus. At first, the rotund Vice Principal helpfully suggested that she call a cab to make the return journey, but a hard stare from the Assistant Registrar was all the convincing that he needed to drive her back to the college himself.

• • •

Not surprisingly, things would turn out to be a lot more complicated back at Northwestern Ohio State, where Azza sat on Dean Miller's sofa, still in shock from the harrowing events of the morning, and awaited her own fate at the hands of the college's chief academic administrator.

During her fleeting moments of mental clarity, she had already convinced herself that she would shortly be deported back to the *banlieues,* that her father's hard-wrought dollars would never be refunded, and that her new life in America was effectively over.

But rather amazingly, it was Dr. Matthews who came to her rescue. For the longest time, Dean Miller had puzzled over just what to do with Azza.

"Until your appearance on our campus, young lady," he informed her, "we hadn't so much as had a fistfight. But now, with everything going on in the world, it's like our own little place in the sun has been upset by the problems in that troublesome Middle East—"

But before he could utter another word, Dr. Matthews had barged her way into the Dean's Office. Staring up at the heavens, as she was so often wont to do, she recounted the scene outside of Faraday Hall.

Azza watched as her professor lambasted the Dean, although in truth she could scarcely register a word of what Dr. Matthews was saying. In her own mind, Azza had already begun lamenting the fact that this might very be the last time she ever saw Dr. Matthews in the flesh. That Azza would shortly be deported for Allah knows what trumped-up reason. And although she had hated Dr. Matthews ever since the Scriptural Anthropology lesson, she desperately wanted to learn the mystery behind the phrase, "When you hear hoofbeats, don't think of zebras." What hoofbeats? Azza thought to herself. And where are those zebras?

Yet as Azza sat there attempting to understand the mystery at the heart of Dr. Matthews's proverb, her professor's tenor took on even darker and more fulsome tones. As Dean Miller sat rigid behind his desk, she really let him have it.

"If you proceed in punishing Ms. Amari here in any way," Dr. Matthews stammered, "you'd be engaging in the worst case of victim-blaming that Northwestern Ohio State has ever seen."

With these last words, Azza had fallen out of her stupor. Perhaps it was because she had heard mention of her own name. Or perhaps she was simply stunned by Dr. Matthews's spirited defense of her cause.

In any event, she was quite suddenly present and accounted for during the great crisis of her life.

And better yet, she had regained her sense of consciousness just in time for Dr. Matthews's big finish—the moment that would alter the Dean's entire trajectory for handling the situation on that fateful morning.

"You know, it occurs to me, Dean Miller," said Dr. Matthews, her eyes gazing ever upwards, "that what this really amounts to is a hate crime."

And quite suddenly, the old anthropologist had gone and done it. She had uttered the two words that obligated Dean Miller to leap into action before the whole incident turned into a federal case, given that a hate crime would, in all likelihood, go federal on him if word got out.

"Now why'd you have to go and say *that*?" Dean Miller groaned, as he began fumbling through his desk for the hate crime pamphlet that he had picked up at a university safety convention some years back. He finally found the pamphlet buried in the bottom of his drawer, where it was hidden under a pile of fading ALICE brochures.

At first, Dean Miller had started rummaging through the pamphlet as if the answer to his dilemma might exist somewhere in its meager pages. But in truth, he already knew what to do.

"Now don't you worry, Dr. Matthews," he announced with as much authority as he could possibly muster under the circumstances. "I will see to it that Ms. Amari's attacker is expelled at once, pending Judicial Review, of course. But that shouldn't be an issue. And the other kid, that high-schooler—you know, Mrs. Beckelhymer's son Kip—well, he'll be Hurley Meriwether's problem. Just remember: they're not as tough over there at Fremont High as we are in Higher Ed—"

But Azza scarcely registered another word that morning in Dean Miller's office—or for the rest of the day, for that matter. The moment that she heard Kip's name mentioned, she fell into a deep terror. Surely, her appearance in this foreign land hadn't led to Mr. Kip's suffering? Surely, nothing horrible would befall him, right? She still hadn't learned to drive, or to do the ALICE. And the pear—the figurine was still missing. How would they ever solve the mystery of its disappearance under this dark cloud of her own making—that had been caused by her mere appearance in this strange world called Ohio? How could she embrace the words of her new American friend Methoataske and learn how to be somebody—to stop talking so much and start *doing* at last?

• • •

That night, Kip struggled to fall asleep—still fuming, as he was, over his traumatic experience back in the quad. Not surprisingly, his mother had been beside herself at dinner, certain that his association with Azza would be the ruination of him, and blaming herself, of course, for bringing the Tunisian woman into his life in the first place.

"It's no sweat," Kip told his mom. "Besides, it's all about the money," he added, compounding the lie.

But now, as he lay awake in the quietude of late evening, he knew differently. He understood that somehow during the few short weeks that he had known Azza, he had become implicated, complicit even, in what had befallen her back in the quad. That virtually everyone he knew was implicated, too: the Skateboard Kid for being, well, terrible; people like Dr. Smyth and his own mom for taking her money and promising her an experience that they could never possibly deliver; Officer Hudgins, for trailing her every move in his police cruiser—*it had to be racial profiling, right?* Kip thought to himself; even people like Ry, Colby, and, *yes,* himself were partially to blame for deigning to act normally around her—to be color blind—as if she were just another young American trying to find herself in an alien adult world.

And that's when he heard it: the plink of a pebble kissing his bedroom window. It was a sound that he thought he would never hear again.

Climbing out of bed, Kip wrenched open his window, and there she was: Birdie. As if she had never left.

As she passed through the open drapes, he stuck his head outside into the nighttime air, looking this way and that. But there was nothing to see, save for Birdie's lime-green VW parked down the street.

"Did you climb up the trellis?" he asked, looking outside yet again to confirm her means of entry.

"Sure did," Birdie replied. She was wearing a yellow plastic raincoat, and her pigtails, as always, were in full bloom.

"Why?" he asked, still in shock over her sudden reappearance in his life. "Why are you here?"

"I had to see you," she whispered, "you know, after what happened today and all."

"It was pretty awful," he admitted. "It was kind of surreal, actually—"

"Everybody's talking about you now," said Birdie, gently interrupting him.

"Because of Azza?" he asked.

"Well, no," she replied. "I mean, yeah—that girl was a big part of it. But they were talking about *you*. About how you just up and took out that guy."

"Why would anyone care?" he asked. "I bet they don't even like her."

"Kip, they don't even *know* her," said Birdie. "They're talking about *you*."

"So I'm notorious?" he asked. "That's different, huh?'

"You're not doing her, right—*that girl*?" Birdie asked.

"No," he said, looking away in embarrassment.

"Good," she said, taking a few steps forward. "Good," she repeated, as she kissed him lightly on the lips.

"Wait," he said, gently pushing her away. "What about Todd from Boston?"

Ignoring his question—or, rather, *answering* it—Birdie allowed her yellow raincoat to fall from her shoulders and onto the old shag carpeting that lined Kip's bedroom floor. Standing naked before him, she closed the space between them yet again, and kissed him once more—and forcefully.

Much later still, as Kip hovered over Birdie in his bed, her body becoming ever more familiar with his own, he winced as he felt her promise ring digging into his shoulder blade, the pain intermingling in new and unaccustomed ways with his pleasure.

CHAPTER 20:
BRADY'S ISLAND

On Saturday morning, Kip drew the Powder Puff to a halt in front of the Holiday Inn only to receive the shock of his life. There, standing on the grey macadam driveway, was Azza. Only it wasn't really Azza. Or at least, it wasn't the Azza that Kip had come to know across that most unusual fall semester.

For a moment, Kip could only sit by and gaze at the unusual figure standing in front of him. He knew that it was Azza, of course. But her headscarf was no longer in evidence. In fact, the only parts of her that were really visible were her brilliant green eyes. Only now they were discernible from within a narrow slit of black fabric. The entirety of her body was sheathed within a full-length silken robe, save for her hands, which peeked out of the long black sleeves of her outfit. And in one of her hands was a letter-sized envelope.

"What happened?" Kip asked, as Azza took her familiar place in the back seat of the Powder Puff.

For her part, Azza stared ahead blankly as Kip piloted the vehicle in the direction of downtown Fremont.

"Seriously," he said, glancing into the rearview mirror. "What gives?"

"It is a burqa, sir," she replied. "I am no longer wearing my hijab."

"Yeah, I gathered that," said Kip. "That's pretty extreme, isn't it?"

"I was trying to fit in before, sir," she said, clutching the envelope tightly with both hands. "Those times are over."

"Wait," said Kip. "When you were wearing the hijab, you were trying to fit in?"

"That is correct, sir."

"You realize, right, that you wouldn't even fit into our fair citizenry if you dyed your hair blonde and spoke with a nasal accent. You're no more an Ohioan than I'm a Tunisian."

"But America is melting pot of diversity, sir," Azza protested, as Kip pulled the Powder Puff into the parking lot behind the museum. The lot was empty, save for an old pickup truck parked a few hundred feet away from the exhibition hall. The driver was standing beside the orange-colored vehicle, calmly smoking a cigarette and staring off in the direction of the Hayes.

"Do you watch the news?" Kip asked.

"I do not, sir," Azza replied, her voice muffled and distant beneath her burqa.

"Well, I do," said Kip, "and just the other night, a guy was removed from an airliner during pre-flight because he had the nerve to speak Arabic. TSA officials escorted him off of the plane out of 'an abundance of caution.' There's your melting pot."

Suddenly, Kip realized that, beneath the manifold layers of her burqa, Azza was weeping. He slowed the Powder Puff to a halt behind the Hayes.

"Oh, hey," he said, glancing up at her trembling image in the rearview mirror, "I'm sorry. I didn't mean to . . . I didn't mean to upset you. You know that, right?"

And that's when Ry wrenched open the passenger's side door and slid into the front seat.

"What's up, slut?" he asked Kip, as Colby strode up and joined Azza in the back seat.

"What are you doing here?" Kip replied, scowling at Ry across the front seat. "And why would you call me *that*?"

"JK, dude," said Ry. "Don't get your panties in a twist. I ran into Colby over at Woody's. Thought I'd come along for the ride. You're getting pretty close, huh?"

"Close to who?" Kip asked.

"Not a who. A *what*," Ry replied. "Colby said that you're getting close to solving the pear thingy."

"Why is Azza crying?" Colby asked from her place in the back seat.

In the same instant, Ry caught a glimpse of the burqa in full flower, its blackness enveloping Azza, save for the fleshy bits about her eyes and hands.

"Shit, you look like a tank, A," he said. "That's hardcore!"

But Azza was undeterred, the sound of her weeping still emanating from within the recesses of her burqa.

"What's this?" Colby asked, gently removing the envelope from Azza's fingers.

"It is from the Judicial Review Board," said Azza, choking back tears.

"What's the charge?" Kip asked. "Walking to class while Muslim?"

"That's pretty close to the truth," said Colby, reading the letter. "Apparently, the student who attacked Azza has alleged that she provoked *him* by creating a disruptive campus climate."

"That's ridiculous," said Ry.

"Agreed," said Colby, "but according to this letter, 'all Northwest Ohio State students who are alleged to have committed a behavioral infraction have the right to be heard in front of the Judicial Review Board.'"

"So Azza's going to trial?" Kip asked.

"FML, sir," said Azza, cradling her head in her hands.

"The letter says that 'the Judicial Review Board will determine whether a preponderance of evidence supports the allegation, and,'" Colby continued, "'if the student is found to be in violation of the Code of Student Conduct, what disciplinary action or academic sanction shall be pursued.'"

"What happened to the skateboard douche anyway?" Ry asked.

"My mom told me that he's going to be expelled for the remainder of the year," said Kip.

"Dude, that's harsh," said Ry.

"Harsh?" Colby asked. "Are you on crack, Ry? That kid committed a hate crime. He should be in *jail*."

"Whoa, whoa, whoa," said Ry. "We're all on the same side here, aren't we?"

"We should drive over to that college right now!" Colby demanded.

"Your mom works there, Kip. She could get to the bottom of this."

"It's Saturday," Kip reminded her.

"Hey, this new outfit probably isn't gonna help your case, A," said Ry. "You would be crazy to wear that to the Judicial Review. You know that, right?"

"I don't care, sir," said Azza. "I give zero fucks."

• • •

With Ry riding shotgun and Azza and Colby seated in the back, Kip piloted the Powder Puff along an old gravel road on the north side of town, searching in vain for 14 Mulberry Street. A few clapboard houses pocked the landscape, which was scarred by an odd assortment of brush-ridden vacant lots and a burnt-out SUV.

"We've been up and down this road, like, five times already," said Kip.

"Yeah," said Ry, stretching his arms out in a protracted yawn, "you probably got the address wrong is all. But that's enough for today, huh? Let's bag this thing and go back to Woody's."

"Maybe Ry is right," said Kip, glancing in the rearview mirror at Azza, who was leaning against the car door, her burqa-covered face pressed against the window.

"Oh, that's rich," said Colby. "It's nice to see you back in each other's good graces."

"Where'd you get the address anyway?" Kip asked.

"While you were slumbering away in your bed last night, I was doing research," said Colby, smiling at Kip as he looked away in embarrassment. "I searched for Edgar Ray Ahrens and found an address through one of those information aggregators."

"Doesn't that cost beaucoup bucks?" Ry asked.

"My mom's PayPal account can handle it," said Colby. "Anyway, the aggregator reported that Mr. Cabbie lives at 14 Mulberry Street in Fremont, which should be, like, right over there," she added, pointing in the direction of the Sandusky River.

"Duly noted," said Kip. "But this is starting to feel like a lost cause."

"No, sir!" said Azza, turning back to face the others from her place by the window. "We must fulfill the bargain and reclaim the figurine. After that, I do not care what the Judicial Review Board will do to me. I have given up my dream of becoming a chemical engineer—"

"Oh, Azza," said Colby.

"And I still cannot drive a car," Azza continued. "But I want to see this pear before they deport me. After that, I will surrender to my fate, Allah be praised."

"Fine," said Kip, groaning audibly as he brought the Powder Puff to a noisy stop beside the river bank. "But you can see for yourself that there are no more houses out that way. We've run out of real estate."

"Hold up a sec," said Ry, studying the electronic map on his phone. "We've been going about this all wrong. 14 Mulberry Street is over there all right. It's actually *over there,*" he said, pointing towards the tree-lined island at the center of the Sandusky River.

• • •

Having abandoned the Powder Puff back on Mulberry Street, the four friends began the short hike in the direction of the river bank.

"Looks deserted to me," said Kip, scanning the opposite shore of Brady's Island. "If Mulberry Street continues over there, I sure don't see it."

"We're going to need a boat," said Colby, staring at the silty river lapping at the bank.

"Nah," said Ry. "We don't need any dumbass boat. All we have to do is take the railroad bridge." Resting against a grassy levee just above downtown Fremont, an old train trestle crossed the Sandusky just a few hundred feet downriver from where they stood.

"Pass," said Kip. "There are about a jillion ways that could go bad."

"Yeah?" Ry asked. "Like how?"

"Like a train comes along and mows us down," Kip replied. "Or worse, we're forced to leap off of the bridge, and we drown to death in the disgusting old Sandusky."

"Yeah, I don't know about this, Ry," Colby interjected.

But Azza simply wasn't having it. As the others stood by on the river bank, she began marching towards the railroad bridge, the jet-black folds of her burqa flapping behind her in rhythm with her footsteps.

"This is crazy, Azza," said Kip, shouting after her as she made her way towards the embankment. "Remember the suicide seat? This is similar to that—only, like, 50 times worse."

As Azza traipsed ever closer to the railroad bridge, Ry fell into line behind her. And moments later, Colby, with a shrug of her shoulders, joined them.

Standing beside the river bank, Kip watched them climb atop the railroad tracks and walk single file, gingerly making their way across the river that churned some 40 feet below.

A few minutes later, they had succeeded in crossing the Sandusky intact. The three friends looked back at him from Brady's Island, with Ry gesturing for him to join them on the other side. With her hands on her hips, Colby began shouting something to him, but by that point her words were inaudible, thanks to the sound of the freight train speeding up from the east. For the next few minutes, Kip watched as several dozen tanker and refrigerated cars whistled by him.

With the sound of the freight train dissipating into the distance, Kip glanced back across the river at Azza, Colby, and Ry. But there was no Azza, Colby, and Ry to be seen—only the tall grass nestled along the Brady's Island river bank, and, just beyond that, the leafy green thickness of the tree line.

CHAPTER 21: FLIRTIN' WITH DISASTER

Kip stood above the railroad tracks, and—looking both ways as if he were crossing a busy downtown street—climbed atop the rail bed and began walking in the direction of Brady's Island.

How unsafe could this really be? he thought to himself. A pretty hefty freight train had just streamed by. It should be at least a good 15 minutes before another one passes through Fremont. *Right?*

As he stepped up to the railroad bridge, it occurred to him that it looked a whole lot safer from his vantage point back on the river bank. A rusting hulk of steel with narrow wooden slats situated along its base, the bridge took on the look of a child's toy—a weathered, rickety toy, in his best estimation.

Well, here goes nothing, he thought to himself.

Stepping onto the railroad bridge, Kip purposefully stared dead ahead, never so much as daring to gaze down at the river that gurgled below. But all the way, he had to move as gingerly as possible to maintain his footing on the narrow slats of wood that formed a flimsy barrier between himself and the Sandusky.

And that's when he heard it: the sound of yet another train streaming up from behind. With a good 40 yards of track standing between himself and Brady's Island, Kip began stepping up his pace, moving as quickly as he possibly could while attempting to keep his balance, precariously situated as he was above the river.

At one point, he fell down to one knee, only to regain his equilibrium in the nick of time and make the last few steps before lunging to safety. As he caught his breath on the Brady's Island side of the river, he heard the sound of the freight train rushing by above his shoulders.

Ambling up to the tree line, Kip tried to catch a glimpse of his friends in the woods, but all he could see were trees and ground cover. So he began calling out their names.

"Azza?"

"Colby?"

And, finally: "Ry, you a-hole!"

And he received absolutely nothing in return for his trouble. The only sounds he could glean were the noise of the train streaming away from Fremont in the distance and the occasional chirp from some random bird. Probably a cardinal, he thought to himself.

With nothing left to lose, he began walking along the base of the tree line, and, spotting the remnants of a trail coursing into the heart of the woodland that made up Brady's Island, he stepped into the forest.

For the first few yards, there was relatively little to see, save for an old tire resting against a tree. But then, quite suddenly, the quietude of the forest was broken by the sound of human agony—and Kip had absolutely no doubt about the identity of that particular human: it was the unmistakable scream of Colby Applegate. In truth, he had never heard her scream before. But he knew her voice just the same.

Kip reflexively broke into a breakneck sprint down the trail. At one point, he slipped on a pile of pine needles and lost his footing, falling head over heels onto the hard ground of the woodland floor, only to right himself at the last possible second and continue on his death-defying trot.

Kip finally caught up with the others in a wide clearing at the center of the island. He arrived just in time to observe Ry and Azza propping Colby up at the base of a tree near the edge of the glade, which was blanketed with a fine bed of pine needles. For her part, Colby was grimacing in pain.

"She twisted her ankle," said Ry, leaning over her for closer inspection.

"What happened?" Kip asked, as he knelt in the clearing, desperately attempting to catch his breath after his life-or-death gallop into the heart of the forest.

"I tripped on that log over there," Colby replied, gesturing towards a pile of rotting timber at the clearing's perimeter.

"Dude, what happened to your face?" Ry asked.

Reaching up to wipe his brow, Kip came away with a stream of blood on his hands.

"Oh, man," he said, staring down at his palms. "How bad is it?"

"It is nothing. I predict a full recovery, sir," Azza replied, stepping towards him for a closer look. But all Kip could see was the rectangular slit that framed her eyes, which had been transformed in the sunlight of the clearing into a brilliant yellowy green.

"I think it's kinda hot," said Colby, laughing through her obvious pain. "You came all this way to rescue me. My hero!"

"Whoa," said Ry. "Get a room, all right?"

"I wasn't so heroic back at the railroad bridge, I can tell you that," said Kip.

"Well, you're kind of an indoor guy, right, Beckelhymen?" Ry asked.

"Takes one to know one," he answered, dusting off his blue jeans from his tumble back in the forest.

"Sirs," said Azza, pointing towards the far edge of the clearing with her robed, outstretched arm, "is that a house?"

And sure enough, they could see it there in the distance: what looked to be an old, broken-down clapboard shack. As Kip and Ry helped Colby to her feet, carefully lifting her by the shoulders, Azza began walking in the direction of the faded wooden structure. With nearly every step, Colby winced in pain as they followed the trail towards the shack.

Up close, the ramshackle house looked even worse than it had from back in the clearing. One of the walls was completely caved in, and all of the windows had been broken down to their sills.

"Let me guess," said Ry, "14 Mulberry Street?"

"This is what you call living off-the-grid," said Colby, staring at the decrepit wooden building standing—*or barely standing*—before them.

"What is off-the-grid?" Azza asked, as the friends walked around the perimeter of the shack.

"It means that you're unplugged from society. No utilities, no electronics, that kind of stuff," Colby replied, wincing from the pain emanating from her foot.

"Aren't you burning up in that thing, A?" Ry asked, pointing at her burqa, which had beads of perspiration running down its lengthy black folds.

"It is very hot, sir," Azza replied.

"I bet you're not gonna take it off, though, are you?" said Ry.

"No, sir," she answered. "I grovel to no one."

"That's probably a good policy," said Ry, laughing to himself.

"That's funny coming from the guy who grovels to just about everyone," said Kip.

"Dude, get outta my shit, all right? I'm out here sweating like a mofo to help you with your little treasure hunt. The least you could do is let me be."

"Ry, nobody asked you to come along, okay?"

"Colby invited me at Woody's, thankyouverymuch," said Ry. "And with all the buzz at school, I figured you wouldn't mind, slut."

"What buzz?" Kip asked, grabbing Ry by the scruff of his lifeguard shirt. "And what's with all this *slut* business?"

"Whoa, dude," said Ry, his hands held up high as he backed away. "You need to *chill.*"

"Seriously, Kip," said Colby, gently patting his back. "We're all friends here, okay?"

"So what's all this buzz, then, Ry?" he asked, as they made their way around the back of the house.

"It's just people talking about what went down the other day on the quad, okay? You're, like, the talk of Fremont High is all. You beat the shit out of a college kid. That's big news among the peeps. Folks were impressed, Mr. Tough Guy."

Rounding the corner of the house, they ambled up to the shack's ruined front door, which was partially ajar.

It was Colby who saw the body first. Recoiling at the sight of it, she fell forcefully back into Ry, who was still acting as her human crutch.

For his part, Kip went white, briefly averting his eyes, as if he had been slapped in the face.

But it was Azza who remained cool and collected, calmly stepping up to the dilapidated front stoop for a closer look.

"Is it Edgar Ray Ahrens?" Ry asked.

"I do not know, sir," Azza replied. "I have never seen this man before in my life."

As the others looked on, Colby inched in for a closer look.

"Oh, yeah," she said. "That's the cab driver all right."

"What do we do?" Kip asked. "Where's Officer Hudgins when you actually need him?"

"Probably rousting Todd from Boston for banging his daughter," said Ry, as Kip looked away in disgust. "What—was it too soon?" Ry asked.

With this last remark, Kip removed his phone from his pocket.

"What are you doing?" Ry asked.

"Seeing if I can get any signal," he replied, as he studied the screen. "It's pretty weak, but I think I can make the call." With a few quick taps of the finger, Kip dialed 9-1-1.

As Kip spoke into his cell phone, Colby inched closer to Azza, hovering above her shoulders.

"What do you think happened to old Edgar?" asked Colby. "I bet it was a heart attack. He was crazy paranoid the other night."

"Sometimes things are not what they seem," said Azza, leaning closer to the body.

And that's when she finally got it: "When you hear hoofbeats, don't think of zebras," Azza whispered to herself.

"Huh?" said Colby.

"I do not think this man expired from a heart attack," said Azza, as she continued to study the body. "No, I believe he has suffered a fatal opioid overdose."

"What is this—*CSI Ohio*?" Ry asked.

"No, sir," said Azza. "It is Chemistry 101 at Northwestern Ohio State College with Dr. Franklin presiding. He taught us that the chemical interactions associated with opioid overdose typically result in a telltale blue coloring around the lips and fingernails. Do you see it, sir?"

And sure enough, as Azza turned back to look at the others, they could see the bluish tinge about the body's lips and fingertips.

"*What* is that?" Colby asked.

"It is cyanosis," said Azza, "which is a result of low oxygen in the blood."

"No shit?" said Ry.

"No, sir," Azza replied. "Absolutely no shit at all."

"Okay," said Kip, "but how do you know it's from an opioid. Aren't there, like, a lot of things that cause your lips to turn blue? Like a heart attack, even?"

"That is correct, sir," said Azza, "but the evidence would seem to suggest otherwise. Do you see the prescription bottle here?" she continued, pointing towards the russet-colored pill bottle just beyond the front stoop. "It is for oxycodone, sir, which is a very popular prescription opioid. We learned that its widespread use has resulted in a deadly epidemic in the Midwest, especially in rural Ohio. Dr. Franklin reported that depressed peoples in the Rust Belt—"

"Jesus God, enough already, A," Ry interjected. "You're starting to sound like a Kip and Colby geek-off on steroids—"

"According to Dr. Franklin," Azza continued, "steroids have also been the subject of pervasive drug abuse, particularly among athletes, sir. It is a good thing, is it not, that you and Mr. Kip are not athletic, correct?"

"Oh, that was a sweet burn, A," said Ry, shaking his head back and forth.

"I'm going inside," said Colby, grimacing in pain with every step into the shack.

"Should we be doing that?" said Kip, as he stuffed his cell phone back into his jeans pocket. "Isn't this, like, a crime scene?"

"Won't hurt to take a quick look, right?" said Colby, as she limped into the cramped, darkened interior of the shack.

"Then I'm going, too," said Ry, following Colby and Azza into the house. With a shrug of the shoulders, Kip brought up the rear.

As Azza began studying the disheveled countertop in the tiny eat-in kitchen, Colby scanned the dusty wooden floor, which was scattered with debris, mostly old pizza boxes and beer cans.

"What a shithole," said Ry, still standing by the front stoop near Edgar Ray Ahrens. Or at least, what used to be him, that is.

"Who are you kidding?" Kip asked, glancing around the shack's narrow interior. "It looks almost exactly like your bedroom. Smells like it, too."

"Dude, chill," said Ry. "Two days ago, you took down a college kid with your bare hands, and now you're turning into my mother."

"Come over here, Kip, and help me look around," said Colby, leaning against him as she continued to poke through the litter on the floor.

"What's that?" Kip asked, pointing towards an object near the base of a decrepit sofa.

"Looks like some kind of watch," said Colby, holding Kip's shoulder to steady herself as she leaned in for a closer view. "Yeah, it's a wristwatch all right," she said, handing the blue plastic object to Kip, who turned it over in his hands.

"This is some sort of electronic device," he said. "Yeah, see here?" he continued, holding up the object for the others' inspection. "This thing's GPS-enabled."

"That's a Fitbit," said Ry.

"What the eff is a Fitbit doing here?" Kip asked.

"A fit-*what*, sir?" Azza asked.

"A Fitbit," Ry replied. "A kind of exercise thingy. Keeps track of your steps. So you can be healthy and shit."

"Wow. Check this out," said Kip, activating the readout on the device. "The user logged 2,389 steps yesterday. That's pretty good, isn't it?"

"Not really," said Ry. "My dad has a Fitbit. He's pissed off if he comes in under 5,000 steps a day."

"Must be good exercise for him," said Kip. "He travels a lot. Probably logs a lot of steps in airports and stuff."

"Do you guys ever hear yourselves talk?" Colby asked, still

hovering over the corpse.

"The cheese apple is right, sirs," said Azza. "We must return our focus to the bargain that we struck. We must locate the figurine."

"Let me have a look-see," said Ry, taking the object from Kip. "So who does this belong to? Doesn't seem like something old Edgar would wear."

"Could belong to the emaciated woman," said Kip, "the one from Turley's."

"You know," said Colby, "since the Fitbit has GPS, we can probably find out where the user has been."

Standing near the shack, they could hear the sirens screaming off in the distance. Not surprisingly, it was Ry who panicked first.

"Why are we out here?" he asked.

"What do you mean, Ry?" said Kip. "We were following up on the cabbie's whereabouts."

"No," said Ry. "You're not hearing me, boy scout. You had to go and call the cops. So I'm asking you: what was our reason for being out here in the first place? What's our explanation going to be?"

"We were hiking in the woods, right?" Colby asked. "That sounds legit."

"It sounds like bullshit," said Ry. "But it may be the best we've got on the fly. All I know is that you and I are out here with those two," he added, nodding towards Kip and Azza. "In case you hadn't heard, they just starred in a hate crime over at the college."

"The Skateboard Kid caused all of that," said Kip, correcting him.

In the background, they could hear the slow whine of an outboard motor veering closer to Brady's Island.

"I didn't say you were the perp," Ry replied. "All's I am saying is that we're not just four kids messing around in the woods. Could look like something else."

Moments later, Officer Hudgins had made his way up from the river back, followed by a second patrolman. Glaring at Kip, he made a beeline for the shack. As the four friends stood around the perimeter, they could hear the cops whispering near the front stoop.

Officer Hudgins strode back over from the shack. "You kids wait here for a sec," he announced. "I'm gonna talk to Mr. Beckelhymer for a bit."

Drawing Kip back towards the clearing, Officer Hudgins didn't waste any time getting to the point.

"What are you doing all the way out here, son?" said Officer Hudgins. "I recognize the Langham boy. And Ms. Amari is already on our radar. Who's the other girl?"

"That's Colby Applegate, sir," said Kip. "She's a junior. Just moved here from Minnesota."

"Officer Rankin over there will escort you kids off the island. This looks like an OD to me, but we'll know for sure after we process the scene. And Kip," he added, clasping him firmly by the shoulder, "you need to start being more careful, okay? I know what happened over at the college, all right? We've known each other a long time, and I don't like much where this is headed. You need to ask yourself if you're hanging out with the right crowd—"

"Ry's just a knucklehead, sir," Kip replied.

"It's not Mr. Langham I'm worried about," said Officer Hudgins. "Now, goddammit, son. You need to start hearing me, okay?"

"If this is about Birdie—"

"My daughter is irrelevant to this conversation," said Officer Hudgins, slowly folding his arms in front of his chest. "Do you understand that, Kip?" he asked. "What you need to be thinking about right now is what's best for *you.*"

But all Kip could think about was his three friends waiting nervously beside the shack. Standing there under the watchful eye of Officer Rankin, they cut an unlikely trio: whip-smart Colby with her All-American good looks; his douchebag friend Ry, who was all talk most of the time, and all heart when it mattered; and Azza, swaddled beneath the black folds of her burqa and silken robing.

Somewhere, deep inside all of that fabric was the beautiful, inquisitive woman whom he had glimpsed on that very first morning back in the Registrar's Office. *But what must she be thinking underneath that robing?* he wondered to himself. *What could she possibly be thinking about her adopted homeland now?*

In truth, Kip didn't have the first idea.

CHAPTER 22:
HEAVYDIRTYSOUL

As dusk fell over Brady's Island, Officer Rankin piloted the police skiff across the Sandusky, shepherding the friends towards the shores of Fremont. Azza stood up front in the tiny boat, like Washington crossing the Delaware, only with her black burqa whipping in the wind instead of a revolutionary tricorne hat. Ry slouched nearby, with his hand dangling in the water, while Colby grimaced in pain as the skiff lapped across the swells of the river. For his part, Kip held up the rear, not far from Officer Rankin, who wordlessly steered the outboard motor, its whine establishing a perpetual drone that echoed between the shores.

Forlorn and dejected, Kip felt strangely trapped, as if he no longer had any options. Or at least none that he could ascertain from within his despondency. He could no more help Azza than he could help himself. Birdie's sudden reappearance in his life had left him confused, at best, and even more uncertain than before, if that were possible. He couldn't stop thinking about Colby, which complicated things immensely. And Ry—well, *whatever,* Kip thought to himself.

As if to make matters worse, as the little skiff neared the opposite river bank Colby reached over and clasped Kip's hand within her own welcoming palm, soft and warm to the touch. Suddenly, he felt as if he wanted to cry. Was it for Colby? he wondered. Or was it something else? Something he couldn't quite determine, yet roiling out there in the ether just the same. Somewhere just beyond his reach.

• • •

After dropping Ry off on Augusta Drive and Azza at the Holiday Inn—albeit only after she had extracted his promise of a Sunday driving lesson—Kip drove Colby home. But then it suddenly occurred to him that he had no idea where she lived. That they had never discussed it before. Isn't it strange, he wondered to himself, that you could hold hands and do something as intimate as kiss another person without having the first clue about them?

"Where to?" he asked, turning to face Colby in the front seat of the Subaru.

"We're renting an apartment in Stony Prairie," she replied. "On Front Street."

"That's funny," he said.

"What's funny?"

"That you didn't mention it when we were over at Stony Prairie Pawns the other day."

"Maybe because it's pretty low rent—that's why. It's kind of embarrassing, to tell you the truth."

"Hey, you don't have to be embarrassed around me—"

"You're all I've been thinking about, you know," said Colby, abruptly changing the subject. "Especially after you kissed me the other night."

"I think it may have been *you* who kissed me," said Kip, as he drove the Powder Puff out of Fremont.

Reflexively, Kip glanced into the rearview mirror, expecting to see Officer Hudgins and his ever-present police cruiser. But he wasn't there, of course. He must be back on the island, Kip reasoned, still processing the scene in Edgar Ray Ahrens's shack.

And that's when Kip happened to notice Colby gazing at him from across the front seat. It was the look of love that he had known so well back when he and Birdie were truly a couple, which was very different from the present, he realized, their night back in his bedroom notwithstanding. No, what he had with Birdie had always been oddly dissimilar from what he was feeling right now with Colby. Which was both different *and* better.

And then Kip being Kip—powered by guilt, no doubt, and his preternatural need to *do the right thing*—went ahead and invited disaster into the interior of the Powder Puff. He simply couldn't stop himself.

"There's something I've gotta tell you," he muttered. He could feel himself reverting into a kind of childlike state. As if he were having to admit to his mother that he had forgotten to take out the trash. Or something similarly insignificant.

For her part, Colby was staring at him across the front seat with a look of near-terror. Now he could feel himself preparing to disappoint her. To let her down for no greater purpose than to service his own insecurities.

"I saw Birdie the other night," he continued.

"No biggie," said Colby. "It's a small town, right? You're bound to run into each other now and then."

"I mean, I *saw* her," said Kip.

"Oh," said Colby, folding her arms across her chest. He could almost see her retreat inside herself, as if she were walling him out. He really couldn't blame her if she did.

Kip realized that there was much more to tell—if he were really aiming for full disclosure. But he didn't have the courage to go any further. How pathetic, he thought to himself.

As he piloted the Powder Puff past Oakwood Cemetery on the outskirts of Fremont, Kip made his move. A last, desperate effort to get back in her good graces while he still could.

"Did you know that President Hayes was originally buried over there?" he asked. "His remains weren't relocated to Spiegel Grove until the early twentieth century. Reminds me of a poignant story about the day of his funeral in January 1893. Did you know that President-Elect Grover Cleveland was there, along with Ohio Governor and future U.S. President William McKinley?"

As he steered the Powder Puff into Stony Prairie, Kip desperately awaited her response. As if her next few words might determine a larger fate.

To his surprise, she broke out laughing, chuckling uproariously as Kip glanced over from his place across the front seat.

"Why . . . why are you laughing?" he asked.

"I don't want to do this anymore, Kip," she said, regaining her composure. "We're past it now."

"This *what*?"

"This game we play," she said. "The one where we try to one-up each other about President Hayes. And Lemonade Lucy. And, you know, history."

For the rest of the drive, Kip and Colby sat in an uneasy silence. Eventually, he pulled up to the address that she had given him: a series of non-descript apartments on the edge of Stony Prairie, a new-build with nary a tree in sight. So much for the prairie, Kip thought to himself. They must have clear-cut this place but good.

After bringing the car to a stop, Kip loped around to the passenger's side to help Colby out of the Powder Puff.

"I'm really sorry about your foot," said Kip, gingerly lifting her out of the Subaru.

"It's nothing," said Colby. "It's not like it's the most painful thing that's happened to me today."

"You mean seeing the body?"

"No, dumbass," she replied, staring up at him. "You just don't get it, do you?"

No, he didn't get it, he had to admit to himself. But he couldn't find the words to explain himself, so he remained mute as he walked Colby to her apartment door, doing his best to help keep the weight off of her aching foot.

As he looked on, she disappeared inside without another word. Only the quiet click of a dead-bolt lock.

Walking away from Colby's door, Kip felt the familiar buzz of his phone from inside his jeans pocket. It was from Birdie, he figured. Just had to be, right? And he knew what the text would say almost before he even read it.

"ILU," she texted.

Sure, he thought to himself. *Now* you do.

• • •

The next morning, Kip fulfilled his promise to Azza, meeting her bright and early in front of that Holiday Inn roundabout that he knew so well. A short while later, as he pulled the Powder Puff into the Hayes parking lot, he fantasized about driving straight over to Colby's apartment building in Stony Prairie. He had absolutely no idea what he would do when he got there, but it seemed like the right thing to do. A kind of heroic gesture after he'd been just about anything but.

For her part, Azza was eager to get started. After the dead end that they had encountered back on Brady's Island, it seemed like their only hope for even partially fulfilling the bargain.

But Azza's enthusiasm appeared to dissipate almost as soon as she took her foreign place behind the wheel of the Subaru.

"I don't know if I can do this, sir," she said, tugging at the sides of her burqa. "This morning, when I knelt upon my prayer rug and said *Salat al-Fajr*, I thought I could do it, Allah be praised. But now, I no longer believe."

"Well, let's start by turning on the ignition," said Kip, reaching over to twist the key in the steering column. After sputtering and coughing, the Powder Puff roared into life.

"It is very hot in here, sir," said Azza, staring dead ahead into the blankness of the parking lot. "Why is it so hot for such a late fall day?"

"I don't know, Azza," he replied. "The AC's running full-blast. Maybe you should go back to the hijab—ditch the burqa for a while?"

For a moment, she turned to face him, staring him down from across the front seat, her olive eyes having transformed into tiny, judgmental pinpoints. And for his part, Kip felt the sting, quickly looking away from her gaze.

"I can no longer do that, sir," she said. "They have already won."

"What do you mean by that?" Kip asked.

"Every day, it just seems to get worse, sir," said Azza. "Sometimes, living in this place makes me feel like I am walking among spiders. Most of the time, spiders leave you alone, wanting nothing to do with humans. They go about their business, spinning webs, laying eggs, trapping insects. But then, out of nowhere, they crawl right up and bite you before you even know that they were there."

"Look," said Kip, banging his fist on the dashboard. "I don't know where you get off being so pessimistic—"

"Pessimistic, sir?"

"Yeah, pessimistic," he replied. "You're acting like the world has ended."

"Oh, but it has, sir," she answered. "Do you know what happens when brown people who are Muslims are subjected to Judicial Reviews? They get deported. *That* is what happens. Do you not understand that this is my last stand? My father saved every last dollar for *years* in order to send me to America, selling irreplaceable family heirlooms in the process. He did it all to save my life and liberate me from the *banlieues.* I am the only member of my family to survive. My brothers, my mother, my aunts and uncles—everyone has succumbed to the ghetto. And now this?" she said, banging her fist on the steering wheel. "I will never take my burqa off. I do not care how hot it gets!"

As Kip looked on—a little fearful, but at the same time, in awe of his friend's newfound spirit—Azza's eyes became even more precise, the green pinpoints even more exacting, if that was possible, than before.

Then she did it: she pushed the gearshift into drive and the Powder Puff lunged forward across the empty parking lot.

"You're doing it!" Kip sang out.

"Yes, sir. I am!" said Azza, as the Subaru lurched across the macadam. "I am doing it!"

"Tap the brakes a little," said Kip. "You're nailing this!"

"Yes, sir. I am nailing this!"

As the car hurtled towards the exhibition hall's massive façade, Azza slowly depressed the brake pedal, bringing the aging vehicle to a halt. She eased the gearshift back into park, before letting out a protracted sigh of relief.

"I can do it now," she said. "I can do the ALICE."

• • •

As Kip drove the Powder Puff across town in the direction of the Holiday Inn, Azza resumed her place in the back seat and basked in the glory of her triumph back at the Hayes. He couldn't see it, of course, but beneath the black fabric of her face-covering, Azza was beaming.

Pulling up to a red light near Woody's, Kip glanced at the dilapidated downtown landscape. *When did this all get so rundown?* he wondered to himself. Was it always this way?

And then he saw it: the Skateboard Kid and another college student sitting in lawn chairs by the side of the road. Beside them was a flagpole planted in the dry sod of a vacant lot. The yellow banner, which depicted a coiled rattlesnake preparing to strike, was emblazoned with the words DON'T TREAD ON ME!

As the car idled at the stoplight, Kip hoped against hope that Azza wouldn't see the boys with their absurd flag waving in the early morning breeze.

But it was hopeless, of course. With the light still burning beet red, Azza caught sight of the banner.

"What is that, sir?" she asked.

"It's the Gadsden flag," he said, suddenly loathing his wide knowledge of American history. "It was a battle cry during the Revolutionary War."

"I know those boys, sir. One of them stole my hijab, and the other is from my Anthropology class with Dr. Matthews. He is terrible. He hates me, sir. I know it."

"We need to get out of here," said Kip, nervously glancing at the stoplight.

"Is that for me, sir?" Azza asked. "I have not treaded on anybody."

"Just ignore them—"

Then it happened: as the light turned green, Azza flung open her door and leapt out of the Powder Puff.

Seeing the woman in the burqa marching across the roadway in his direction, the Skateboard Kid stood up from his lawn chair and held the banner high. The sloucher tried to follow suit, but couldn't negotiate his way out of his chair. An absurd display followed in which he stood up, hunched over with the lawn chair still clinging to his backside.

"Is that flag for me, sirs?" Azza barked, as she joined the two boys along the roadside. "I have never treaded on you!" she added, thrusting her index figure in front of her like a weapon.

"We can do anything we want out here," the Skateboard Kid snarled. "We're not on campus anymore. You're fair game now. Nobody gets expelled downtown, bitch!"

As Azza accosted the boys, Kip jumped out of the Powder Puff, the engine still idling at the stoplight, and joined her by the curb. By this point, the slouscher had managed to extricate himself from his lawn chair, angrily hurling it onto the ground beside the roadway.

"Come on, Azza," said Kip, grabbing her by her robed arm. "These dudes aren't worth it."

"*You're* not worth it, shithead," said the sloucher, giving the lawn chair one last angry kick.

"Hey, that's the asshat who attacked me on campus," said the Skateboard Kid, glaring at Kip.

"I didn't attack anyone," said Kip, still tugging at Azza's arm.

"Sure, you did," said the Skateboard Kid, inching closer to him. "You were with the raghead. Now, you're *both* provoking me."

That's when Kip stepped in front of Azza, pulling himself face-to-face with the Skateboard Kid.

"So, are we gonna go again?" the Skateboard Kid asked, tossing the flagpole aside like it was a stray piece of kindling.

For a moment, it seemed as if something might happen as Kip and the Skateboard Kid stood toe-to-toe on the roadside. But the crackle from the loudspeaker in the police cruiser, which had pulled up just behind the Powder Puff, left all that for naught.

"Get back into the vehicle, Mr. Beckelhymer," said Officer Hudgins, holding the transmitter in his fist. "*Now.*"

As Kip and Azza climbed back into the Subaru, the police cruiser pulled up alongside the hatchback.

"Get a move-on," said Officer Hudgins, speaking to them through the open passenger's side window.

"What about those guys?" Kip asked.

"They're exercising their right to free assembly," Officer Hudgins replied. "Move along. *Now.*"

As Kip pulled the Powder Puff away from the stoplight, Azza straightened the folds of her burqa.

"I am exhausted by all of this nonsense, sir," she announced from her place in the back seat. "Now I've gotta *do.*"

"Gotta do *what*?"

"Whatever it takes, sir," she replied. "I will never grovel before anyone again."

CHAPTER 23: ALTERNATIVE FACTS

"Oh, it just gets better and better," said Kip, stepping into the kitchen later that afternoon.

There, sitting at the dinette table, was Ry, with a broad smile creeping across his face. Kip's mother stood nearby, pulling a tray of freshly baked chocolate chip cookies out of the oven.

"Dude," said Ry, "you're just in time. Your mom made cookies!"

"Yeah," said Kip, sitting down at the table. "She does that sometimes."

"Ryan was just telling me about your project with the missing pear," said Mrs. Beckelhymer.

"Then he probably told you that it's a figurine, right?" Kip asked.

"If Fletch Clawson has wrapped you up in his shenanigans, he's going to have to answer to me," she said. "You don't have any more time for distractions. You're retaking your SATs next weekend—"

"That's totally bogus," said Ry, scarfing down a handful of cookies. "Kip doesn't need to retake his SATs. He's good to go!"

"I'm good to go as far as enrolling at Northwestern Ohio State," he replied. "I'm trying to aim higher, if that's okay with you."

"Oh, come on, dude," said Ry. "You're way smarter than I am, and I got, like, a 1,350."

"FML," said Kip, holding his head in his hands.

"FML?" Mrs. Beckelhymer asked as she set glasses of milk on the table.

"Is that bad?" Ry asked.

"Not at all," said Kip, shaking his head back and forth. "In fact, it's way better than my 1,200."

"Huh," said Ry, beaming from ear to ear. "How do you like that? I outplayed the brainiac."

"I'll finish these upstairs," said Kip, glumly standing up from the table and fumbling with a handful of cookies.

"Oh, come on, dude," said Ry. "Don't leave angry!"

• • •

A few minutes later, as Kip cracked open his SAT study guide to practice for the algebra section, Ry appeared at his bedroom door.

"Wanna study, buddy?" he asked.

"Seriously, Ry," Kip replied, "I've got to buckle down and work on this if I'm going to have any hope of getting into a good college."

"Shit, why bother?" Ry asked. "I'm not going."

"To college?"

"Hell, no."

"Ry, you have an awesome score. You probably even qualify for scholarships."

"I've got something better than that."

"Than scholarships?" said Kip. "I doubt it."

"What if I told you I knew someone who could help us crack the code?"

"The code for *what*?"

"For this," said Ry, removing the blue Fitbit from the bowels of his jeans pocket.

• • •

"Where are we going anyway?" Kip asked, as he drove the Powder Puff across downtown Fremont. When he reached the stoplight in front of Woody's, he took a long look around the streetscape. But there was nothing to see. The Skateboard Kid and the sloucher were long gone by then.

For his part, Ry remained strangely mute as he sat in the passenger's seat.

"Seriously, Ry," Kip said, "we're not going to get anywhere if you don't give me an address."

"Okay, dude," said Ry. "But you're not gonna like it."

"Try me," said Kip.

"Fine," said Ry, sighing loudly from his place in the front seat. "It's not very far from my house, actually. Steer this puppy to 2014 Pebble Beach—"

"Oh, bullshit!"

"I told you that you weren't gonna like it," said Ry, waving his hands in the air.

"No way," said Kip. "I don't care if he's the last person on earth who can help us with the exercise thingy—"

"It's a Fitbit," Ry interjected.

"I don't give a shit what it's called—"

"Chill out, dude," said Ry. "Hey, what's up with Colby, by the way? You guys making it work?"

"You are the worst, Ry. Do you know that?" said Kip, banging his hands on the steering wheel. "Why am I always driving you places anyway? You're the one who lives by the golf course. When did I luck out and become your chauffeur?"

"About the same time my mom took away my car."

"Your Mini-Cooper's in lockdown again, huh?" said Kip, making the wide turn in front of the Fremont Bible Church. "What did you do this time?"

"Smoking weed in the house," Ry replied. "Can you believe it?"

"Yeah," said Kip. "Sounds like a bum rap to me."

"That's what I said."

"I'll drop you off on Pebble Beach," said Kip, "but there is no way I'm going into that dude's house."

"Oh, come on, Beckelhymen," said Ry. "We're almost there."

"Let me spell it out for you," said Kip. "No. Fucking. Way."

"No wonder I outplayed you on the SATs," said Ry. "Even I know that's not spelling—"

"Get out of the car," said Kip, bringing the Powder Puff to a screeching halt on Master's Way.

"Dude—"

"Right now, Ry. We're done."

"I'm sorry, dude," he replied. "*Seriously.*"

"Sorry?" said Kip. "For which thing? There are so many. Frankly, I wouldn't even know where to begin—"

"For being such a fucker," Ry replied.

"You mean 'fuckup.'"

"A fucker, fuckup, *whatever,*" said Ry. "I'm going to stop screwing up your life. Right now—I promise."

"Honestly, Ry," said Kip, "I don't think you've got what it takes to accomplish that level of real and abiding change."

"'Real and abiding change'?" Ry asked. "Sometimes, I feel like I'm in school when I talk to you—"

"That's exactly what I mean," said Kip. "I can't live in the Ry ecosystem anymore—where everything's a wisecrack and nothing has any real meaning. Now get out of the car. *Please.* I'm begging you, dude. I can't take this anymore—"

"Kip, listen to me," said Ry. "I can change—really, I can. I want to be more help to you and not such a pain in the ass all the time. I can do this. *I swear.*"

"Oh, really," said Kip. "Why the change of heart?"

"I guess it started when I saw you back on Brady's Island with Officer Hudgins," he replied, as he gazed at the verdant green lawns on the golf course. "You've got a lot on your plate."

"Oh," Kip answered, "so you're doing it all for me? That's mighty charitable of you—"

"No," said Ry, staring at Kip from across the front seat. "I'm doing this for me, too. I'm being selfish here—"

"Well, of course, you are. That's what you do best, isn't it?"

"I'm being selfish," Ry continued, "because you are—absolutely, without a doubt—the only friend I've got."

"What about sexy tattooed Cheyenne?"

"You're not gonna believe this," said Ry, "but there is no Cheyenne. Never has been."

"Well, there's a newsflash," said Kip, laughing to himself.

"I made her up," said Ry, choking up. "'Cause I thought if I was this cool guy, you might stick around."

"Oh, good God."

"I know, I know," said Ry. "It turns out that after all this time, you were the cool one—"

"And you were *my* entourage?" Kip replied.

"Kinda sad, isn't it?"

"Let's get this over with, sidekick," said Kip, plunging the Powder Puff into gear as he sped off in the direction of Pebble Beach Road.

• • •

As it turned out, the homes on Pebble Beach were decidedly more opulent than the ones on Augusta and St. Andrews, which were only a few blocks away. And 2014 Pebble Beach, with its circular driveway and its detached double garage and pool house, was at least twice the size of the Langham place.

As Kip and Ry approached the front stoop of the multistory Tudor home, the massive oaken door creaked open. And there he was: lanky, good-looking Todd from Boston.

"Sup," he said, looking away as he ushered them into an enormous marble foyer. "Be right back."

As Todd from Boston disappeared into the far reaches of the house, Kip turned on Ry with a vengeance.

"I cannot believe you are doing this to me!"

"I told you I was going to stop being such a screw-up," said Ry. "I'm trying to help here."

"By bringing me to Todd from Boston's freakin' mansion?"

"He knows technology, dude. He can help out with the Fitbit."

"You realize, right, that he's about the last person I wanna see?"

"Let T from B work," said Ry. "You'll see."

"We're calling him 'T from B' now?" said Kip, holding his head in his hands. "FML! And *eff* your life, too, while we're at it."

"I wonder what's keeping him?" said Ry, as he peered down one of the long corridors snaking away from the foyer.

Pulling his phone from his jeans pocket, Kip ripped off a text.

"ARE YOU THERE?" he typed.

A few moments later, Todd from Boston reappeared from some faraway corner of the house. He was carrying a laptop under his arm and nodded for Kip and Ry to join him—presumably, in some other faraway corner of his family's manse.

After climbing down a set of steep stairs, they finally alighted in a basement rec room dominated by a pool table.

"Oh, dude, we gotta play!" said Ry, suddenly forgetting the point of their mission.

"Uh, the Fitbit, Ry?" Kip muttered, as his friend began selecting a pool cue from a rack on the wall.

"Feel free to shoot a round," said Todd from Boston, as he nonchalantly opened up his computer on top of a ping pong table in a distant corner of the basement. As Kip stood nearby, Todd from Boston began typing commands, spitfire-like, into the laptop.

"Let's see it," he hollered, as he looked up from the table.

"See what?" Ry asked, as he tried, unsuccessfully, to bank the three ball into one of the center pockets.

"The device," said Todd from Boston. As Kip looked on, Ry dug the Fitbit out of his jeans pocket and lobbed it to Todd from Boston, who made a clean underhanded catch.

"Where do you plug it in?" Kip asked, as Ry busied himself with another pool shot.

"You don't," Todd from Boston replied. "Bluetooth."

"Right," Kip answered, as he watched Todd from Boston rap another series of commands into the laptop.

"You and I are cool, right?" Todd from Boston asked, still staring intently at the screen on his laptop.

"Uh, yeah," said Kip, uncertainly. "We're, uh, totally cool."

"That's good," Todd from Boston replied, "'cause Birdie broke up with me, you know."

"I didn't know that," said Kip. "Did you know about that, Ry?"

"Yeah, T told me about it yesterday," said Ry. "It's total bullshit, right?"

"Yeah," said Kip, glaring at Ry from his station by the pool table. "I'm really sorry to hear about that."

"Don't be," said Todd from Boston. "She's a fuckin' bitch. Just called me out of the blue yesterday and ended it."

"Man," said Kip. "That's brutal."

"Brutal is right," said Ry, after taking another shot—and missing badly—from his place at the pool table.

"Birdie's really heartless, you know," said Todd from Boston, pausing to look up from the laptop. "Do you realize how mean she can be? I mean, like, evil," said Todd from Boston, staring at Kip searchingly, as if the other boy might be able to provide some kind of answer to the misery that currently ailed him.

"Heartless is right, dude," said Ry. "Birdie sucks Smurf dick. Forget about her."

For a moment, Todd from Boston stared off into the distance, as if he were waiting for Ry's guidance to sink in and reap its reward. Shrugging his shoulders, he went back to work on the laptop. After a few minutes, he looked up from his laptop with a grin spreading across his face.

"Boom!" he shouted, as Ry dropped his pool cue to join the other two by the ping pong table.

"Do you have something?" Kip asked.

"Mos def," said Todd from Boston. "This thing has been, like, everywhere. Take a look for yourselves."

As Kip and Ry stared at the laptop, Todd from Boston highlighted the Fitbit's travels on an electronic map of the greater Fremont area.

"The device started out here, see?" he said, gesturing towards the blip pulsing on his laptop screen.

"That's Spiegel Grove, where the Hayes is located," said Kip.

"Must be when the perp lifted the pear," said Ry. "Shoulda gone with the sword, I always say."

"Then it went a few miles northeast to Brady's Island," said Todd from Boston, as he pointed to the green space in the middle of the Sandusky River. "Whoa, then it went *way* down south to here," he added, highlighting a location in Fort Seneca.

"Must be Turley's," said Kip.

"Then the device went back up north for a while," said Todd from Boston. "Back to Brady's Island, I guess. And then it traveled to Spiegel Grove and made a return trip to the island. All in the very same day."

"Dude, this thing is making me dizzy," said Ry.

"Huh, that's weird," said Todd from Boston.

"What's weird?" Ry asked.

"Well," Todd from Boston replied, "it looks like the trail runs cold at that point. Back at the island. That's where you guys must've found this, right? 'Cause that's the last known location."

"That doesn't make any sense," said Kip, gazing ahead of him as if he were lost in some sort of stupor.

"Oh, and there's something else," said Todd from Boston, looking up from the laptop. "Whoever you're looking for must not be very healthy."

"Why's that?" Ry asked.

"They barely logged any steps," said Todd from Boston, chuckling to himself. "Almost all of the Fitbit's movements were in a car. I mean, what's the point of having one of these thingies if you're not getting in your steps? Am I right?"

"Dude, you're not only right—you're righteous," said Ry, fist-bumping Todd from Boston.

• • •

Later, as the two boys climbed back into the Powder Puff, Kip turned to face his friend across the front seat.

"You might have mentioned that Birdie and Todd from Boston had broken up, Ry," he said, as he turned the key in the ignition and fired up the Subaru. "Would have been useful to know before I went down to the guy's basement."

"I don't think I follow you, dude," said Ry. "Useful in what way?"

"Never mind," said Kip, laughing to himself as he piloted the Powder Puff towards nearby Augusta Drive. "Let's worry about the figurine for now."

"Yeah, like, where is it?" Ry asked. "You heard T from B back there: the trail goes cold right where we found the Fitbit back on Brady's Island."

"And if we didn't find it near the shack, then where is it?" Kip asked.

"Liam!"

"That's right," said Kip. "It's gotta be."

"Fucking Liam!" said Ry.

"What do you say we pay a little visit to Turley's tomorrow after school?" Kip asked, pulling the Powder Puff up in front of the Langham house.

"I'm down with that," Ry replied, as he climbed out of the vehicle.

As his friend made his way up the front walk, Kip glanced down at his phone to check for any incoming messages.

But there was nothing there to see

CHAPTER 24: MUSLIM BAN

Early the next morning—so early, in fact, that she had not even said *Salat al-Fajr*—Azza roused herself from sleep, crawled out of bed, and fired up her ancient Anova laptop. Drowsily logging into Little Tunisia, she negotiated her way into the "Lifestyle and Tourism" subthread. As her familiar alter-ego Anna Karenina, she was determined to learn her father's fate. And his latest message quickly laid her fears to rest:

منزل آمن

Safe home indeed. With her father having returned to the city of their birth—having finally escaped the horrors of the *banlieues* for himself—she would no longer obscure her elation behind something as pedestrian as an emoticon: "Vive la Tunisie!" she wrote.

With a full heart, she loped into the tiny Holiday Inn bathroom to prepare for the new day. There is nothing in this life or the next that could possibly ruin this day, Azza thought to herself. Allah be praised!

• • •

"I don't understand, sir," said Azza, sitting in her usual place in the back of the Powder Puff.

"The Fitbit is a GPS-activated wearable object," said Kip, as he made the wide turn onto College Avenue.

"No, sir," said Azza, "I understand that part. But I do not

understand why you have to go back to Turley's. That was an unsuccessful visit, sir, was it not? Have you spoken to the cheese apple about this development?"

"Not exactly," said Kip, glancing in the rearview mirror, as was his habit, for any signs of Officer Hudgins.

"That sounds like evasion to me, sir," Azza replied. "You must talk to the cheese apple at once to obtain her perspective."

"That may be a problem," said Kip, "'cause she doesn't seem to be speaking to me right now."

"You must have done something very bad to merit such treatment, sir," said Azza. "Very bad indeed."

"I couldn't have done much worse, actually," said Kip, as he pulled the Powder Puff up in front of Faraday Hall, which was teeming with commuter students and faculty on their way to class.

"If you want my advice, sir," said Azza, gathering up her valise, "you should act now and act quickly. If you have wronged her, then apologize. You have got to *do*, sir. Less talking, more doing. Do you understand me?"

"I think so," said Kip, observing Azza as she climbed out of the Powder Puff.

"No more thinking, sir," said Azza, her eyes gazing softly at him, the glaring olive pinpoints having long since disappeared. "You must start doing."

As he watched Azza loping off towards the quad, Kip liked to imagine that, beneath the black fabric of her burqa, she had been smiling warmly at him. That he had been a source of comfort to her, and not a hindrance—just as she had been a healing source of comfort for him. That, finally, the trials of her short life in America were somewhere behind her now.

• • •

Any comfort that Kip may have felt had dissipated the second he stepped into Miss Pearson's first period AP English course. His trusty desk in the far corner of the classroom was empty and waiting for him, but sitting nearby, just one desk over, was none other than Birdie. And the scowl across her face indicated that she was none too happy to see him. Even stranger still, her pigtails seemed to have become aligned with her mood, angrily framing her face like a pair of menacing stiletto blades. Kip's long experience in her orbit told him that if he wasn't careful, he just might get cut.

As Kip took his seat, Miss Pearson announced that the day's assignment would be a group project devoted to performing a dialogue from *Who's Afraid of Virginia Woolf?*

"So I guess that makes me George and you Martha?" Kip asked Birdie, hoping that his attempt at breaking the ice would quell her anger.

No such luck.

For her part, Birdie could only stare at Kip—wordlessly, as if she were sizing him up. And while he remembered how she had looked at him with disgust in front of Domino's on that fateful afternoon not so long ago, now she looked at him with real pity, verging on something else: something like anger, although for what he had no idea.

"Did I do something?" said Kip.

"No, you didn't do *anything*," said Birdie. "You didn't text me back, even though I texted you that I loved you—"

"Actually, you texted 'ILU,'" said Kip.

"Same difference," said Birdie. "And you didn't tell me that you were still seeing the towel-head—"

"The 'towel-head'?" Kip asked. "Seriously, B?"

"You didn't think that would get back to me?" said Birdie.

"I thought you said that nobody was talking about Azza."

"Kip, the whole fucking town is talking about her. You didn't need me to tell you that."

"Well, maybe the whole fucking town should mind its own business?"

"*Azza*?" said Birdie, raising her voice. "What kind of name is that anyway?"

"It's Arabic," said Kip. "Did you like Todd from Boston 'cause everybody was talking about him as the new kid? Was that the attraction?"

"Well, I sure as fuck didn't like him because he was a goddamned terrorist!"

But before Kip could answer, he looked up to see Miss Pearson, the smell of mothballs having suddenly permeated the far corner of the classroom.

"Ms. Hudgins and Mr. Beckelhymer, if you would be so kind as to begin practicing your dialogue," she instructed, as the nauseating aroma of old clothes and stale closets swirled about her.

Birdie and Kip may have been having words with each other, but they hadn't qualified for AP English by accident. Good students to the core, they began practicing their dialogue with a vengeance.

It was Birdie who piped up first, playing the role of Martha.

"Truth or illusion, George. You don't know the difference," she said, reciting her part with an especially acidic tone.

"No," replied Kip, adopting the wistful sound of George's resignation, "but we must carry on as though we did."

"Amen," said Birdie, channeling Martha.

"Oh, amen, indeed!" said Miss Pearson, who smiled with great approval as they completed the dialogue. Still hovering over them, she gave her hands a tiny clap to signal her unfettered delight with their performance.

But that was exactly what it had been: a performance.

As he stared at Birdie there in the corner of the classroom, Kip began to realize just how far afield he had roamed. Perhaps he didn't want to be with Birdie anymore. That he didn't know whom he had become, but he certainly didn't like who she already *was*. That maybe he hadn't wanted to be with her for a very long time, only he hadn't realized it before. That he simply wanted to have a girlfriend, and that who it was hadn't really mattered before now.

Staring at Birdie's pigtails as they dangled beside her face, Kip had to admit that, painful as it may be, he was starting to agree with Ry: he no longer cared for them very much. In fact, the pigtails were starting to annoy him on a much deeper, more elemental level. Or maybe it was just that he didn't really care for Birdie all that much either, her hairstyle be damned.

As Miss Pearson ambled away to harass another pair of students about their dialogue, Birdie finally spoke up, breaking the spell.

"I wish I never met you," she said, twisting the heart-shaped ring off of her finger and handing it to him.

"Oh," said Kip. "Thanks, I guess."

• • •

Making his way to second period that morning, Kip walked out of AP English with a renewed sense of purpose. Birdie *does* suck Smurf dick, Kip thought to himself. Maybe now he would finally be able to start forgetting about her once and for all?

But as it happened, Kip would never make it to second period. He had barely eked out a few steps into the dour corridors of Fremont High when he came face to face with Burly Barrelhead, who was waiting to intercept him.

"What did I do now?" Kip asked the Vice Principal.

But Burly Barrelhead wasn't having it, staying mum for the entirety of the long march from Miss Pearson's classroom to the Principal's office. And there, sitting forlornly on the threadbare sofa in the anteroom, was Ry. And standing behind him, with grim looks plastered across their faces, were Officer Hudgins and Officer Rankin.

"Who died?" Kip asked, in an absurd attempt at breaking the mood.

• • •

Things hardly fared any better as they sped across town in the back of Officer Hudgins's squad car. With Birdie's dad behind the wheel, Officer Rankin manned the radio, periodically checking in with dispatch.

"Where are we going?" Kip asked. For his part, Ry sat next to him in the back seat—white as a sheet with fear and utterly wordless. His friend's abnormal silence had Kip just about as worried as anything else.

"We're heading to the campus, son," said Officer Hudgins, as he drove the cruiser along College Avenue.

And suddenly it hit him: "Did something happen to my mom?" Kip asked, lunging forward and digging his fingers into the wire-mesh barrier that separated the front and back seats.

"I'm sure she's just fine," said Officer Hudgins. "But listen here, boys. Time is of the essence. We need to ask you a series of questions. And we need straight answers—and we need 'em fast. Now Bill, do you have that card ready?"

Setting the transmitter down on his lap, Officer Rankin began reading from a cardboard checklist.

"Now, boys, I need to ask you some questions about Ms. Amari—"

"Azza?" Kip asked. "What does she have to do with this?"

"Do you think that she is in jihad?"

"A's not in jihad," said Ry, rousing himself from his stupor. "That's ridic—"

"Just answer the questions," said Officer Rankin. "We need to ascertain if the subject has been radicalized—"

"Radicalized?" said Kip. "Are you kidding?"

"Have you ever observed the subject speaking in Arabic or citing Allah?" Officer Rankin asked.

"Well, yeah," said Ry. "She's Muslim, dude. It's always 'Allah this' and 'Allah that.' It's no different from my mother's dumbass friends saying 'Praise the lord' and shit, right?"

"Okay," said Officer Rankin, "next question: has the subject been attempting to learn how to operate any motor vehicles that may be unfamiliar to her—like, say, an automobile, an airplane, or a big rig?"

"She asked me to teach her how to drive, I guess," said Kip.

"Do you *guess*, or do you *know*?" asked Officer Hudgins from his place behind the wheel.

"Has the subject ever shown any interest in firearms or weaponry of any kind?" Officer Rankin continued.

"We looked at guns in a pawn shop once," said Ry. "But that doesn't mean anything, does it? I mean, it's not like we took her out for target practice."

"Have you ever witnessed the subject engaging in any unusual internet activity, especially social media of any sort?" Officer Rankin asked.

"I saw her logged into a chat room once, but who doesn't surf the net?" Kip asked.

"Have you ever witnessed the subject attempting to radicalize yourselves or others?" Officer Rankin asked.

"No way," said Ry. "Not A. She mostly just goes on about her classes and shit. Well, that and eating halal. Or was it haram?"

"Haram's the bad one," said Kip, correcting him.

"Yeah, that's right," said Ry. "She basically just seemed like she wanted to fit in."

"By wearing a burqa, son?" Officer Hudgins asked.

"Yeah," said Ry. "I hear you. But remember: she's still, like, a girl. She got really pissed off about the Skateboard Kid and wanted to up the ante."

"Well, she definitely accomplished that," said Officer Hudgins.

"You boys need to understand the way we work in law enforcement," said Officer Rankin, as his partner brought the squad car to a screeching halt in front of the Registrar's office. "If it looks like a duck, swims like a duck, and quacks like a duck, then we've probably got a duck on our hands."

As they climbed out of the vehicle, it was Mrs. Beckelhymer who got to them first, followed closely by Dr. Smyth, who was wringing his hands in fear.

"Oh, Kip, I am so glad you're safe," she said, hugging him tightly beside the police cruiser.

With his mom in tow, Officer Hudgins led the group to a makeshift barricade at the edge of the quad. Yellow police tape blocked off the entrance to the parklet, and a dozen or so of Fremont's finest were training their rifles on the rolling lawns of Northwestern Ohio State. Peering over the barricade, Kip scanned the quad for any signs of life. But there was nothing to see. The only thing in evidence was the unfamiliar quiet that had descended over the college.

Kip felt a nudge at his arm. It was Ry, directing his attention to Officer Rankin, who was standing near the entrance to the Registrar's office. He was reading from the cardboard checklist as he interrogated the Skateboard Kid and the sloucher. For their part, they were silent, save for an occasional shrug of the shoulders.

"Is it true what they've been saying?" Mrs. Beckelhymer asked Officer Hudgins. "There's no way this is happening in Fremont, right?"

"I'm afraid so, ma'am," he replied, as Officer Rankin joined him by the barricade. "Here's the 4-1-1: a short while ago, we began receiving alerts from the vicinity of Faraday Hall about an active shooter. Now, at this point, that's the sum total of everything we know. But we're not ruling anything out. There're a lot of lives at stake, and I am duty-bound to protect them."

"Everyone locked and loaded?" Officer Rankin shouted to the other policemen who had gathered behind him. "All right now, shit's gonna get real."

And that's when Officer Hudgins turned to Kip and gave him a lengthy stare—not of disgust or derision, but of fear.

"No way," said Kip, folding his arms in front of his chest. "There's no way it could be Azza."

CHAPTER 25: JANNAH

For Azza, the campus had never appeared more serene, more bucolic, more welcoming, even. With her burqa on full display, she strolled around the quad with nary another student in sight. The only sound came from the American flag, which was noisily whipping in the wind high atop its silvery pole. For a while, Azza sat on one of the park benches just outside of Faraday Hall, where she basked in the glory of her Anthropology class earlier that day.

For once, Dr. Matthews had seemed to understand her. "To get where she was coming from," as Azza's fellow students liked to say. During their morning class, Azza had delivered her oral report about meeting Methoataske, and when she was finished, a couple of students even clapped. But Dr. Matthews was radiant, staring up towards the heavens, as was her usual posture, with unchecked jubilance.

During her presentation, Azza told them all about how Methoataske admired Chief Tecumseh and the idea of living life on your own terms without worrying about the fear of death. How the esteemed and honorable leader of the Shawnee nation was really a great American—that he belonged to everybody's history now, and not just the descendants of the United Remnant Band of the Shawnee Nations.

And Azza didn't even mind when the other students had begun to snicker after she said, "we gotta *do*." It was just a saying, after all. And she didn't care when they laughed even louder after she quoted Methoataske's parting words of wisdom: "Don't take any shit out there, ya hear? Show respect for all men, but grovel to none."

And the other students seemed to listen—*really listen*, even the sloucher, no less—when Azza shared Methoataske's greatest philosophy for living, exhorting them to live in the here and now. To find a place to be somebody.

Oh, it had been a great triumph for Azza that morning in Anthropology, it truly had. It was all she could think about as she lounged on the park bench near the center of the quad. There was a late fall chill in the air, a light breeze that played at the tufts of her burqa. Folded open on her lap was her well-worn copy of *First Lady*, which she had consumed twice through already. She was rereading the part where Lucy Hayes made her 1880 West Coast tour, meeting Sarah Winnemucca, the Native American activist, along the way. Known by her Palute name as Thocmentony—meaning "shell flower," which Azza liked a great deal, although admittedly not as much as "turtle laying its eggs"—Winnemucca would deliver rousing tales about the plight of the nation's rapidly waning native population and the loss of its tribal lands.

During one of Winnemucca's lectures, the First Lady had been so moved that she openly wept. At the time, the press had dubbed Winnemucca the "Palute Princess," sometimes mockingly, and Azza admired Mrs. Hayes for her willingness to share her empathy with the Native Americans when so much of the rest of the country seemed bent on stamping them into oblivion. It was little wonder, she thought to herself, why Mr. Kip and the cheese apple seemed to admire Mrs. Hayes as much as they did. Azza liked to think that, had she still been alive, the First Lady would empathize with her own plight, would understand how difficult it was to live with dignity in a world that would rather see her kind locked away in some awful reservation. *Or a ghetto.*

Azza still had a few hours to kill before her next class, Chemistry 101, one of the gateway courses for her Northwestern Ohio State major, was set to begin. Isn't it ironic, she thought to herself, that her favorite class at the college ended up being Anthropology? On her very first day on campus, she had all but cursed Mr. Skakel over the reality of having to enroll in gen-ed requirements, of the ostensible need for some common body of knowledge instead of concentrating on chemical engineering, her major field of study and the reason that she had emigrated to these United States in the first place. Well, that and her father's abiding wish not to see her die like everyone else they had ever known in the enforced poverty of the *banlieues*. But here she was, living in a foreign land as an almost-American. Sure, it had its ups and downs—more downs, she had to admit, of late—but it was never boring.

And that's when Azza saw him: one of her fellow Northwestern Ohio State students poking his head out from behind a row of thick azalea bushes. What a strange thing to behold, she thought to herself. *Was he playing a game of hide-and-seek?* she wondered. *Or was he caught up in some kind of fraternity prank?*

With her curiosity having gotten the best of her, Azza stood up from the park bench and began inching her way towards the hedgerow. As she moved ever closer, she caught the student's eye. Startled, he began waving her away, as if he were afraid she might join him in his secret place among the azalea bushes. With a shrug of her shoulders, she reclaimed her place on the park bench and went back to reading her book.

It was the red dot flittering atop the book's front cover that first caught Azza's attention. She cherished Colby's gift above all of her earthly possessions, and most especially the book's elaborate cover art, which depicted the First Lady as portrayed in the famous engraving by John Sartain. To Azza's mind, it was odd how the red dot seemed to dance, wavering a bit now and then, upon Lucy Hayes's scalp, darting up and down amidst the dramatic parting of the hairline above the First Lady's delicate forehead.

The first shot might have hit Azza squarely in the chest had she not inadvertently dropped the book, entranced as she was by the red dot's unexpected appearance in her world. The high-powered tactical round bored into the back of the wooden bench and flew clean out the other side, finally lodging in Faraday Hall's limestone exterior. For her part, Azza fell face forward onto the freshly mown grass that graced the quad. But she wouldn't stay there for very long, quickly scrambling onto her feet and running headlong towards the azalea bushes—her body a jet-black blur as she leapt into the shrubbery beside the frightened student, the very same kid who had shooed her away only moments before.

"Get the fuck out of here!" he screeched.

"But why, sir?" she asked.

"Because you're the one they're after!" he replied.

"Why me?" she asked.

But her words would fall on deaf ears. By that point, the boy had already sprinted in the direction of the kiosk at the edge of the quad, where he dove into a flower bed thick with mimosa ground cover.

Peeking out from within the azalea bushes, Azza scanned the quad, eventually settling her eyes on the makeshift barricade near the Registrar's office. She could just make out the headgear of the armored police officers from her vantage point in the shrubbery.

Before she could so much as catch her breath, the red dot had begun homing in on her yet again. She observed as it flitted about the bush's rosy buds, seeking out its target among the campus flora like some kind of hungry laser pointer.

But by this juncture, Azza knew better than to stick around. Summoning all of the energy that she could possibly muster, she made a beeline for the nearest entrance to Faraday Hall, leaping into the vestibule a microsecond before the second rifle shot burrowed its way into the side of the building.

Inside the first-floor corridor that bisected Faraday Hall, Azza lay prone against the cold linoleum floor, her heart racing as she attempted to regain her wits. Eventually, she sat upright, resting her head against the hard cinderblock walls and biding her time until the red dot found her again.

Like the quad, the interior of Faraday Hall had become oddly silent. With the heat billowing inside her robed body, Azza took advantage of the solitude to wrench the burqa from her head, allowing her face and neck a chance to cool down.

As it happened, Azza's heart barely had a chance to recover from its relentless pace when the quietude in the corridor was exploded by the distinctive sound of a shotgun blast in some distant quadrant of the building. Standing up with a start, Azza hastily pulled the burqa back over her head, reflexively dashing towards one of the classroom doors to seek refuge.

Only the door wouldn't budge.

Determined to make her way inside, Azza turned the knob over and over again in her hands, but it wouldn't give an inch. Peering through the beveled glass above the doorknob, she could glimpse shadows moving about inside, followed by the sound of furniture scraping across the linoleum floor and slamming headlong into the door.

And then Azza heard a female voice whispering from somewhere just inside the classroom, its words unmistakable and clear: "Go the fuck away," said the voice, suffused with fear and without a hint of malice. "He's coming back."

And sure enough, there he was all right.

Azza could see the shooter's eerie visage at the far end of the corridor. He was going from door to door, blasting his way into each classroom, only to return to the corridor moments later with even more fury, if that were possible, than he had before blasting his way inside in the first place. She could tell this by the manner in which he screamed in disappointment as he ambled up to each new doorway, reloading his shotgun in anticipation of something—or *someone*—that never quite materialized.

And that's when Azza realized that that something was *her*. And that the shooter was none other than the stocky guy—the very same man whom they had seen during their visit to B&C Super Pawns. The one who made the gun sign with his fingers. Only now, he had a real gun, with real bullets—the whole shebang. Instinctively, Azza hid among the shadows at the far end of the corridor near the vestibule. Pressing her body as tightly as she could against the cinderblock wall, she could feel the perspiration slithering down her back and congealing with the gauzy material of her robe.

As the stocky guy blasted open the very next classroom door, with a cigarette dangling from his mouth, he scanned the interior before emptying the second barrel into the ceiling tiles above the doorway.

"Where's the camel jockey?" he shrieked, as clumps of fiberglass rained down upon him.

For a moment, he leaned against a bulletin board in the middle of the corridor, as if he were catching his breath. But then Azza realized that he wasn't resting at all, that he was only pausing to reload.

With each step, the stocky man shifted ever closer to Azza's place at the end of the corridor. As she waited there—her doom becoming ever more certain as he made his way further down the Faraday hallway—she felt the fear growing inside her, taking hold of her, and rendering her unable to move.

With each new shotgun blast, Azza took comfort in the words of the Prophet Muhammad: "Seek help from Allah, and do not lose heart."

FML, Azza thought to herself. There was simply no way, *Allah be praised,* that she would be losing heart now.

And then suddenly Azza had it: ALICE would see her through. She just knew it would. That brochure—the selfsame pamphlet that she had received during her very first week at Northwestern Ohio Statue—would be her saving grace. Only, try as she might, she couldn't remember the acronym. Or more precisely, she couldn't remember *all* of it.

Sure, Azza could recite *part* of the ALICE. For example, she already had the first part, *Alert,* down to a tee. If Azza knew anything, she knew that she was on high alert.

But that's when things got dicey—and fast.

As for what L meant, she didn't have the first clue. She was drawing a blank on I, too. But no matter: she had C and E down pat: *Counter* and *Evacuate.* She reasoned that C and E were all that was left to her now.

As the stocky guy with the shotgun made his diabolical progress down the corridor, Azza realized that she would have to shuffle the ALICE order a bit to accommodate her circumstances.

If she tried to carry out C at this juncture, he would almost definitely ferret out her hiding place in the shadows at the far end of the corridor. No, it had to be E at this point. It was time to attempt to *Evacuate* for sure.

Or was it?

How long would it be, she reasoned, before he stopped blasting the ceiling panels and began shooting the other students over his frustration at not finding her—"the camel jockey"? *What does that even mean?* she wondered to herself. She'd never so much as glimpsed a camel outside of the illustrations on Wikipedia.

This was it, she reckoned: the time when she had to quit caring so much about herself—*to give zero fucks*—and start worrying about the welfare of others. You gotta *do*, she thought to herself. And now's the time.

Stepping out of the shadows, Azza calmly stood in the center of the corridor, waiting for the stocky guy to register her presence. But he was too busy terrorizing the other students to even notice the woman in the burqa at the far end of the hall. So she did the only thing she could think of, screaming "Allahu Akbar!" at the top of her lungs.

Oh, he saw her now, turning to face her with vengeance in his eyes. And what seemed like a giant shotgun cradled in his arms.

And then she did it: she ran like the dickens through the vestibule and back outside into the stillness of the quad. And quite suddenly, she realized that she was actually *doing* it:

She was Countering!

Azza couldn't see him, but she knew he was back there somewhere, lumbering down the corridor in the direction of the vestibule. He was a few seconds behind, at best. And with her robe sticking to her skin after the deluge of perspiration back in the corridor, she found it difficult to break into a full-on trot, forcing her to resort instead to a series of stutter steps as she circled around the back of Faraday Hall, not far from the very same spot on College Avenue where Mr. Kip had dropped her off earlier that morning. Only it seemed like days ago at this point, as the seconds of her life peeled off in a kind of slow-motion—as if they were destined to be her last.

But the Powder Puff was no longer there, of course. Sitting in its place instead was a burnt-orange pickup truck. The vehicle was parked at a strange angle against the curbside, with the driver's side door flung open, as if its occupant had been forced to exit the vehicle in a hurry.

By this point, Azza was only a few awkward stutter steps away from the truck. And the stocky guy was gaining on her now, having made his own progress around the back of Faraday Hall.

Leaping into the front seat, Azza scanned the dashboard, only to discover that the keys were still lodged in the ignition. Firing up the engine, she slid the gearshift from P into D, and the truck lurched forward, hopping the curb, and chewing up the pristine lawn behind Faraday Hall.

"I am doing it!" Azza proclaimed from her perch inside the cab. "I am doing the ALICE!"

CHAPTER 26: THE SUICIDE SEAT

As the truck's engine roared into life, Officer Hudgins and his contingent of policemen in full body armor saw their opportunity to make a break for it, charging across the quad in the direction of Faraday Hall. They were followed closely on their heels by Kip and Ry.

Fremont's finest arrived just in time to see Azza speeding across the lawn towards the stocky guy wielding a shotgun. As the truck bore down on him, he managed to get off one more blast. The majority of the buckshot sprayed onto the vehicle's massive steel grill, which blunted most of the discharge, save for the loose bits that survived just long enough to penetrate the windshield itself. Inside the cab, Azza could feel the pellets piercing through her burqa and burrowing into the soft skin about her face. But she never let up on the gas, barreling into the stocky guy with the full force of the truck's grill, which catapulted his lifeless body several yards into the quad.

With her adrenaline raging, Azza held her foot firmly on the gas. And the truck might have kept moving inexorably forward had it not been for one of the park benches stationed at the edge of the quad. After Azza succeeded in ramming the wooden bench head-on, the truck came to a sudden, imperiled halt. Absorbing the full force of the collision, Azza bounced back and forth in the cab, cartoon-like, as her body careened between the steering wheel and the driver's seat.

When she had finally, mercifully come to a rest, Azza stared blankly through the shards of the ruined windshield. Overcome by shock, she barely noticed the posse of police officers who had taken up positions around the truck. As with the barricade by the Registrar's office, one of the officers trained his laser sight on the subject inside the cab, with the red dot flittering about Azza's burqa-covered forehead. As they would later testify in the public hearings devoted to the matter, the policemen still believed that their chief suspect was behind the wheel and that the stocky guy must have been some innocent bystander attempting to bring the standoff to an end. At least, that's what they testified.

While things may have been over for the stocky guy, Azza was still in the throes of a life-or-death situation—although she could barely comprehend it, of course, given her state of shock. At this point, the police contingent began shouting for Azza to step out of the vehicle immediately or risk being shot. But in her stupor, their voices had transformed into an unintelligible cacophony. Azza could see their lips moving and could hear their shouts, yet it all seemed surreal.

Why would they need all these policemen, she wondered to herself, if the stocky guy had been subdued? She could see his body lying prone several yards away in the quad. Couldn't they see him, too? Wasn't that evidence enough? In that moment, if she had had the ability to break out of her stupor and speak, she would have told them, "When you hear hoofbeats, don't think of zebras." But she doubted that anything, or anyone, could help her now. From what she could tell from her vantage point in the cab, her longevity had been reduced to a matter of minutes, possibly less. There was simply no time for riddles anymore.

As it happened, Azza finally came out of her stupor when she heard the crackle of Officer Hudgins's voice. "You have 10 seconds to vacate the truck, Ms. Amari," he shouted through the megaphone. He was standing only a few yards behind the phalanx of police officers, with Kip and Ry nestled by his side.

But Azza wasn't moving, frozen with fear even though she had finally regained her wits. Glancing up into the truck's rearview mirror, she could see the red dot homing in on her forehead for the kill shot. And that's when she executed her most significant tactical maneuver of the day—even more significant, if that were possible, than knocking the stocky guy into oblivion—by slowly raising up her arms as if she were preparing to announce her surrender. With her right hand, she carefully removed the burqa from her head, revealing a stricken, vulnerable face, her olive skin pocked by the rosy blemishes of the pellet wounds.

"I am Lemonade Lucy," said Azza, her eyes ablaze and her voice clear and commanding. "I grovel to no one."

Not surprisingly, Officer Hudgins and his armored contingent were confused by the spectacle that had unfolded before them. They would later admit at the hearings that they had no problem blowing away a suspected Islamic terrorist swaddled in black robing, but there was no way they could kill the beautiful girl with the green eyes and the speckles of blood mottling her face. They just couldn't bring themselves to do it.

And then Kip leaned towards Officer Hudgins and whispered, "It wasn't Azza, sir. *Please*. You have got to believe me."

Slowly raising the megaphone up to his mouth, Officer Hudgins barked out his order. "Stand down," he informed the policemen who had congregated, weapons drawn, around the truck.

"Are you sure about that, Matt?" Officer Rankin asked, as he steadied his sidearm.

With his chin held up in defiance, Officer Hudgins nodded in his direction.

"I mean, are you really *sure*?" Officer Rankin asked.

"I got this, Bill," Officer Hudgins replied. "Stand down!" he barked into the megaphone once again. "The situation's been contained," he added, glancing over at Kip. "The suspect is down."

Meanwhile, back in the cab, Azza let out a protracted sigh of relief. Staring into the rearview mirror, she watched the red dot as it finally disappeared from its place in the center of her forehead.

With Ry by his side, Kip looked on as the policemen and the other first responders gathered around the truck to assist Azza, to gather her in their arms and liberate her from the disaster that had befallen the college on such a beautiful late fall day. For his part, Kip liked to think that it was all going to end there, that there would no longer be any need to hold a Judicial Review meeting. Not just about the hijab incident—but about *anything*. That Azza was going to be accepted into the community—not just on the sacred groves of Northwestern Ohio

State, but all across Fremont. Throughout the great state of Ohio, even.

That very same day, the whole of Fremont learned that the stocky guy had murdered his family—his young wife and infant son—before driving his truck to the campus and wreaking havoc on Northwestern Ohio State. Pretty soon, rumors began buzzing that perhaps he hadn't actually meant to terrorize the "radical Muslim girl," as she came to be described in the Fremont *Daily Register*, but instead had been playing out the last, tragic act of some domestic psychodrama. That he had only brought his demented personal malaise to the college because he was hell-bent on committing suicide-by-cop.

"Turned out to be suicide-by-Azza," Ry joked at the time.

• • •

But there was nothing funny about the Judicial Review meeting, which was held a few days later in Thayer Hall. Kip and Azza arrived early, having met up with Ry in the sculpture garden near the main entrance to the building. Sitting on a park bench amidst a whimsical series of stone-cut representations of the characters from A.A. Milne's *Winnie the Pooh*, the three friends observed as members of the Judicial Review Board, an assortment of campus faculty and students, made their way inside.

As they waited on the park bench, Kip slyly removed his phone from his jeans pocket and glanced at the screen. Still nothing, he lamented. *What was with this wall of silence?* he wondered to himself. *Would he ever be able to break through?*

For her part, Azza was still smarting from the traumatic events earlier in the week. Donning her burqa over her wounded face, she walked with a limp as a result of the truck's violent collision in the quad. With each step, she felt wracked by an intense pain. When she finally settled onto the park bench beside Kip and Ry, she propped her feet up on the Eeyore statue, using it as a makeshift ottoman to ease the ceaseless throbbing that emanated from her ankles.

As it happened, Kip had managed to worm his way into the Judicial Review meeting, which was public—but only, that is, for members of the Northwestern Ohio State community. Kip owed his mother for making his attendance possible. He had promised her virtually everything he could think of—doing the dishes, getting straight A's—which he planned to do anyway, but whatever. He even relented and said that his mom could refer to him as "monkey" for the remainder of the calendar year. For all Kip knew, that may have been what did it, what prompted Mrs. Beckelhymer to talk Dr. Smyth into sneaking her son into the Judicial Review—what with the Registrar being a member of the board and all.

"What's with all this Winnie the Pooh shit?" Ry asked. "Did Northwest Ohio State used to be an elementary school?"

"Don't look now," said Kip, pointing to the blond student ambling into Thayer Hall, "but there's the Skateboard Kid."

"What an asshat," said Ry. "I'd like to knock that shit-eating grin right off of his face."

"No," said Azza, grimacing in pain. "Do not attack the asshat, sir. There has been enough violence already."

As the friends waited there in the sculpture garden, Dr. Smyth strolled up from the direction of the Registrar's office. Making his way towards the entrance to Thayer Hall, he motioned for Kip to join him. Still smarting from the pain that wracked her body, Azza sauntered up behind Kip. Each step had become a miniature trial in itself, as she attempted to beat back the agony that was throbbing inside of her.

"You got this, A!" Ry sang out, as his friends disappeared inside.

• • •

By the time that Azza had hobbled upstairs to the boardroom, most of the Judicial Review membership had already assembled. Dean Miller was seated in front of an imposing wooden desk, complete with a gavel laid out before him. Dr. Smyth sat nearby, along with Dr. Matthews, with whom Dean Miller could barely make eye contact. He was still smarting over her nerve at bringing forth the idea that a hate crime could actually transpire at Northwestern Ohio State—even if the events of the past few days would seem to suggest that it could.

The board was rounded out by student body president A.J. Grant, a senior Poli Sci major with dreams of one day becoming district attorney, along with Penny Rae Hoover, a sophomore Communications major who chaired the yearbook committee. Old Agnes from the Registrar's office was there, too—acting as scribe on behalf of the Judicial Review Board. As for the audience, there wasn't an empty seat in the room. Mrs. Beckelhymer sat in one of the front rows in contrast with her son, who had taken the last available seat in the back of the room.

An additional row of four chairs was situated directly in front of Dean Miller's desk, and three of them were already occupied by the sloucher from Dr. Matthews's Anthropology class, Officer Rankin, and the Skateboard Kid himself, whom, it turned out, actually had a name: Allen Thurman. For Kip, this seemed like a terrible omen. He was all too aware that one Allen Granberry Thurman had been President Hayes's Democratic opponent in the hotly contested gubernatorial election of 1867, in which the future president eked out victory by a margin of fewer than 3,000 votes. Worse yet, Thurman had been a virulent racist, raging against granting African Americans the right to vote in those early post-civil war years. Just thinking about the coincidence made Kip's heart sink, although it may have been because he wished he could share this particular historical insight with Colby, who was still nowhere to be found. By this point, Kip was genuinely wondering if he would ever see her again.

When Azza finally made it to the doorway to the boardroom, Dean Miller leapt to his feet and escorted her inside.

"Take your place right here up front, Ms. Amari," he said, pointing towards the empty chair across from his desk. "That's what we call the hot seat." But for Azza, the chair seemed more like a suicide seat. In its own way, it appeared even more dangerous and more foreboding than the passenger's seat in a moving vehicle. Or the driver's seat in a hate-monger's truck, she thought to herself.

CHAPTER 27:
FAKE NEWS

Looking around the room, her face shielded within the cocoon of her burqa, Azza felt like she had descended into her very own hellish tribunal. As far as the witnesses went, she didn't like the looks of things. She wasn't entirely sure about Officer Rankin, but she knew beyond a shadow of a doubt that the sloucher and the Skateboard Kid were trouble. She was surprised to see that they hadn't brought their DON'T TREAD ON ME! flag along for the occasion.

Startled by the sound of the gavel, Azza looked on as Dean Miller called the proceedings to order.

"Ladies and gentlemen," he recited from a yellowed notepad, "as you are no doubt aware, all Northwest Ohio State students who are alleged to have committed a behavioral infraction have the right to be heard in front of the Judicial Review Board. In this case, Mr. Thurman here—who has already been expelled for his recent violation of the Code of Student Conduct—is counter-alleging that Ms. Amari provoked him by creating a disruptive campus climate. In keeping with college policy, the Judicial Review Board will determine whether a preponderance of evidence supports this allegation, and, if the student is found to be in violation of the Code of Student Conduct, what disciplinary action or academic sanction shall be pursued. I now ask that Mr. Thurman present his allegations for the board to consider," Dean Miller continued, "and about which we will subsequently hear testimony. Mr. Thurman will have approximately 10 minutes in which—"

"Dean Miller!" said Dr. Matthews, interrupting him as she stood up in front of the assembly.

"Yes, Dr. Matthews," he replied, casting his eyes downward. "Did you have anything to share?"

"I, for one, would like to register my resentment regarding the audacity of our institution, which persists in requiring that we hold this Judicial Review in the first place," she said, staring heavenward, as always. "We must remember that all of this ugly business was instigated by Mr. Thurman's commission of a hate crime against Ms. Amari."

"Hear! hear!" said Dr. Smyth, standing up from his seat to join her.

And with that, the audience broke into a mêlée of shouts and murmurs, which Dean Miller quickly rapped into silence with the sound of his gavel, startling Azza yet again.

"Please proceed, Mr. Thurman," said Dean Miller, glaring at Dr. Matthews as if he were daring her to interrupt his proceedings yet again. Apparently, she got the message.

Not surprisingly, it turned out that the Skateboard Kid was a man of very few words.

"I could no longer perform—you know, like, academically," said Thurman, as he succinctly presented his case, "what with her running around campus in that . . . in that weird-ass getup."

"Mr. Thurman, please try to refrain from hyperbole," said Dean Miller. "In any event, if I understand correctly, you're saying that the observance of her religious freedom mitigated your ability to effectively carry out your studies?"

"Yeah, that—that's exactly what I meant," Thurman replied. "I felt, uh, mitigated."

"Do you have anything else to add?" Dean Miller asked.

"Nah," said Thurman. "That's pretty much it."

"At this time, then, I will turn over the proceedings to our student representatives," said Dean Miller.

"Thank you, sir," said A.J., with his freshly coiffed blond hair and neatly pressed three-piece suit. "Hey there, Al!" he continued, with a wide, beaming smile plastered across his face. "It's kinda weird seeing you without your skateboard! Anyway, can you tell me, specifically, how Ms. Amari's presence has impacted your environment here at

Northwestern Ohio State?"

"Sure, A.J.," Thurman replied. "It all started, I guess, on the first day of school. I bumped into her over at Faraday, and I was, like, 'what the eff is this doing here?' I mean, think about it: if this were some hoity-toity place like—I don't know—Harvard, then it would make some kinda sense. But here—at a state school?—that's pretty bogus in my book."

"I got this, A.J.," said Penny Rae, who was sporting a black bodysuit, along with a conspicuous nose-piercing, for the occasion. "Okay, Mr. Thurman. I only have one question—and it requires you to provide a yes-or-no answer. Think you can handle that?"

"Yeah, sure," Thurman replied.

"Yes or no," said Penny, "do you understand that you were the one—not Ms. Amari—who started all this? That you were the one who decided to make *his* presence known in *her* life, and not the other way around?"

"Oh, come on," said Thurman. "That's not a fair question. That's total bullshit, and you know it!"

"It was a yes-or-no question, Mr. Thurman," said Dean Miller, banging his gavel. "Please answer. And by all means, please watch your language."

"Here's my answer," said Thurman, turning to face Azza. "Why the fuck did you come here anyway?"

"Mr. Thurman!" said Dean Miller, banging his gavel yet again.

"It is okay, sir," said Azza. "I will answer. I came here to study chemical engineering and to experience the American Dream."

"That's garbage!" said Thurman. "If you weren't born here, then you're not from here. Which means you can't be an American."

"I didn't say that I wanted to become an American, sir," said Azza. "I said that I would like to experience the American Dream. To experience life, liberty, and the pursuit of happiness."

"That sounds like propaganda, Dean Miller!" said the sloucher, standing up in the middle of the boardroom.

"Please identify yourself for the record, young man," said Dean Miller.

"Ronald Jones," he replied, as old Agnes dutifully noted his name for the record. "People call me RoJo."

"Please proceed," said Dean Miller.

"Okay, so how about this, *Ms. Amari*?" RoJo asked, pronouncing her surname with an audible sneer. "Do you feel bad about killing that guy—you know, 'cause of your almighty religion and all?"

"That question is out of order, Dean Miller," said Dr. Smyth.

"I'll allow it," Dean Miller replied. "Please repeat your question, Mr., uh, RoJo."

"Do you feel bad about killing that truck-driver guy?" RoJo asked, as he sat down and resumed his customary slouch right there in the boardroom.

"Allah has decreed," Azza replied. "And what He wills, He does."

"What does that even *mean*?" RoJo asked.

"It means that as long as it is Allah's will, sir, I am perfectly fine with it."

"The dude is *dead*," said Thurman. "At least, you could be a little, you know, sympathetic. I mean, think about his family—"

"Apparently, they are dead, too," said Azza.

"Did everybody hear that?" RoJo asked, turning to face Dean Miller. "This chick is heartless. And now, some people are even saying that the truck guy was some kind of crazy wingnut. But nobody really knows that for sure—"

"I don't think we should speculate about facts not in evidence," said Dean Miller, banging his gavel once again. "We don't really know what was in the perpetrator's heart, and we're not qualified to speak to his psychological state."

"Oh, really?" Dr. Smyth asked. "Did any of you happen to see his truck? I watched the police tow it away yesterday afternoon. The man had a SAVAGE NATIONALIST sticker pasted across his rear bumper. That sounds pretty heartfelt to me!"

"All right," said Dean Miller, "I think we've heard enough *ad hominem* attacks for one day from both sides of the aisle."

"'From both sides of the aisle,' Archie?" said Dr. Smyth. "This isn't your American Congress, where everything's so relentlessly partisan!"

"I'm sorry, Dr. Smyth," Dean Miller continued, "but you're out of order here. I've tried to accommodate your interjections. At this point, though, I am going to have to ask you to refrain from any further upsurges—"

"*Upsurges*?" said Dr. Smyth, standing up from his seat. "Are you even deploying that word correctly, Archie? Try using it in a sentence."

"You're out of order, Dr. Smyth!" said Dean Miller, banging his gavel with a newfound fury. "We're moving this proceeding forward this instant," he added, clearing his throat. Meanwhile, as Dr. Smyth resumed his seat, he began tapping his fingers furiously into his phone.

"Now, you all may have noticed Officer Rankin's presence here today," Dean Miller continued. "I've asked him to share his observations for the record. This should help us round out the picture a bit more."

"Thanks for giving me a chance to speak today, Dean Miller," said Officer Rankin. "I may have a slightly different perspective here. But don't get me wrong. I'm not like that numbskull over there," he added, pointing to Thurman. "I mean, what he did could net him a simple assault charge."

"Assault?" Thurman asked. "I never touched her!"

"Oh, it's simple assault, all right," said Officer Rankin, his face growing red along with his wrath. "Assault, by definition, doesn't have to involve physical contact. It can be anything that causes the victim to be in fear of imminent battery."

"Please continue, Officer Rankin," said Dean Miller.

"Thanks, Dean Miller," he replied. "Like I said, I don't have anything in common with Mr. Thurman. But I think you all know where I'm coming from, don't you? All these terrorist attacks keep happening. And these Middle Easterners—they're inevitably the culprits. We've all seen the news reports. It's always the same: somebody mows down a bunch of people on a boardwalk with a big rig, and it's like waiting for the other shoe to drop until you learn the perp's identity. And then you find out that it's Ahmed Something or Aziz So-and-So. I've got nothing against Ms. Amari. From what I can tell, she seems like good people. But where there's smoke, there's fire, right?"

"You're damned right, there is," said RoJo. "I have plenty more questions, *Dean*. For one thing, why is she always in the computer lab, logging onto chat rooms with the funny-looking words made up of all those squiggly lines?"

"It's called *Arabic*," said Dr. Smyth, interrupting him. This time he remained seated, with his arms folded across his chest in defiance.

"And what's with all the driving, *Ms. Amari*?" RoJo continued, sneering Azza's surname yet again. "Everybody knows you've been hanging out with that dude over there," he added, pointing towards Kip.

As Kip would remember it years later, this was the moment when things began to happen in a kind of discomfiting slow-motion haze, not unlike the morning in which Thurman rode his skateboard across the quad and tore the hijab away from Azza's body.

"Haven't you seen enough already, Archie?" Dr. Smyth asked. "You heard the copper, right? She's good people. The real McCoy. Do we really need to go any further with this travesty?"

And that's when, without warning, Azza abruptly stood up to face Kip from her place near the front of the boardroom.

"I am very sorry, Mr. Kip, sir," she said, her voice breaking into a sob. "At first, I only wanted to do the ALICE. But I have not been as truthful as I could be. Whether my family had stayed in Tunis or in our adopted home in the *banlieues*, it didn't matter: I was never going to be allowed to drive."

For his part, Kip could scarcely comprehend what she was saying. He was still trying to make sense of what Dr. Smyth had said only moments before. The real McCoy, huh. Did he hear that correctly?

"See, Dr. Matthews? That's what I meant back in class," said RoJo. "It's always the same with these people. There is nothing equal about men and women in the Middle East. The women are always some dude's property—"

"I admit it, sir. I wanted to drive a car," said Azza, her voice choking up. "I wanted to be like my father and my brother, like the men from the *banlieues*. It made me feel . . . powerful."

"That may be true, Ms. Amari, but I think we need to get back to the squiggly lines," said Dean Miller. "I mean, the *Arabic*. Please resume your seat. I believe I have some additional questions."

"Yeah," said Officer Rankin, nodding his head. "And I'd like to hear about those chat rooms."

But nobody would be hearing any more testimony—at least, not on that particular evening. The boardroom lapsed into silence as the door abruptly opened to reveal the tall, withering personage of Dr. Graham Alexander, the college's wizened president, who had recently been inaugurated into his eighth consecutive four-year term at the helm of Northwestern Ohio State.

A tiny smile crept across Dr. Smyth's face as President Alexander strode across the room.

"I'll take it from here, Dean Miller," he said, carefully lifting the gavel from its place on the desk and cupping it gently in his hands, as if he were extinguishing a candle.

"Ms. Amari," said President Alexander, "we've taken up quite enough of your time here tonight. These proceedings are hereby ended. Godspeed to you and your studies."

For a moment, nobody knew what to do. Even Dean Miller seemed uncertain about how to behave, as if he were acting in a stage play and had suddenly forgotten his lines. But then just as suddenly, the assemblage seemed to remember that Dr. Alexander was the president of the college and all. If he deemed the Judicial Review Board to be concluded, then it must be over, right?

In short order, members of the campus community had begun filing out of the room, making their way downstairs, and walking out of Thayer Hall and into the night air, where they could feel the chill of impending winter.

As it turned out, Kip and Azza were the last to leave the boardroom that evening.

"Is it really over?" Azza asked, as if the relief that she had sought from her new life in America might actually be on the verge of becoming her reality.

"If President Alexander says so, then it must be over," said Kip. "Let's go find Ry and tell him the good news!"

• • •

Kip and Azza found Ry all right. Waiting right where they left him in the sculpture garden outside of Thayer Hall, Ry was leaning on the statue of Tigger, frozen forever in mid-bounce, his pantherine expression brimming with mischief and whimsy.

But before Ry could so much as congratulate Azza for her victory up in the boardroom, the three friends were joined by RoJo and Thurman, who—President Alexander be damned—were in a fighting mood.

"This is a bad idea, dude," said the Skateboard Kid, trying to hold back RoJo. "The raghead's not worth it."

But there was no stopping RoJo that evening. Staring Azza dead in the eyes through the narrow slit in her burqa, he leaned back, arching his spine as far as it could possibly go. It was quite a scene to behold, really: all of RoJo's years as a dyed-in-the-wool sloucher had clearly transformed his vertebrae into machines of perfect elasticity. And that's when he thrust his body forward, as if he were releasing a shot-put, and spit in Azza's face, with his sputum splattering across the whole of her burqa.

Ry, of course, was beside himself. Now it was Kip's turn to hold back his friend, and it took everything he could possibly muster to stop Ry from attacking RoJo, who gazed at Azza with a leering, wicked smile.

Then she did the most remarkable thing, nearly as extraordinary as if she had thrown off all of her clothing right there in the sculpture garden—with Winnie the Pooh, Rabbit, and the whole menagerie from the Hundred Acre Wood as her witnesses:

Azza stepped up to RoJo, as close as she could possibly get, and said, "As-salāmu ʿalayki." She was so close, in fact, that he could smell her sweet breath, redolent of jasmine and a hint of coriander. And then, lifting up the folds of her burqa, Azza exposed her lips and kissed him gently on the cheek. For his part, RoJo was frozen in place, as if he no longer knew what to do or how to act.

But it was Azza who acted first, turning on her heel and quietly walking away into the night. As RoJo and Thurman looked on, still unsure about what exactly had transpired in that sculpture garden, Kip and Ry followed after her into the darkness.

CHAPTER 28:
NEVER LET ME DOWN AGAIN

The next afternoon, the very moment that school let out for the day, Kip drove over to the Hayes. He was on a mission—head down, eyes straight ahead as he piloted the Powder Puff across Fremont.

This was destined to be the day! Kip thought to himself. Today would mark the end of their mind-numbing search for the figurine. As he motored along Hayes Avenue, he could see Spiegel Grove looming up ahead. And just beyond it, the museum itself.

Kip couldn't wait to tell Fletch about the Fitbit and his suspicions regarding Liam's shady role in the whole bloody business. Heck, maybe they'd even confront him together. He could just see it: the two of them, Fletch and Kip, as they blew into Turley's and demanded that Liam hand over the pear. Maybe they'd even bring Marv along to give Liam an extra jolt of fear. Oh, this is gonna be great! Kip thought to himself.

Passing through the vestibule and into the exhibition hall, Kip nodded as Marv offered his customary greeting—"Well, if it isn't President Rutherford B. Hayes, Junior!"—before heading straight back to Fletch's office. Kip had no time for pleasantries today, flashing the security guard a quick smile as he brushed past him in the entryway. Kip was on a mission, after all.

A few moments later, Kip was standing in Fletch's sad and disheveled office. Only it wasn't so disheveled anymore. Fletch's belongings were neatly packed away in a pair of banker's boxes stacked beside his rolltop desk.

"Going somewhere?" Kip asked, startling Fletch, who had been lost in thought.

"I'm afraid so," said Fletch, who looked far more broken and distraught than Kip had ever seen him before. Which was saying something.

"Donahue came in late last night," Fletch continued. "He completed the audit even earlier than expected. He was royally pissed, as you might imagine. And he had accounted for everything, I tell ya. The figurine was only the tip of the iceberg. But let's face it: the car dealer was always looking for an excuse to can me."

"Because of Emily?" Kip asked.

"Possibly at some level," Fletch replied. "But that road has been closed for a long time. She'd never leave Donahue for a wreck like me. I had my chance with her years ago, and I blew it. It's probably for the best, really, that the car dealer is finally sending me packing. They were gonna take my directorship sooner or later. If it hadn't been for you, I'd have been out of here much earlier. Your vote saved me during the executive session last spring. Bought me some time."

"I'm really sorry to hear all this," said Kip. "You were always the lifeblood of this place."

"Well, like you said a while back: It'll roll on without me, that's for certain. Too bad you couldn't find the figurine, though. Would've been nice to see it again, wouldn't it?"

"That's just it," said Kip. "I've never actually *seen* the thing before in the museum. And let's face it: outside of you and Marv, nobody has spent more time roaming these halls than I have."

"Well, that's simple," Fletch replied. "I never actually put the figurine on display. I recognized its value almost immediately, so I stowed it away for safekeeping."

"Stowed it away for safekeeping?" Kip asked. "But why? It couldn't be worth that much."

"See, that's where you're wrong," Fletch replied. "It's actually worth a great deal."

"Because it was a gift to Lemonade Lucy from the French president?" Kip asked.

"No," said Fletch, "although that bit of history makes for a nice backstory."

"Then why?" Kip asked.

"'Cause of Bonheur."

"What's a Bonheur?"

"It's not a what, but a *who,*" said Fletch. "Isidore Bonheur was the premier French sculptor of his day. His work is in all of the world's finest collections—primarily, Musée d'Orsay in Paris. But you see, what makes the figurine even more special is that Bonheur typically worked in animalia. So the pear was a real departure—and at the behest of the President of the Third Republic of France, which makes it even more valuable."

"Okay," said Kip, "but why a pear, then? What was the significance for the French?"

"For many cultures, the pear symbolizes immortality and prosperity," said Fletch. "Wouldn't that be a perfect gift from one nation to another—particularly, if there's, say, an international canal involved?"

"Well, how about that?" Kip asked. "I had no idea that the Hayes was in possession of such a prized artifact."

"And now, I suppose it will be irrevocably lost," said Fletch. "If you can't find it, I doubt that anyone can. It's just another nail in my coffin, another regret to add to a whole sea of the things."

"I may take one last stab at finding the figurine on my own," said Kip. "Unless you object, that is."

"Suit yourself," Fletch replied. "I can't see any good coming of it, but I'd never be the one to stand in your way, kid. But I guess you already know that."

"So what now?" Kip asked. "Where do you go from here?"

"I don't rightly know," said Fletch, patting his ample belly. "My health is still a gigantic fiasco, that's for sure. But there's no way I'm staying in Fremont. Good riddance to that, right?"

"Can't say I'm not jealous," Kip remarked. "My own plan has been to find the pear, graduate from Fremont High, and win a scholarship to some school far, far away from here. At least one of those things won't be happening now—"

"Don't be so down on yourself, young Kippers," said Fletch.

"You've got your whole life splayed out in front of you. Forget about the figurine, I say."

As Kip looked on, Fletch broke into one of his coughing fits.

"You really should get that checked out, Fletch," he told the older man.

"Maybe in my next life," said Fletch. "For now, I'm all packed up and ready to go. Marv will be sending my stuff along before you know it. As for me, I'll be in greener pastures wherever I happen to land."

"You know that's true," said Kip, flashing him a warm smile.

"I doubt that old Marv will miss me much," said Fletch. "And let's be honest: I've become an annoyance as much as a friend to you over the past few months."

"Oh, don't say that," Kip replied, choking up right there in Fletch's soon-to-be-former office. "I'm sure going to miss you. You've been a huge part of my life."

"That's awful nice of you to say, Kippers," Fletch remarked as he gingerly stood up beside his desk and enveloped the younger man in a warmhearted embrace.

• • •

If Kip could have responded—if his throat hadn't closed in on itself with unexpected emotions of heartbreak and nostalgia—he might have hung back a little longer. He might have even summoned up the nerve to tell Fletch that he'd been like a father to him—a rare thing, indeed, for a young man who had never really known that kind of relationship. But as it was, he gently withdrew from Fletch's bear-hug and ambled back towards the exhibition hall.

Felled by his grief, Kip waved Marv away as he headed for the vestibule. But the old security guard, always game for a little fun and frivolity in the workaday world, didn't miss a beat. As the museum board's junior member exited the Hayes that afternoon, Marv broke into a spirited rendition of "Hail to the Chief." Even in his heartbreak, Kip had to admit that he was impressed with Marv's effort. Somehow—amazingly, even—the security guard seemed to know all of the words:

Hail to the Chief, we have chosen for the nation!
Hail to the Chief, we salute him, one and all!

As it turned out, Kip's emotional gauntlet was only just getting started. Passing through the vestibule, with the sound of Marv's voice still ringing in his ears, he made a beeline for the parking lot behind the exhibition hall. There, leaning against the Powder Puff in the heat of the afternoon sun, stood Colby. Radiant with her pageboy haircut and her youth, she cut an exacting presence in the parking lot. Perhaps Kip was luckier than he had previously thought? But as he loped ever closer to the Subaru, Kip could tell that Colby was none too happy. In fact, she seemed downright pissed.

With the first flush of adrenaline, Kip's throat began to open up once more. But it wasn't just that he was beginning to feel better after leaving Fletch back in the Hayes. He realized that he was really glad to see Colby. That she could say the most dismal, degrading things in the world to him, and he wouldn't care a whit. Am I so far gone, he wondered to himself, that I am buoyed by the mere sight of her, no matter how much she loathes me?

Any stress that he may have felt about the unexpected reunion dissipated in an instant, as they apologized to each other in almost perfect simultaneity.

"I'm sorry!" said Kip, breathlessly.

"I'm sorry, too!" said Colby.

"Wait, why are *you* sorry?" Kip asked.

"For not responding to your texts," Colby replied. "I was being a real baby about everything. At first, I deleted them, but then I just turned off my phone altogether."

"Did you know that Hayes was the first president to have a telephone installed in the White House?" he asked.

"Oh, dear God, Kip, don't do that now. *Please*. I just wanna get through this, okay?"

"Yeah, I get it," said Kip. "I'm really, really sorry."

"Why are *you* sorry?"

"For the same thing as you, I guess."

"Hold up," said Colby. "*You're* sorry that I didn't respond to your texts?"

"Well, yeah," Kip replied. "For sure. I mean, I wish you had texted me back and all. But I'm . . . I'm also sorry for the way I acted. For Birdie—"

"Yeah, but that's over," said Colby.

"How do *you* know that?" Kip asked.

"It's all around school," said Colby. "Birdie's like a one-woman bullhorn. You must have wronged her, but good."

"Birdie and I don't see things eye-to-eye anymore," said Kip.

"'Cause she's a mighty bitch?" Colby asked.

"More like a mighty racist bitch," Kip replied. "But yeah, that covers it, more or less."

"I'm also sorry for one other thing," said Colby. "I've realized that I'd been sort of throwing myself at you."

"Well, then I'm sorry, too," said Kip, "because I sort of liked it."

"Then we're kind of back where we started, aren't we?" Colby asked.

"I guess we are," said Kip. "In a way, it's just like starting over."

"Then remember this above all things, Kip Beckelhymer," said Colby. "I am warm and powerful. You don't wanna cross me again."

"I definitely don't want to do that," said Kip. "I mean, I wouldn't dare."

And then Colby went and did it again: standing high up on her tippy toes and kissing him full on the mouth right there in the Hayes parking lot.

"I'm glad we got that out of the way," said Colby, smiling up at him.

"Me, too," said Kip. "Hey, are you here for the Young Docents program?"

"Yeah," said Colby, "but I'm not feeling it today. I'm thinking of skipping out, actually."

"And you can just do that?"

"Sure, I can," said Colby. "I'm a volunteer!"

CHAPTER 29: PYRUS COMMUNIS

With Colby riding shotgun, Kip brought the Powder Puff to a halt outside of Woody's Drive-In. Parked next to the Subaru was a gleaming, metallic red Mini-Cooper.

Well, how about that! Kip thought to himself.

As he and Colby made their way inside, Ry stood up and ushered them over to the table that he shared with Azza.

"Beckelhymen!" he shouted. "I'm back behind the wheel!"

"I saw that," said Kip, as he and Colby sat down to join them. "Your mom must've relented."

"Yeah, she cut me a break," said Ry. "I promised no more weed in the house, and she was fine with it. I mean, shit, it's legal all over the place now, right?"

"Perhaps we could continue my driving lessons today, sir?" said Azza. "I would like to practice braking some more. And besides, we are so close to completing our bargain."

"I'm happy to help you with your driving," said Kip. "But we may have to give up on the figurine. Fletch was fired last night. He's no longer the director of the Hayes. He figures that we might as well bail on the search. I mean, what's the point now anyway?"

"Bullshit!" said Ry. "It's too bad about Fletch's job and all, but as far as I'm concerned, that freakin' pear is still out there waiting to be found, and we should be the ones who find it."

"I hate to say this," Colby added, "but I'm with Ry, which is a truly painful thing to admit. I owe Fletch a lot. If it hadn't been for the Young Docents program, I doubt that I'd know any of you guys. But we're close, right? The Fitbit data seems to indicate that the object could be over at Turley's right now. And if it's not there, maybe we'll go and find another lead."

"Are you guys with me?" Ry asked. "Are we in it to win it?"

"Sure am," said Colby.

"I am in it to win it, too, sir," said Azza. "Please count me in. Our bargain is still incomplete."

"So what do you say, Kip?" Ry asked. "Are you ready to hit the trail again? Remember what Fletch himself said: this isn't just some bogus paperweight we're after. This pear's the real McCoy!"

"It is, isn't it?" Kip asked. "You know, Dr. Smyth dropped that phrase at the Judicial Review meeting. And I've been thinking about it ever since. It occurred to me that if something is the real McCoy, then other things, by contrast, must be cheap knockoffs or, worse yet, outright fakes."

"So where does that leave our search?" said Colby.

"Do you know the origins of the phrase 'the real McCoy'?" said Kip.

"Can't say that I do," Colby replied.

"Oh, no," said Ry. "Here comes Rain Man again."

"The real McCoy refers to the innovations of Canadian inventor Elijah McCoy," said Kip. "In his day, McCoy was so ingenious that other firms began pirating his ideas. The problem was that they were never as well-made if they hadn't sprung from the hands of the inventor himself. So thoughtful consumers took to saying, 'Make sure it's a real McCoy.'"

"What did he invent?" Colby asked.

"Oh, a whole bunch of stuff," Kip replied. "The lawn sprinkler, the ironing board."

"Now that you're done with your lecture," said Ry, "can I ask what the eff you're getting at?"

"I believe that the pear was the real McCoy," said Kip, "and the replica of the lease and all the other stuff that Fletch and Colby couldn't find were a bunch of red herrings."

"Wait," said Colby, "why is the pear suddenly so valuable?"

"'Cause it's a Bonheur," Kip replied.

"Bonheur means happiness," said Ry.

"Really?" Kip asked. "How do you even know that?"

"I always figured that French would come in handy with the ladies."

"Oh, right, 'cause you're a playa and all," said Kip.

"What is a playa, sir?" asked Azza.

"A dude who's got lots of game," Colby replied. "It's kind of gross, if you really think about it."

"That's one way of looking at it," said Kip. "Most people think of a player as a cool guy who has a bunch of different girlfriends."

"Oh!" said Azza. "I know what is a player, sir. He is a man who has a harem, right?"

"I guess," said Kip. "But here's the thing with the pear—"

"It's a *figurine,*" said Ry, correcting him.

"That's my line, asshat," Kip replied. "But when it comes to the *figurine,* Bonheur is a famous sculptor, not a state of being."

"Where'd you learn that?" Colby asked.

"Fletch told me about Bonheur back at the Hayes," said Kip. "Apparently, Bonheur's pretty famous, and anything he made is worth, like, a gazillion bucks."

"So that's why it's the real McCoy," said Colby. "I get it now. But hold up: if the figurine is the big-ticket item, why were the cabbie and the emaciated chick only trying to pawn off the replica?"

"How would they know the difference," said Ry. "They're a couple of heroin addicts. They only care about their next fix—"

"Yeah, how could they possibly know the thing's value?" Kip asked. "If they did, they wouldn't be wasting their time with the replica. So what gives?"

"Remember the words of Allah, sir," said Azza. "Beware of this world, for it is sweet and tempting."

"Okay," said Kip, nodding as he took in the essence Azza's words. "So we're looking for someone who's more worldly, who would have the knowledge to be tempted by the pear."

"Dear Jesus," said Colby. "It couldn't be, *could* it?"

"Allah be praised," Azza added.

"FML!" said Ry.

"I'll drive," said Kip, who leapt out of his seat as the waitress, carrying their menus, watched as her customers made their mad dash to the exit.

"Thanks for coming to Woody's," she muttered in their wake.

• • •

As Kip drove the Powder Puff across Fremont, it was Ry, not surprisingly, who spoke up first.

"I still don't get it," he said from his place in the passenger's seat. "I mean, I get that it was Fletch who stole the damned thing. But why did he go to all of the trouble of sending you on a wild-goose chase if he was the dude who lifted it in the first place?"

"Fletch must have been trying to fence the stuff," said Colby. "That explains the cabbie and the emaciated woman—and even why they approached Liam with the replica, right? Maybe Fletch was testing the waters?"

"Yeah, that makes sense," said Kip, as he negotiated the wide turn onto Hayes Avenue.

"But then he goes and makes the mistake of picking a couple of heroin addicts to round out his gang," said Ry.

"That is kinda weird," said Colby. "How does a guy like Fletch even meet those two druggies?"

"Because he was desperate," said Azza, bracing herself in her usual place in the back seat. "I know about desperation, and it can drive you to go to any lengths to find relief."

"And Fletch was worried about getting fired by his archrival for letting the museum go to pot," said Kip. "It's all starting to make sense."

"Except that you're being way too kind to him, Kip," said Colby. "He wasn't fearful about losing his job. He was worried about getting busted. Remember, it's not just the figurine now, but also the President's pocket watch and the First Lady's diamond brooch that went missing. Fletch was clearly stepping up his game."

"So why does he rope Beckelhymen into this whole mess?" said Ry, as Kip made the final turn into the parking lot behind the exhibition hall.

"That is an easy one, sir," said Azza. "Mr. Fletch needed to devise an alibi for his behavior. In my experience, frightened people often resort to all manner of behavior. And their alibis frequently give way to scapegoating other people for their offenses."

"So if he hadn't been fired, he likely would have scapegoated the druggies?" Ry asked.

"Oh, Jesus," said Colby, as the Powder Puff screeched to a halt. "Kip might've been next!"

• • •

Marv couldn't believe his eyes when the four kids jostled through the vestibule, spilling right out in front of him into the Hayes entryway.

Leading the way, Kip sprinted by the security guard, followed closely on his heels by Ry and Colby. For her part, Azza brought up the rear, moving as quickly as she possibly could, given the constraints of her burqa.

When he finally arrived at the doorway to the director's office, huffing and puffing from his wild jaunt across the museum, Kip was stunned to discover that Fletch was no longer in evidence. And neither were the banker's boxes that contained his belongings.

Within a matter of moments, Kip was joined by his friends, along with Marv who had been trailing them across the Hayes.

"What the hell are you kids doing?" Marv exclaimed.

"Where's Fletch?" Kip asked, still struggling to catch his breath.

"Old Fletch was relieved of his duties. He's on his way to his new digs, I guess."

"And the boxes?" Kip asked. "He said that you'd be sending them along later."

"That's hogwash," said the security guard. "Fletch took the whole lot over to Fed-Ex right after you left. I thought he was gonna up and die trying to move those boxes, but somehow he managed to get them into his station wagon."

"And then?" said Kip.

"Well, then he came back, dropped off his keys, and we said our goodbyes," Marv remarked. "What's so special about all that? You got to see him off earlier, didn't you, President Rutherford B. Hayes, Junior?"

• • •

Things were a lot less harried as the kids made their way back towards downtown Fremont. And there certainly wasn't as much talking this time around as Kip powered the Powder Puff in the direction of the Fed-Ex store, which sat just across the street from Tal's Bait and Tackle Shop.

As the friends entered the store, a tiny bell above the doorway signaled their entrance.

"Can I help you kids?" the clerk barked from her place behind the cash register. As she pawed at the wrinkles that lined her leathery face—having grown coarse, no doubt, after too many years of sunbathing on the banks of the nearby Sandusky—she couldn't take her eyes off of Azza.

"You're that girl from the campus, ain't ya?" she asked, with a quizzical look overwhelming her face.

"I am she," said Azza.

"Is it true what they say?" the clerk asked. "That you're a terrorist and everything?"

"You don't have to answer that," said Kip, stepping in front of her.

"It is okay, sir," said Azza. "I will answer. I am only a student," she told the woman, staring at her, unblinking, right there in the shop. "I am majoring in chemical engineering for now, but I am seriously thinking about changing my course of study to Anthropology."

"So they're wrong, huh?" asked the clerk. "You're not one of those ISIS people?"

"I am only a student," Azza repeated. "If it assists you in understanding me better, you should know that I am like Lemonade

Lucy. I am tough as the nails," she added, glancing over at Colby, "and I grovel to no one."

"That's reassuring, I guess," said the clerk, laughing nervously to herself. "So what can I do ya for?"

"A friend of ours brought by some boxes earlier today," said Kip. "His name's Fletch Clawson."

"I remember him all right," said the clerk. "His packages are sitting right over there," she said, gesturing towards a palette piled high with boxes near the rear entrance to the store.

Kip and Ry were on the palette in no time, quickly ferreting out the banker's boxes that Kip had seen earlier that day over at the Hayes.

Glancing at the first box, Kip easily recognized Fletch's elegant handwriting. But what surprised him was the shipping address, which was listed as a post office box in Toronto.

Ry didn't waste any time, as he began tearing open the first banker's box.

"Now what in tarnation are you doing?" the clerk asked. "I said you could look at the boxes, I didn't say nothing about opening them up."

By this point, Ry was already rifling through the contents of the first box, which consisted of veritable reams of paper.

"Looks like the museum's inventory," said Colby. But by then, Ry had already begun pulling the second box off of the palette.

"Wanna take a gander at an honest-to-goodness plaster of Paris pear?" Kip asked his friends, as he prepared to tear open the box.

"Don't you mean *figurine*?" said Ry, smiling as he wiped the sweat from his brow.

"You're pretty confident there, aren't you, Kip?" said Colby, standing alongside him with her hands playfully resting on her hips.

"I believe that the cheese apple is flirting with you again, sir," said Azza.

"I think you may be right," Kip replied. "Gather around, folks. I think we're about to see ourselves a pear!"

And with that, Kip ripped open the banker's box. Nestled just inside, swathed in a trio of old pillowcases, were the artifacts: first, the pocket watch, then the brooch, and, *finally*, the plaster of Paris pear that once belonged to the First Lady herself—the selfsame woman whom many derided in a new and different century as Lemonade Lucy.

Turning over the figurine, Kip pointed to the name of the famous sculptor that was embossed upon the object's base.

"Happiness!" said Ry.

"Enjoy it in immortality and prosperity," said Kip, with great ceremony, as he placed the artifact in Colby's outstretched hands. And there it was: Bonheur's exquisite execution of a European pear, complete with its shiny, 24-carat gold stem rising up out of the artist's ivory-colored rendering of the fruit.

"Why don't you just return it to the Hayes yourself?" Colby asked, gazing at the object resting in her hands.

"You take it," said Kip. "You're the Young Docent, after all."

"But you're the junior member of the executive board," she replied. "In my book, that carries a lot more clout."

It all might have ended right then and there, if the bell above the store's entryway hadn't rung again, this time ushering in none other than Fletch himself. Sweating profusely, he was lugging a third banker's box into the store.

"Hey, look!" said the clerk. "Your friend's come back. Ain't that something?"

As his friends stood behind him, Kip stepped towards Fletch, who was standing in front of the cash register now, nearly doubled over from his exertions.

"Didn't expect to see you guys here," said Fletch. "I guess you probably found what you were looking for, huh?"

"We sure did," Kip replied, as he closed the space between himself and Fletch.

"I should be making my exit, then," said Fletch, as he took a step towards the door.

"Remember the time that Liam thought you were my dad?" Kip asked. "Over at Turley's?"

"Sure, I remember it," said Fletch.

"I think about it a lot," said Kip.

"Is this the part where you tell me what a disappointment I've become?" Fletch asked. "That I should have been a better father figure for you?"

"No," said Kip. "I won't be saying those things to you, Fletch. I'm starting to realize that there are two kinds of people in this world. The first kind are the ones who study the past and learn from the mistakes of our forebears. As a confirmed history geek, I'd like to think that I am that type—and that, just possibly, it might have even made my father proud. But then there are the others, the ones who believe that history can teach us nothing. That our lives in the here and now are the only ones that matter, the past and the future be damned. And I'm beginning to learn that those people make up almost everyone I know. That they're everywhere—like a plague."

"So I guess you're telling me that I'm in the latter category," said Fletch, "that I'm one of the selfish, unthinking ones. Well, I'm just fine with that—guilty as charged."

"You're just about the last guy on earth who should be running a place like the Hayes," said Kip, the fury rising up from his gut. "You know that, don't you?"

"I think I'll be leaving now, Kippers," said Fletch, who had begun walking back towards the door again.

"You know," said Kip, choking up right there in the Fed-Ex store, "you were kind of a hero for me for a little while. You were an annoyance, too, but I liked the idea that you were out here in the hinterlands of Fremont, fighting the good fight for American history."

"See, that's just it," Fletch replied, staring down at his belly and then back towards Kip. "You're 17, kid. You get to believe in those kinds of things. But take my word: it looks a whole lot different 30 years on. Here endeth the lesson," he said, before breaking into a coughing fit.

After Fletch's cough had finally subsided, Ry stepped towards him, and, reaching deep into his jeans pocket, produced the blue Fitbit.

"I believe this belongs to you," said Ry, wiping the lint off of the device as he handed it to Fletch. "You should probably start using it, dude."

And with one more ring of the bell, Fletch passed back through the entryway, Fitbit in hand, as he disappeared into the blinding sunlight of another ordinary afternoon in Fremont.

CHAPTER 30: PRECIOUS SNOWFLAKES

As Kip looked on nervously from the passenger's seat, Azza steered the Powder Puff across downtown Fremont. It was a Friday morning on the day after Thanksgiving, a holiday for the students of Fremont High and Northwestern Ohio State alike, and Azza had taken to wearing her hijab again. She had done it up in the College Girl Look, her personal favorite, with its billowing folds carefully arrayed like the glamorous models who lived in the pages of *Aquila Style.*

For Azza, the journey marked her first experience on the open road. She was thrilled to discover that when she pressed down on the pedals, the ache in her feet was no longer in evidence. And as she glanced at her reflection in the rearview mirror, she was delighted to note that the wounds on her face had been reduced to a few rosy blemishes.

Not surprisingly, Azza had proven to be an overly careful and exceedingly conscientious driver. When she pulled the Powder Puff up to a stop sign, for example, she would diligently count to three in her head before entering the intersection. And when it came to stoplights, she was always careful to lean forward and look both ways—watching defensively for any other drivers who might be running the opposing light.

If Azza had a failing as a driver, it may have been her approach to the speed limit. If a street sign indicated that the speed limit was 45, that was exactly what she did—depressing the accelerator until the needle hit 45 miles-per-hour and holding it there until it was time to slow down again for a mandatory stop.

But the other kids didn't mind the way she punched it after pulling away from a stop sign. They were just happy that she was once and truly doing the ALICE. That she had finally found her mettle on the streets of Fremont. And, perhaps most important, that she had recently earned her driver's license, which she would giddily show off to anyone who revealed even the slightest interest.

"You're nailing it, A!" said Ry from his place in the back seat next to Colby.

"Yes, sir," Azza replied. "I am nailing it very much!"

As Azza steered the Subaru in the direction of Woody's, something in the next lane caught her attention. It was the turban-clad Sikh again, riding his metallic blue motorbike as it purred alongside the Powder Puff. For a moment, they locked eyes, and then, just before riding off ahead of her, the Sikh lifted his hand and rewarded Azza with a tiny salute.

After eating an early lunch at Woody's—where Azza studiously avoided the calamari—the friends strolled for a while along the banks of the Sandusky, walking among the dilapidated buildings nestled by the riverside. It may have been late November, but the first blush of winter cold was only just descending on the region, leaving a faint chill in the air. With Ry and Colby walking just ahead of them, Kip and Azza brought up the rear, strolling at a slightly slower gait.

"I think Ry may have a crush on you," said Kip.

"How can you tell, sir?" Azza replied.

"He's started brushing his teeth regularly. And just the other day, I think I saw him tuck in his shirt."

"It is flattering, sir. But he is still a boy."

"Now hold on a sec," said Kip. "He'll turn 18 next month, and I'm only a couple of months behind him. You're not that much older than we are."

"Really, sir?" Azza asked. "How old do you think I am?"

"I don't know—18, I'd guess. Maybe 19?"

"I am 26-years-old, Mr. Kip."

"Wow," he replied. "I would never have figured you to be that old. Maybe Ry likes older women?"

"That must be the source of the attraction, sir," said Azza.

"Hey, don't kid yourself about Ry," said Kip. "He's not easily dissuaded. Remember that night in the sculpture garden, when those two idiots followed us out of Thayer Hall? I thought he was going to go absolutely ape-shit on those guys."

"What is ape-shit, sir?" Azza asked.

But before Kip could answer, they were interrupted by the sound of Ry's voice, booming just up ahead, where he and Colby stood, mouths agape, staring at the crumbling brick façade of an old church.

And there, scrawled in giant red lettering, were the words DEATH TO ISLAM.

Kip and Colby were predictably aghast, and Ry, for his part, was ready to go to war. But looking around the empty streetscape, he quickly realized that there was no one available for him to play out his rage.

Not missing a beat, Azza stepped up to the wall to get a closer look at the graffiti.

"Does anyone have a pen, please?" she asked.

Rummaging through her handbag, Colby produced a magic marker and dutifully handed it to Azza, who began forming a series of elegantly-arrayed Arabic letters.

When she was done, Azza stood back from the wall, admired her work, and nodded resolutely at the finished product.

سلام

"What does that mean?" Ry asked, his face scrunched up in confusion.

"Peace, sir," Azza replied.

"You know, right, that the same dudes who wrote that other shit won't even know what the Arabic means?" Ry asked.

"And they aren't going to bother trying to translate it either," Kip added.

"That is okay by me, sirs," she said. "They cannot possibly know what they don't know anyway. And they probably never will."

"Why is it so easy to hate, do you think?" Colby asked.

"Because loving is so much more difficult," said Azza. "If you really love someone, you must love the whole person, just as they are, and not merely as you would like them to be."

"That's beautiful," said Colby.

"Alas, it is not mine," Azza replied. "I read it somewhere."

"Yeah, but don't you just wanna find the guys who pulled this shit and teach them a lesson?" Ry asked.

"That would not be holy, sir," Azza replied. "Allah teaches us not to transgress limits, to deploy violence only as a means of self-defense. To do otherwise is forbidden, and Allah loveth not transgressors."

"Let me guess," said Ry. "Anyone who violates Allah's teachings will enter the fire?"

"Very good, sir," said Azza. "You are learning."

"So what then?" Colby asked. "Do we just give up, say 'haters gonna hate,' and go merrily on our way?"

"I have no idea," said Azza, laughing to herself. "When you find out, please tell it to me, too."

• • •

For a while, the friends paused by a cement outcropping at the edge of the river. Kip sat close to Colby, taking her by the hand, while Azza and Ry sat nearby, gazing across the Sandusky, which flowed down from Lake Erie, to the north, past Brady's Island, and onto the shores of Fremont down below.

"Dude, that graffiti really has me creeped out," said Ry, breaking the ice as usual. "When did this town get all racist and shit?"

"Maybe it always was," said Kip.

"I think the only thing that's changed," said Colby, "is that everybody's become way too obsessed with anyone who doesn't quite fit in. How some people insist on being different from one another and not the same."

"I hear that," said Kip.

"It is all so ridiculous," said Azza. "We are not precious snowflakes.

We are animals. We are all made out of the same stuff."

"That's deep, A," said Ry. "You shoulda laid that on those Judicial Review bastards."

"I am not sure that would have been a winning strategy, sir," Azza replied.

"I've been meaning to ask you about the Judicial Review Board, Azza," said Kip, clearing his throat.

"Yeah, me, too," said Ry. "The whole thing seemed pretty bogus."

"What are you talking about, Ry?" Kip asked. "You weren't even there."

"I was right outside with Winnie and the gang the whole time," said Ry.

"Is there a question in the offing or are we just going to listen to you two bicker?" Colby asked.

"Right," said Kip. "Anyway, it was that whole bit about the chat rooms that I can't seem to get out of my head. The RoJo kid appeared to be accusing you of something—I don't know what, but something sinister, right?"

"He was certainly implying something, wasn't he, sir?" Azza replied.

"Like some kind of underground terrorist network, maybe?" Ry asked.

"That would seem to be the inference," said Azza, matter-of-factly.

"See, that's the part I don't understand," said Kip. "I've watched you working away on a computer—visiting chat rooms, like RoJo said. What are we supposed to think after hearing something like that?"

"You have come to know me very well, Mr. Kip, have you not?" Azza asked. "How sinister could I really be?"

"I know," said Kip, "But he made such a big deal about it."

"Who am I to know what lives inside of that boy's heart?" she asked. "Or how it got there?"

Kip had to admit, if only to himself, that he had no idea how to respond to Azza. She was right, of course: who really knows what anybody thinks? *Or why*. But he pressed on nevertheless, going for broke right there along the riverside.

"What lives inside of your heart, I wonder?" Kip asked.

"I will say only this, sir: my heart is uncomplicated, save for a daughter's love for her dear father and a fervent desire to give meaning to his sacrifice."

Kip had to admit, if only to himself, that somewhere in Azza's words was an uncomplicated sentiment that he, too, could genuinely understand. And he realized, sitting there by the riverside among his friends—even Ry, with his wisecracks and his bravado—that he had never felt so content, that he was exactly where he belonged.

And in Fremont, no less.

• • •

For a long time, the friends sat together in silence, watching as the sky became overcast, as if a storm were brewing somewhere on the horizon.

This time, it was Colby who spoke up first.

"My, aren't we talkative?" she asked. "Come on, guys, we can do better than this! Does anybody know any good jokes?"

"I do, actually," said Azza.

"Whatevs, A," said Ry. "Is this gonna be another cannibal joke?"

"Yeah," Kip added, "it's not like Azza has a sense of humor."

"What do you mean, sir?" Azza replied. "I am very funny."

"*Right*," said Ry, laughing uproariously.

"Girl-toy. Cheese apple. Slaking his lust. Laughing My Hijab Off. Zero fucks," she replied, looking back and forth between the two of them for any possible hint of recognition. "How did you miss that, sirs?"

"Oh, sweet Jesus," said Kip. "Deadpan!"

"*What*?" Ry asked, glaring at Kip.

"You heard me," said Kip. "She's been deadpanning us this whole time!"

Kip and Ry looked back at Azza, who was beaming at them, her face aglow as the sun briefly peeked through the storm clouds.

"So let's hear the joke," said Colby.

"Okay," said Azza, "but I am not sure that you are going to like it."

"Tell us anyway," said Colby. "We can take a joke, right, fellas?"

"We'll like it if it's funny, A," said Ry, good-naturedly.

"Very well, sir," said Azza. "What do you call an employee in America who will work hard for unreasonable pay and never whine?"

"I have no idea," said Kip. "What do you call them?"

"An immigrant," Azza replied, her College Girl hijab gleaming in spangles wrought by the sun. And in that moment, she allowed herself a tiny kernel of hope that there might yet be an American Dream in her future.

ACKNOWLEDGEMENTS

I am grateful to the many friends and colleagues who shared their encouragement and advice throughout this project, including Isabel Atherton, Steven Bachrach, Harry Burton, John Carlberg, Eileen Chapman, John Christopher, Lynne Clay, Todd Davis, James Decker, Maegan Dibble Elliott, Donald Erwin, Mike Farragher, Jack Ford, Laura Ginsberg, Jennifer Hom, Bryan Jenner, Teodora Kamburov, Jason Kruppa, Cheyenne Mayernick, Nancy Mezey, Analise Mifsud, Dinty W. Moore, Judy Ramos, Joe Rapolla, Barbara Collins Rosenberg, Peter Rubie, George Severini, Lee Stringer, Michael Thomas, and Fred Womack. I owe a debt of gratitude to Azza Zagouani for her inspiration and many acts of kindness. I am particularly grateful for the heroic efforts of Nicole Michael, my indefatigable publicist, who kept me on track throughout the writing process. Black Rose Writing's Reagan Rothe deserves special mention for his goodwill and encouragement, as do Dane Low and Jason Kruppa for their assistance with the cover art for *I Am Lemonade Lucy!* along with Takamin for his line drawing. Special love and thanks, as always, go to Becca, PMo, Ryan, Chelsea, Emma, Landon, Tortle, Josh, Justin, and especially to Jeanine Womack, who makes all things possible.

Finally, it is difficult to imagine a place in the ether for this novel without the vital, pioneering work of Mathieu Kassovitz, whose film *La Haine* continues to resonate, nearly 25 years later, with lacerating images of hate and the insidious ways in which it inevitably begets even more hate in its terrible wake. Even now, well into the twenty-first century, we continue to grapple with the corrosive nature of prejudice and xenophobia, which travel the globe with increasing velocity in our interwebbed world. Our work to stem the tide of hatred has only become more vital—and even more urgent—in the intervening years.

ABOUT THE AUTHOR

Kenneth Womack is the author of three previous novels, *John Doe No. 2 and the Dreamland Motel, The Restaurant at the End of the World,* and *Playing the Angel*. He has also written several books about the Beatles, including *Long and Winding Roads: The Evolving Artistry of the Beatles, The Beatles Encyclopedia: Everything Fab Four,* and, most recently, an acclaimed two-volume biography about the life of Beatles producer George Martin. He is Dean of the Wayne D. McMurray School of Humanities and Social Sciences at Monmouth University, where he also serves as Professor of English. He lives in West Long Branch, New Jersey, with his wife Jeanine.

Thank you so much for reading one of our **Mystery** novels.
If you enjoyed our book, please check out our recommended title for your next great read!

K-Town Confidential by Brad Chisholm and Claire Kim

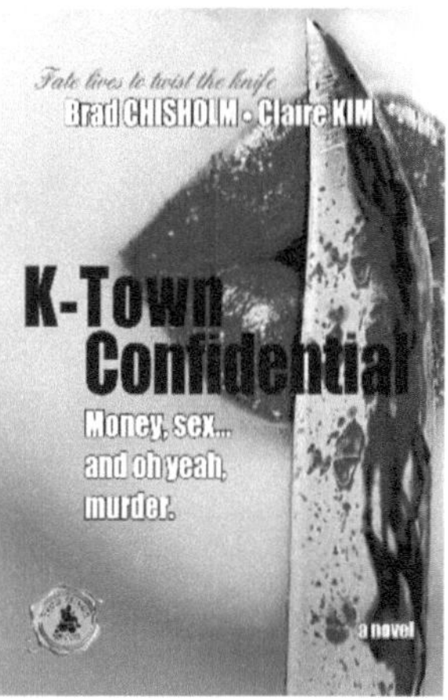

"An enjoyable zigzagging plot." –***KIRKUS REVIEWS***

"If you are a fan of crime stories and legal dramas that have a noir flavor, you won't be disappointed with *K-Town Confidential*." –***Authors Reading***

www.ingramcontent.com/pod-product-compliance
Lightning Source LLC
Chambersburg PA
CBHW030358310726
48979CB00001B/355

* 9 7 8 1 9 4 4 7 1 5 3 8 0 *